ON THE RUN

WHISPERING KEY
BOOK 2

MAY ARCHER

Cover Art: Cate Ashwood Designs
Cover Photo: Wander Aguiar
Editing: One Love Editing
Beta Reading: Leslie Copeland, Lucy Lennox, Eden Finley, Neve Wilder,
Chelsea Bell, Shay Haude
Proofreading: Lori Parks

All the good bits are theirs, and any mistakes are my own!

1

———

TOBY

Help Me Hagatha (Issue #2394)

Dear Aunt Hagatha:

I'm dating a woman who's slept with twelve different guys including me. It's not that I'm judging her, it's just that this seems like a lot of guys for one woman. How many sexual partners should a person have?

Randy in Richmond

Dear Randy,

That *is* rather a lot. I personally sleep with a maximum of ten. My mattress is king-sized, you see, and with more than ten, men start falling off here and there, and elbows end up in places where elbows do *not* belong. The whole thing gets rather awkward.

Oh! Oh, wait. Did you mean in a lifetime? Hmm. While I'd

ordinarily hesitate to provide a one-size-fits-all response to such a deeply personal question, your assurance that you're "not judging her" has swayed me, so I've undertaken hands-on research to arrive at the correct answer. I'll let you know when I hit it.

In the meantime, if Randy's girlfriend is reading this, the answer is at least thirteen. Make of that what you will.

Love,
Aunt Hagatha

"For the love of God, Mason, pick up," I muttered for the fourteenth time in as many minutes.

If my best friend was trying to make a point about me ducking his calls and texts for the past week or so, message fucking received. I regretted all the life choices that had led me to this place—every single one—and I'd happily beg his forgiveness once he answered the goddamn phone.

The blue-haired lady standing in front of me in hell's own rental car line turned around to give me a pursed-lipped cranky sigh, possibly because my muttering had grown increasingly sweary and increasingly loud and there was a family of kids behind me... or possibly because she realized she was wearing a blue plastic sun visor indoors at night-time, and she, too, regretted her life choices.

Okay, probably not that.

Fact Number One: I was supposed to be headed to the Maldives right now, to the grand opening of a gay-friendly resort whose tagline read "Adventure Travel for the Unadventurous," which was so perfectly on-brand for me, I'd known it was destiny.

It was meant to be the trip of a lifetime—a trip I'd been talking about for over a year since my name had been drawn in a lottery to take part in the opening week festivities. A chance to frolic on sandy beaches with nearly naked, well-oiled celebrity chefs, actors, and musicians, while social media influencers and the mainstream press cavorted around us, documenting the whole experience. My private villa had cost approximately five mortgage payments, but I hadn't minded.

I'd had my suitcase packed and my passport ready. I'd started day drinking by eleven—because who doesn't love a salon that offers rosé whilst threading your brows and waxing your unmentionables?—which had flowed nicely into a boozy lunch with my editor, Jeanette, at a little café not far from her office at HiWire News, and was *supposed* to segue into a twelve-hour nap on the first leg of my first class flight to Malé, give or take a frisky hand job if my seatmate was cute (and male and heteroflexible).

But then, at some point after my first celebratory martini but before my crab cakes arrived, Jeanette's chatter had segued into celebrity gossip—a part of HiWire's revenue stream I wasn't generally involved in—and I'd felt the first little frisson of concern.

"Have you ever heard of a bar called Dive?" she asked with a wolfish smile. "It's a gay bar."

I rolled my eyes. "Obviously." But some hind-brain-ish form of self-preservation had made me bite my tongue rather than inform her I'd been there just two nights before. "Why?"

"The latest scandal, Tobias, darling! Turns out, a certain rock star was partying at Dive and hooked up with a man."

I'd gripped the stem of my martini glass. "Some of us do that regularly, Jeanette. It's hardly scandalous."

"Don't be naïve, Tobias. *You're* not famous. Half the female population of America is in mourning this morning. So much for that actress Jayd dated last year, hmm?" She'd snorted. "Of course, his people refuse to comment on their client's sexuality and blah blah. But the pictures tell the tale." She'd pulled up the HiWire website on her omnipresent tablet and slid it across the white linen table-cloth with an absolutely gleeful smile. "The poor sod on his knees in the picture is about to become famous, too, for approximately fifteen minutes."

After one glance, I'd signaled the server over, canceled my crab cake order, and ordered another martini.

"Hard to make him famous," I'd croaked, my throat gone dry, "when his entire face is hidden."

She'd pointed at the picture again. "It's only a matter of time until someone figures out his identity. How many men have a tattoo of Where's Waldo wearing a string bikini? Honestly, why would anyone do that?"

"It's more of a Speedo," I'd whispered. "And it was probably at a low point in college. Drinks were probably consumed. Decisions were made."

"What?"

"Just speculating. I can't see why you want to find this guy." I chuckled uncomfortably. "He's a nobody."

"We want to find him to get a statement about Jayd, clearly," she said slowly, like she was talking to a very young child. "Everyone has a price... or a breaking point. And if HiWire doesn't find him, the cretins at BlazeNewz will."

I'd cleared my throat. "But Tattoo Guy is a victim of circumstance. An innocent. Who clearly spends lots of time in the gym. And has an amazing head of hair."

She'd tipped her head to one side. "Honestly, Tobias, listen to yourself. Should you be having another martini? I'm afraid you're losing your killer instinct."

I was losing something, for damn sure. Possibly my mind. As evidenced by...

Fact Number Two: I was right then in freakin' Florida, at Sarasota-Bradenton International Airport, having a low-key panic attack and trying to avoid my fifteen minutes of fame at all costs.

I'd canceled my once-in-a-lifetime trip to the place where every reporter and celebrity gossip hunter in the solar system would be hanging out this weekend, grabbed my already packed suitcase, and fled the city, imagining I was mere seconds ahead of a SWAT team of camera-toting paparazzi closing in on my location. I'd headed for the most remote place I could conceive of and the *one* man I could trust to hide me, no matter the cost to his own health and safety, my best friend, Mason Bloom... who apparently had his phone on silent, with *zero* regard for my crisis.

Furthermore, I was being auditorily assaulted by a maintenance dude riding a Zamboni-esque floor cleaner around the linoleum of the baggage claim area with wanton disregard for my eardrums, which was unacceptable.

I also may have been hungover at 8:00 p.m., but that was neither here nor there.

Why, yes, I *was* given to slight overdramatization. I liked to imagine that, along with my complete inability to think logically under pressure, were delightfully amusing quirks of my personality.

My phone rang in my pocket, and I answered immediately.

"Mason, finally! Thank fu—dge!" I amended when Blue Hair gave me a death glare over her shoulder. I widened my eyes in the universal gesture for "Back off, sis," and when she harrumphed and faced forward again, I continued. "I need you to come get me. As in, posthaste."

"Uh. Tommy? *Mi angel*, it's Aron. From the bar. And, uh, from Dive the other night, too. Remember?"

I huffed. Did I remember? Did George Washington remember Benedict Arnold? Did Jesus remember Judas Iscariot? Did Britney remember whoever the heck had provided her with those hair clippers?

It wasn't likely I'd forget the instrument of my downfall, especially when it came packaged as a hot bodybuilder I'd flirted with at a bar last weekend who'd invited me to the exclusive backroom VIP party Wednesday night at Dive.

"Come on, Tommy," Aron had said, flexing all his muscly muscles and smiling with every one of his professionally whitened teeth, which had been such a welcome change from his blathering about his chances in the upcoming Muscle Man of Manhattan competition that I'd agreed without thinking and hadn't even bothered correcting him when he'd used the wrong name.

I hadn't understood that he'd meant we'd attempt to party with an *actual* rock star, and had therefore not comprehended the possibility that I could be caught on camera with said rock star in what appeared to be a very compromising position.

This would be the last time I was a fool for a muscle-bound guy with a perfectly sculpted ass, I vowed to myself. The very, very last time. I'd officially hit rock bottom.

"I am not your *angel*, and of course I remember you, you dick—ens," I corrected, in deference to the children. I added in a furious, accusatory whisper, "You staged that whole scene and sold me out for forty pieces of silver."

"No way, man, it was twenty-five thousand dollars." Aron's voice was both sincere and sincerely awestruck, and the confirmation infuriated me. "And I didn't sell you out... exactly."

"No? What do *you* call pushing me to the ground at the exact moment a photographer snapped the picture?" I whisper-hissed.

I wasn't sure which was more mortifying: that I'd been so busy plotting my escape from another deadly boring night at a club with young try-hards, I hadn't seen the move coming, or that I'd been so incensed by Aron's braying laughter and his insistence that it was a "harmless prank" to notice a photographer was even there until Jeanette showed me the picture earlier.

I hadn't lived a blameless life by any means, but I had one rule that was inviolable: I kept my shit *contained*. No gossip, and sure as fuck no scandals.

Thanks to Aron, I'd broken that rule, and now everything I'd spent the last ten years working for was in jeopardy...

And I was almost positive that wasn't me being quirkily dramatic.

"It's me making lemons outta lemonade," Aron insisted. "Look, Tommy, the story's gonna come out one way or another, it's only a matter of time. That singer dude wasn't acting like any virgin I've ever met, so we can't be the only ones he's fooled around with."

"We?" I demanded. "Nuh-uh-uh. *We* were not involved in any fooling, Aron. You were the one kissing him. And then you stood up and pushed me so *I* was the one who got caught in the picture."

A picture which not only showcased the aforementioned shoulder tattoo, but also Jayd's hands reaching out to embrace me and his chart-topping face, complete with beard burn and kiss-swollen lips, contorted in what appeared to be incredible pleasure—and, let me just say for the record, totally *would* have been incredible pleasure, had I actually been doing what it looked like I was doing, because blow jobs, especially with me, were fucking *life-changing*.

Only Jayd, Aron, the photographer, and I knew poor Jayd had actually been yelling and trying to grab me because I'd tried to break my fall by bracing a hand on his nuts.

"What's done is done," Aron the punk-ass philosopher reasoned. "You can't change it now, so you might as well tell your side of things on the record. Control the narrative, Tommy. Don't be the victim in your own story. I read that the other day."

"Yeah? Truly inspirational," I muttered. "Thanks oodles."

"Don't thank me, thank the advice lady. What's her name? Aunt Something."

Don't say it, Aron.

"Aunt Aggie?"

Don't you do it, boo.

"Aunt Agatha!" he said triumphantly.

"You mean Hagatha," I corrected flatly.

"You sure?"

"Very."

"Huh. Well, that bitch is fierce, whatever her name is, and she knows what the fuck she's talking about, so you should listen to her."

I rolled my eyes. Little did Aron or the rest of America know, America's favorite advice columnist, Aunt Hagatha, was a total fraud who didn't know shit about shit, and she was only able to comment on other people's poor choices because she'd made one or two of her own.

Life advice for you, precious: should you find yourself in a competitive job market looking to put your state school communications degree to use, and you accept a part-time gig answering advice letters at minimum wage for a silly tabloid, and your boss, Jeanette, is so blown away by the public response to the silly, snarky, Twizzler-loving, romance-reading, middle-aged agony aunt you created that she offers you a full-time job with benefits and a salary so extremely cushy you'll be able to afford the mortgage on an Upper West Side one-bed with a gorgeous view of the park, it's important to ask questions.

For example, "Will my identity be more closely guarded than most CIA operatives'?"

And, "How will I show my judgy, homophobic parents back in Ohio that I've made it if I can't tell them about my column?" along with the slightly more positive but no less crucial, "Wait, what will I tell my best friend I do for a living?"

Then I'd suggest you follow it up with a humdinger like, "How can HiWire Entertainment News be both entertainment *and* news, anyway?" Because that might be illuminating.

Alas, I hadn't had an Aunt Hagatha to consult about becoming Aunt Hagatha, so after agreeing to take the job Jeanette offered at America's most-read tabloid, HiWire News, I'd signed contracts.

Reams of them.

Entire ironclad forests of them.

Which was part of the reason my fleeing from Manhattan had been so perilous.

I didn't only care about the inconvenience and embarrassment of being found by the paparazzi (though no one dreams of being famous for a blow job), and I wasn't *just* trying to help Jayd by refusing to confirm his identity and his presence at the club (though there were lines I wouldn't cross, and outing someone who deserved the right to tell his family, friends, and fans whatever he wanted to tell them, whenever he wanted to tell them, even if he *never* wanted to tell them, was one).

No, my fear of being found out could best be summed up in just three tiny letters: N. D. A. As in, the one I'd signed that showed I'd be responsible for damages—likely equivalent to the gross domestic product of a small nation—should my identity as Aunt Hagatha be divulged, *even if it was an accident*.

If I left documentation lying around for my apartment cleaners to find, that was my fault. If a coffee shop patron looked over my shoulder and saw me working on Hagatha business whilst drinking a latte, that was on me. And if some soulless paparazzo who wanted to make a quick buck was able to connect Tattoo Guy to Mr. Toby Elford—not unlikely, given that my existence was hardly one of monk-like abstinence and I was quite prone to removing my shirt at clubs—and that paparazzo started digging into my life? Honey, you'd best believe HiWire would make that *my* problem.

Jeanette and HiWire's stars had risen along with Aunt Hagatha's rise to popularity, and they were devoted to keeping up Hagatha's persona as a harmless, eccentric *woman*.

As for myself, I was growing more ambivalent to Hagatha by the day. The secrecy was annoying, the responsibility of advice-giving was surprisingly heavy, and I was pretty sure no one read my columns for anything but a laugh.

I was not ambivalent enough to give up the salary, though. That was the mercenary truth. And I was sure as fuck not ambivalent enough to pay HiWire a bajillion dollars for breach of contract—I was slightly bored, not criminally insane—hence my panic.

If I were thinking logically, I might have reasoned that it was just as easy for an industrious reporter to suss out my identity while I was in Florida, and this whole mad dash had approximately the same coherence as an ostrich burying his head and thinking no one could see him…

But logic was not my strong suit in times like these.

Quirky, remember?

"Alright, Aron. Well, fun as it's been to catch up—"

"Alright? Does that mean you'll do it?" He sounded relieved. "Good, 'cause BlazeNewz said they'd give me an extra five large if I got you to come forward, so I gave them your phone number. I'll split it with you."

BlazeNewz? Literally the only scammy tabloid that was scammier and tabloid-ier than HiWire?

"You *what?*" I screeched, drawing the ire of Bathilda Blue Visor, who turned around and gave me a gimlet glare.

"You could step out of line to take your call, you know." She pursed her lips. "It's extremely annoying."

I pressed the phone to my chest. "Excuse you, I am having a *crisis* here," I informed her. "I am surrounded by liars and betrayers, my very best friend is not answering my calls, my entire life is about to be ruined, and I really need a rental car, so if you wouldn't mind?" I flipped a hand in the air to indicate an open spot at the rental desk, and as she flounced away, I seethed into the phone, "There is no way, in this reality or any other, that I will take their call, Aron."

"Fine, fine," Aron relented. "It was five thousand apiece—"

"Oh, well, that's a whole different ball game. For an extra five thousand, I'd be happy to sell off the last vestiges of my soul and harm an innocent man irreparably! Why didn't you say so?" I scoffed.

"Wait, really?"

"No, you piece of... toast." I smiled hard at one of the blond snot monsters standing near my elbow watching me steadily. "Of course not really. I said no, and I meant no."

Aron heaved a put-upon sigh. "They're gonna find you, Tommy. You either tell the story or you *are* the story. You can't just wait around to see what happens, you've gotta— wait, what's that noise?"

That noise was the combined sound of the whiny floor Zamboni and the arguably whinier sound of the rugrats busting out a mother-freakin' hymn right there in the rental car line.

"That's 'Jesus Loves Me' in three-part harmony. You see, Aron, this whole business has caused me to rethink my life and repent my club-hopping ways. I'm joining a convent. I've taken vows of poverty and chastity. Please don't attempt to look for me. Goodbye."

I jabbed Disconnect, then tapped the phone against my lip and tried to quell the dread gripping my chest.

I needed Mason. I needed someone who was coolheaded in a crisis. Mason would know what to do, I was almost positive. And even if he didn't, he'd still hide me in his brand-new house tucked away on a little island off the Gulf Coast, and I could stay there until a hot new story came along or Jayd finally made a statement and the media speculation evaporated.

I'd be golden. As soon as Mase answered his damn phone.

I could admit I'd been a less than stellar friend for the last couple months since Mase moved to Florida and, yes, especially in the last eight weeks or so, since he and the love of his life had discovered a motherfucking, yo-ho-ho, coins-in-the-ground treasure whilst cavorting on some rainy evening adventure. It was possible that I was being slightly immature and feeling left out of his shiny new life. It was possible I'd missed a call or six. It was possible that Aunt Hagatha would tell me to get over myself, and that she might even be right.

But we'd been friends for seventeen years, so he wouldn't stage a friendship breakup over something that minor, right?

The fates wouldn't be cruel enough to heap yet more tragedies upon me.

"Oh, Jebediah, no!" the woman behind me yelled. The singing broke off abruptly, and I turned to see what the ruckus was about... just in time for the screaming baby to projectile vomit all over my shoe.

My open-toed Armani shoe.

I was wrong. The fates might, indeed, be that cruel. I needed to get out of this airport immediately.

"Oh, goodness gracious!" the mother cried, scrambling through her purse. "Oh, sir, let me get you a baby wipe! Let me—"

"Next!" the woman at the rental counter called.

"No worries," I told the mother tightly. "Baby vomit is good luck."

"I think that's bird poo," one of the many other ragamuffins piped up.

I nodded once. "Same thing."

"*Next!*" the woman at the counter yelled again. "Sir?"

I threw my head back with all the dignity I possessed—which, legit, was like, a *lot* of dignity—and squelched my way over to the counter.

"Good evening. Reservation for Elford. I requested—" I removed my credit card from my Ferragamo crossbody and set it on the counter with a click "—a convertible. Something red if you have it, white if not."

The woman—Sofi, per her name badge—did not bat an eyelash nor touch a key. "We don't have one."

"Fine, then." I tapped the credit card again. "Any color convertible is—"

"Don't have one."

"But I have a reservation number—"

"Sorry. Our reservation system is down at present." Her lips twisted to one side, and she shrugged. "I can't look anything up."

The vomit on my toes grew colder.

"A sedan, then." I waved a hand and scooted the card closer to her. She took it but shook her head. "A compact?" She shrugged. "A *sub*compact?"

"We don't have any of those, sir. And our reservation system is—"

"Down at present? So you said." I sucked my top lip between my teeth. "Well, what do you have?"

"I've got..." Sofi tapped the screen idly. "A fifteen-passenger cargo van. It's the last thing in our lot tonight. You can exchange it tomorrow."

"Fine. I'll—"

Behind me, a baby laughed, and I glanced back at the Vomitous von Trapps. The mother clutched a packet of baby wipes and bounced the human projectile launcher, who was now giggling merrily, having deposited his unhappiness on my shoe.

I sighed.

"I think someone needs the van more than me. But surely there must be something else, Sofi," I told her with my widest, most charming smile. "Maybe if you check with a different company here at the airport?"

"Can't." She grabbed a piece of dirty-blonde hair and twirled it with one finger. "Their reservation systems are down too. Catastrophic outage," she said, and it was the happiest she'd looked during our whole interaction.

I set my jaw. "Fine. *Fine.* I will catch a cab. Thank you so much for your exemplary customer service and willingness to go the extra mile."

"Welcome!" she said with no irony at all.

I huffed out a breath. It was impossible to slay someone with my rapier wit when they didn't realize we were dueling.

I grabbed my suitcase and dragged it toward the closest bathroom, hobbling along in my sticky shoe until I got some damp paper towels to clean off the worst of the damage.

Didn't bad things come in threes? First there'd been the photographer at the nightclub, then the puke, then the rental car. Surely that was enough.

I dragged my phone out of my pocket one more time as I left the bathroom and jabbed Mason's number. It was time to play hardball and actually leave the man a voicemail.

"Mason, sweetness," I said when it clicked over. "Toby here. *Again.* You, ah, may have seen my many missed calls? You may have wondered why I didn't text? Ahem. Well. The thing is. I find myself in a bit of a sticky situation. A situation best explained in person. You might remember that time a few months back when you said, 'Come visit! Anytime you like for as long as you like'? Well, today might be your lucky day, precious. I sincerely hope you're not having some kind of epic tantric sex marathon with your boy toy right now. Or that you've left room for me, if you are. Ha ha." I swallowed. "But, um, seriously. Call me."

I clicked off the phone, rubbed it against my forehead, and

sighed, then scooted out of the way as the floor scrubber headed right for me.

Lovely. Here I was, being stalked by a guy with a floor scrubber, in need of a cab and possibly another strong drink. But the important thing about hitting rock bottom was realizing you were there, right?

I put my phone on top of my suitcase and dug through my bag for my credit card so I could pay for my ride, but I couldn't find it.

Fuck. I'd left it at the car rental place. Which I now saw had turned its lights off while I was in the bathroom, like it had closed up for the night. Sure enough, Sofi was disappearing through the door to the back room.

I grabbed my suitcase handle and ran for it, only remembering why that wasn't a good idea a second too late. I turned and watched in horror as my phone fell off my suitcase and slid across the slick floor... right past the whirly thing on the side of the floor scrubber and then—with a sickening crunch—underneath its back tire.

"No no no no no! My baby!" I screeched, running after the machine, which was dragging the carcass of my phone along inside it, leaving a trail of phone pieces stuck to the linoleum in its wake. "Stop! Halt immediately!"

But it was too late, and the floor scrubber guy drove on, blissfully unaware thanks to his noise-protecting ear-thingies.

I dropped to my knees like Demi in that scene from *Ghost*, gathering the remains of my darling, perfect, life-giving device in my tiny hands and cradling them tenderly.

"Oh, you were so young," I sobbed, squeezing my eyes shut. "You had so much left to give!"

Like... my payment app. And my email. And all my stored passwords for everything in my life.

I gasped. And Mason's phone number. And his address in my address book.

"I'm going to pinch myself," I whispered calmly. "And when I wake up, I will be on a plane over the Atlantic. I will ask the attendant for some electrolyte water, for clearly the martinis have caused me dehydration, which in turn caused this terrible fever dream in which the paparazzi have hunted me to Florida, and I am stranded here with no phone, no credit card, and a vomit-stained Armani sandal. I will repent henceforth and live a blameless life." I opened one eye and saw linoleum. I quickly closed it and added, "And I will give to charity. And... and not have sex for a week." Another quick peek and I offered desperately, "A month?"

But of course, no divine intervention happened. And by the time I'd counted out the cash in my wallet—a hundred twenty-seven dollars in small bills—I realized I probably had just enough cash to pay for a cab to Whispering Key, and literally no other options. I would throw myself on Mason's mercy, whether he liked it or not, because that's what friends were for.

I was proud that I remembered Mason lived on Bougainvillea Boulevard and I sort of remembered the address began with a 1. Or possibly a 3. But the place was tiny, right? Mason made it sound like a ghost town from the 1950s, so how hard would it be to find him?

As it turned out, it was much harder than expected, which was really the tagline for my life these days, and when I got a moment of free time, I was going to trademark it and put it on a T-shirt.

Bougainvillea Boulevard was long and winding enough to feature house numbers that started with both 1s and 3s, and Umar, my cab driver, was unamused when I asked him to drive me up and down the street—just to see if Mason was conveniently standing outside any of them, in the dark, as one does—even before the ridiculous fat raindrops started smacking the windshield, because fuck my life.

"It's gonna be coming down buckets any minute," Umar predicted. "You could call your friend and ask—" He winced, possibly remembering that my grief for my lost phone was very fresh, since he'd had to lend me his own phone a minute ago so I could figure out how to cancel my credit card. "Or maybe we could stop at one of these houses and a neighbor could direct you to your friend's house?"

I sighed. Only *I* would try recreating Hugh Grant's iconic scene in *Love, Actually* on a ghost-town tropical island in a fucking monsoon, but the meter was literally ticking me to the end of my cash reserves, and I couldn't think of anything better, so when Umar pulled over at the smallest house on the block, which coincidentally had the brightest porch light, I got out and ran up the path in the drenching rain to bang on the door.

It was thrown open almost immediately by a fiftyish man wearing a Pabst Blue Ribbon hat, a bathrobe, plaid boxer shorts, white athletic socks, and plastic sandals. It was, as they say, a lewk.

"Dang it, Lorenna, I said I'm not joinin' your fool— Oh. You're not Lorenna."

I smiled winningly. "No, sir, I'm not. I'm actually here to—"

"I didn't order any pizza." He narrowed his eyes. "Besides, you don't have a pizza."

"Good detective work there," I agreed. "I wanted to ask—"

"I'm not lookin' to find Jesus," he warned. "I'm real spiritual, but not religious."

I looked down at myself, not sure how I'd been mistaken for a missionary. In addition to my slightly odiferous Armani sandals, I wore a short-sleeved, pink button-down jumpsuit that ended at midthigh, and the closest I'd come to finding Jesus was when I blew a guy by that name at the Puerto Rican festival last month.

"I'm not trying to convert you," I assured him. "I just need to find Mason Bloom's house. Dr. Mason Bloom. I'm afraid I forgot the address—"

The man blinked, and his suspicion cleared. "Well, damn! You're a friend of Doc Mason? All you had to do was say so! I'm Littlejohn Jennings, but folks on the key call me LJ. You babysitting for Mason while he's gone? Last I heard, one of the Goodman boys was doing it."

I swallowed. "Gone" did not sound promising. Not at all. Neither did the rest of it. "Babysitting?"

"Babysitting the contractors tearin' up his house while he and Fenn are in New York this week." LJ chuckled. "No actual babies. Well, 'cept the baby Doc's sister delivered last week, of course, which is why they went up north for a visit now. That and his brother got married. So, Fenn and Mase are gonna meet the little one, and celebrate the wedding, and introduce Fenn to the whole family, and whatnot." He scratched his stomach idly, like we were making polite chitchat. "Say, did you know, New York is a city *and* a state?" He shook his head in disbelief. "Mason said he and Fenn won't see the Statue of Liberty at all from where they are. Crazy."

"Shocking," I agreed, slightly panicked.

Fact: I had no transportation, other than Umar, who was rightly impatient. I had no credit card. I had no phone. I had very little money. And there was no one I could call to obtain any of those things except Mason, because in my entire life there was no one else I trusted. But Mason was up with Micah and Constantine in O'Leary, and I had no way of getting there.

Also fact: my family—who were not really family anymore—wanted nothing to do with me. My friends back in the city—who were likewise not really friends—would sell me out in a heartbeat. It was almost enough to make a man start channeling Eponine and busting out an a capella *"On My Own"*... which indicated I was still more than a little hungover, damn it.

Aunt Hagatha would probably say something pithy, like "when you figure out you're in a hole, stop digging," but then Aunt Hagatha had never been stranded on a semi-inhabited island with no cell phone or credit card.

Until now.

"So." I cleared my throat. "Funny thing about me staying at Mason's house, Mr. Jennings. I don't, um, have a key to get in. I don't suppose..."

"Ah, don't worry about that! Tell your cabbie to scram, bring your bag in, and take a load off. *Wheel of Fortune*'s about to start, and it's your lucky day, 'cause I got some SpaghettiOs on the stove *and* Pizza Bites in the oven. Soon as the rain passes, I'll getcha sorted."

"Get me sorted." That could mean so many things, and none of them good.

As an occasional listener to true crime podcasts, I'd often wondered how the hell some victims wound up in the truly sketchy situations that led to their deaths. Did they have no sense of self-preservation? Surely there was *always* another option besides taking a shortcut down a dark alley... or being lured into a complete stranger's home with the promise of a canned pasta dinner, the likes of which I had not eaten since leaving my childhood home in Ohio. Yet, mortifyingly, my stomach growled, and Umar honked the horn behind me.

"SpaghettiOs with meatballs?" I asked hopefully.

"The best kind," LJ confirmed. "What'd you say your name was again?"

"T—uh, Ray," I said, supplying my middle name because cloak and dagger was really not my specialty.

"Trey," LJ repeated, like he was committing this to memory. "Welcome to Whispering Key."

2

BEALE

Czarina's StarCharts for Today
Poor Virgo! Your yearning to be understood holds you back from meaningful connection. Don't be shy—allow people access to the deeper levels of your emotions and accept help when it's offered!

"You want another lemon water, cutie?"

I looked up from checking my horoscope on my phone and found Blue Smoke's hot new bartender watching me. Again.

"Oh, uh... Yes, please." I smiled a little. "Thanks, Silvio."

"Or maybe I could interest you in something... *harder* this time?" Silvio peered up at me through his eyelashes, and he blushed a little, just in case I didn't get his double entendre. "I could drive you home, if you were worried about that. It'd be my pleasure."

The guy was really cute, with dark hair, sparkling eyes, and a lean, toned body. That, combined with the way he looked at me—like pandas look at bamboo, as if he wasn't sure whether he wanted to climb me or consume me—made it impossible not to feel a tiny tug of awareness, a little zing of attraction, but... that was all.

And it wasn't nearly enough.

"I'm good with water for now," I said with genuine regret. "But thank you."

Silvio's smile faded, but he shrugged like it was all the same to him. "Your loss."

"Definitely," I agreed.

Silvio's smile brightened again, and he rolled his eyes and filled my water glass before moving away.

"God, you're thick, Beale," the grumpy guy on the stool beside me leaned over and whispered. "He was totally coming on to you, and you didn't even notice."

"Hey! Of course I noticed," I told my brother as I slid my phone back into my pocket. "Look, contrary to popular opinion on Whispering Key, I am not totally unintelligent, okay? I recognize flirtation."

"So what's your problem?" Rafe demanded. "I'm not saying you need to fuck everything that moves, but there's such a thing as having too high a standard when it comes to hookups, you know?"

"So you've said." I sipped my water. "Many times. But I don't do hookups." Which I'd also told him many times.

"Yeah, but Silvio's seriously hot."

"I know."

"As in, out-of-your-league hot."

"I know that too." After all, Silvio was gorgeous and interesting, while I was the middle Goodman brother, the guy my cousin, Fenn, had once described as a cross between G.I. Joe and a Teletubby—probably the red Teletubby, or whichever was the gay one—and whose height was generally considered bigger than his IQ.

"And did you see his ass in those pants?"

"I definitely saw his ass." It was, objectively, an incredibly nice ass. I was not unmoved by it.

"And that doesn't qualify for an exception to your self-imposed celibacy? God, back in the day, if a guy like that flirted with me, I'd have had him out back so fast I—"

"Lemme stop you right there. Rafael, I love you, but please don't make me take a stroll down Bisexual Memory Lane," I pleaded. "I do *not* wanna get a visual of what you'd've done out back."

Rafe laughed out loud, and it made him look years younger. He'd been doing that more and more often over the past few weeks since we'd found the Whispering Key treasure—laughing, flirting, showing off his dimpled smile, acting carefree—and I hadn't truly understood how much responsibility and resentment he'd been carrying, trying to keep our family afloat, until I saw him smile again. "But we're brothers, Beale. Aren't we supposed to tell each other everything?"

"Nope." I lowered my voice. "Especially not when Dale Jennings is two stools down from you, ready to overshare about his favorite sex positions and offer us some of his *ferrymone* supplements—" I tilted my chin toward the beer-bellied older man currently cussing out Pat Sajak and the contestants on *Wheel of Fortune*. "—and Mrs. McKetcham's at the table behind us, ready to offer me a condom-rolling demonstration and a lecture on safe sex." I flicked my head behind me, at Whispering Key's favorite sex-positive octogenarian, Lorenna McKetcham, who sat with my old kindergarten teacher, Ms. Pepper, and the rest of the Whispering Key Mahjong Society, enjoying their monthly Mahjong and Margaritas Night.

I hadn't looked at Ms. McKetcham the same since Doc Mason told me how she'd decimated the condom stash at his medical clinic and invited him to her swingers group.

"Besides," I continued, "would you really wanna hear about *my* sexual experiences?"

Rafe narrowed his eyes for 0.5 seconds like he was thinking about it, then shook his head vehemently. "Shit, no. You're absolutely right. I don't need to stroll down Gay Boy Alley."

I nodded firmly.

And it was just as well since my end of Gay Boy Alley looked like one of those towns in the old westerns Grandma Goodman used to watch—nothing around but ghosts and tumbleweeds, especially for the last few years—not that I was going to tell my brother that. In fact, I occasionally pretended I'd gone on a date or two, just to throw him off.

Rafe already thought I was ridiculous for being too picky; if he knew the truth—that I was a virgin—he'd probably have me committed.

"But just to say," Rafe went on, like the Taurus he was, "if you were gonna cut yourself a break and have some no-holds-barred monkey sex, now would be the time to do it."

"Why? Is the world ending and I wasn't told?"

"No, dumbass. Because you've finally moved out of Dad's place."

Oh, that.

"Temporarily," I reminded him. "Crashing in someone's guest bed for a few weeks while Dad's tearing down walls and redoing the house isn't like actually moving out. Oh, but speaking of—" I dug his keys out of my pocket and slapped them on the counter. "Thanks for loaning me your shiny new truck so I could haul my shit. I promise, I didn't stop for a single injured possum, though I was sorely tempted."

"I appreciate your restraint." He got out my car keys—the keys to the old, beaten-up Jeep he'd passed down to me when he upgraded—and exchanged them. "Did you get all moved in?"

"Sort of? My boxes are stacked in the closet. Couple things in the kitchen cabinets. Haven't gotten the crystals out yet, 'cause I didn't want Marjorie breaking them in a fit of anger."

"Satan's feline hell muppet," Rafe said with a little shudder. "I hope your cat behaves herself while you're staying there."

"Of course she will," I said loyally. "She's perfectly behaved. She just takes a minute to adjust to new situations. And settings. And... people."

"Can't think who she reminds me of," Rafe said blandly.

I rolled my eyes. He wasn't wrong, though.

"Seriously, though, this move will be the best thing for you," Rafe predicted. "I know it's temporary, but it's not like there's any hurry for you to move back when Dad's house is redone. You're twenty-eight, Beale. I know you're a creature of habit, but you're gonna enjoy having some privacy. Dad and Gloria have only been with me for six hours so far, and I already called you to meet me here just so I could get out of the house. They're very... loved up, aren't they?"

I snorted. "That's one way of putting it." For Rafe's sake, I was hoping our dad and his fiancée would remember to be a little more chill about their sexual exploits while they were staying with Rafe. Or at least a little quieter.

"It *is* weird, though, I'll grant you." Rafe twirled his beer bottle on the bar top.

"What, Dad having a fiancée?"

It had been three years since our mom died, and in some ways it felt like three very long years—three whole *lifetimes* —but other times I picked up my phone to text her and remembered I couldn't.

Rafe pursed his lips and shook his head. "Nah, not that. Or not *only* that. I meant the way everything is changing all at once. Us finding the Whispering Key treasure and finally having money for a change. Dad getting remarried and renovating the whole house so he can give Gloria the craft palace of her dreams. Fenn and Mason falling in love and moving in together, then tearing up *their* house. Which begs the question, what is it about love that makes some people wanna do home renovations?"

I laughed. "I wouldn't know."

"Yeah. Well. Me neither, apparently." He smiled, but the smile looked forced, and I winced.

"Do you wanna talk about—?"

"Aimee leaving me?" He shook his head again as the *Jeopardy!* theme song began to play from the television over the bar. "Oooh, I'll take 'Not just no, but hell no' for a thousand, Alex. Besides, that's old news."

"But I thought we were *brothers*," I teased. "I thought we were supposed to tell each other everything."

"*Your* everything," Rafe clarified. "Not *my* everything. Older brother's privilege."

"Hmm. That sounds suspiciously like bullshit."

"I don't make the rules, Beale," he said mock-seriously. "The Universe does, and I am merely a pawn at her mercy. Isn't that what Mom used to say?"

"I'm sure that's what you *heard*." I rolled my eyes again, because I knew he was teasing... mostly. But beneath the bar, I ran my hand over the bracelet of protective stones I'd worn every day since my mom had given it to me four years ago. As always, feeling the cool lapis lazuli, moonstone, and sapphire beads under my fingers centered me.

Despite the fact that we'd all grown up side by side, I was the only one of Mary Goodman's three sons to understand her view of the Universe—to understand how energy flowed around us and connected all living and nonliving things, to believe that energy could be seen, and felt, and changed, and predicted, to know we were all intended for a higher purpose.

I believed we had to visualize the future we wanted, and trust that the Universe would manifest it for us. My younger brother, Gage, meanwhile, tended to be pretty skeptical of anything he couldn't logic his way around, and Rafe... well, Rafe thought if you didn't Hulk-smash your way to happiness, you were cheating somehow.

"You'll know the right paths when they're revealed, honey," Mom had said the day she put the bracelet on my wrist. "The Universe will guide you to the things that are meant for you. You'll see the signs. Don't settle for less." I'd promised her I wouldn't. And every time I looked down at the bracelet, I reminded myself of that promise.

"And speaking of thinking we're pawns at the mercy of the Universe—"

"Were we speaking of that?" I shook my head. "'Cause I don't recall—"

"—when do fall classes at the community college start?"

I blew out a breath. "I don't know, and I haven't decided whether I care or not."

"Uh-huh."

"It doesn't feel right," I insisted. "Not at this moment. Besides, I have plenty to do. I volunteer at the Nature Center and with Fish and Wildlife. I still do boat tours with Dad. I'm not unhappy! And look, I know you and Gage operate differently than I do. You determine the right thing logically, and then it feels right because you *decided* it's right.

But that's not my way, okay? I wait to see if it *feels* right, and then I know it *is*, even if it's not logical. And that's the way I work, whether you're talking about me going to college, or buying a house"—one of Rafe's other favorite things to nag me about—"or dating a guy. I'm not gonna settle for something that's not right, just because it makes *you* antsy." I nodded once, with a confidence I didn't feel, and caught sight of the question on the television. "The answer is Vienna, Alex!"

Predictably, Rafe turned to glance at the television to check my accuracy. "Nope, Salzburg." He turned back to me and wiggled his eyebrows. "No matter how *right* Vienna might feel."

I laughed. "You were the one pointing out that everything is changing. I don't think there's a damn thing wrong with waiting until the dust clears to make some big life choices."

"Just don't wait too long. Remember, there's only so much you can control, Beale. I know the easiest way to prevent yourself from getting hurt is to not act... but then you're not really living either."

I shook my head sadly. "Man, the whole point is that I'm *not* controlling it. I'm open to the messages I'm getting from the Universe, and I believe there's a great future out there for me. I wish I could make you believe that. The answer's ligament," I told the television.

Rafe turned for half a second. "Tendon," he corrected.

"Know-it-all," I muttered, bumping my shoulder into his.

"Not *all*. Just most." He gave me a one-sided grin. "I wish I could make *you* believe *that*."

"Uh-huh." I sipped water and assessed him—his tired eyes, the strain of his muscles. "And this advice about not missing out on life. You've applied this to yourself?"

"Once again, we're discussing you and not me." Rafe finished his beer and set his bottle down with a hollow thunk, then motioned to Silvio for a second one.

I whistled. "More big-brother privilege? Shit. Wait until Gage comes home for the weekend and hears about my new rules."

"Dork." But after a sip of his fresh beer, he continued relentlessly, "Okay, now just think about this for a second…"

I stifled a sigh.

"You wouldn't know if pizza was right for you if you never knew it existed, right? So how can you possibly decide that college isn't for you if you don't try? How can you decide you weren't—" Rafe hesitated, then finished like the word caused him physical pain "—*destined* for a career in real estate, if you've never explored it?"

"The same way I know I'm gay even though I've never had sex with a woman. There's zero appeal there, Rafe. And I told you, I'm happy—"

"But volunteering at the Nature Center's not a career, Beale. It's a hobby." He swiped at the condensation on the side of his beer bottle. "You know, the life you want isn't going to break into your house at night, hide under your blankets, and wait for you to find it. At the very least, you have to get out and live a little, try some new things."

I opened my mouth instinctively to protest, then narrowed my eyes.

I was used to him being dismissive. I wasn't used to him being persuasive. "As much as I hate to admit it, the words you're speaking... make a certain sort of sense. For once."

Rafe snorted. "I like to change it up every so often, just to keep you on your toes. I won't let it go to my head." He clapped his hands once, then rubbed his palms together. "So, I think what you need to do is have a party. Invite a nice guy or two. See where things go."

I stared at him in concern. "Okay, I take it back. You're making zero sense again. Clearly one good piece of advice is your limit for the year."

"I'm being serious."

"I know you are! That's what's so funny. Sure, I'll throw a party, Rafe. Then I'll stand in my underwear in front of all the guests, just like the *other* half of my recurring nightmare. Solid plan. 'Dear Aunt Hagatha, my brother's lost touch with reality. What should I do?'" I rolled my eyes. "I have no idea how we got back on the subject of my sex life. Let's go back to me taking a class. Or, like, auditing a class, maybe. That'd be—"

"A party," Rafe insisted, folding his arms over his chest. "The more I think about it, the more I like it. Why *not* start there? If you want to find your one true *destined* love, you're gonna need to meet more guys."

Wait, what? "Meet guys? For what?"

"For playing checkers, Beale." He shook his head like he doubted my mental stability. "To see if you're compatible, obviously."

I laughed again, a wheezing, desperate sound. "You're out of your goddamn mind. That's not how it works. And I am *not* throwing a party," I said way too loudly.

"Party? Who's having a party?" Dale asked loudly.

"No one." I gave Rafe a challenging look.

"I'm not saying a *rave*." Rafe lowered his voice and rolled his dark eyes like I was the one being unreasonable. "I'm suggesting you have a small, intimate get-together with a couple folks you're comfortable with. Fenn and Mason, me, Gage, Taffy, Maddie. You. Silvio. A select few of my gay friends—six, eight, maybe ten—"

"Ten!"

"We'll see how it goes! Then, once you've met them all, you wait and see which one the Universe *vibrates* for you, or however the heck it works, and boom. Eternal happiness." He drew a circle in the air with both hands. "How silly would you feel if you just haven't been trying hard enough all this time and let something special get away?"

"But—"

Rafe tilted his head toward Silvio significantly, and my eyes slid in that direction. I bit my lip. The guy was really good-looking. Small and slender, with high cheekbones and a tip-tilted nose, and I was a sucker for a man with intelligent eyes... but I didn't feel any kind of connection to him.

Not a single whisper from the Universe.

Dead radio silence.

"No," I whisper-hissed. "I told you, I'm not into Silvio. For real, for real. And you're making it sound like some weird

Bachelor thing, where I meet a bunch of gay dudes and pick one lucky guy to fall for." I made a fake-vomit noise.

"I mean—"

"Plus," I continued in that same voice, "recall please that even if I somehow lost my mind and agreed, I don't own a house where I can throw a party! Dad's house is under construction, so is Fenn and Mason's, and yours is gonna be full since Dad and Gloria are staying there. The more I think about it, the worse this sounds." I tried to adopt his authoritative tone, but it didn't seem to work.

"What if you have the party at Mason and Fenn's! They gave you the key."

I tilted my head to one side. "Because I'm staying there to keep an eye on the contractors while they're out of town and so I don't have to pile into your house while Dad's house is getting fixed, not so I can have a party."

"Or maybe it's because it's *destiny*!" Rafe said excitedly. "You can have the party in the yard by the pool."

"No, I could *not*."

"Wait, I know! You can make it a surprise *for them*, for the day they get home! A 'Congrats on Shacking Up' party, to celebrate them cohabitating—"

"Think they call that a housewarmin'. I'm down!" Dale shouted so loudly that people on both sides of him flinched.

"The man has superhuman hearing," Rafe muttered.

Dale yelled out to the bar in general, "I got a friend who makes toilet covers outta seashells and resin! Doc Mason'll love 'em. Really liven their place up. Who wants to go in on a set with me for the housewarmin' party?"

"Me 'n' Tammy," Mac Horne pronounced from the corner where he and a bunch of other bikers had congregated. "The Stallions MC'll bring a keg to the party. Doc Mason was real helpful when Bobo burned his leg the other week."

A blond guy wearing a patch on his leather vest that read "Bobo" lifted a beer in salute, and a couple of brothers made noises of agreement.

"I can bring a pasta salad!" Lorenna McKetcham called from a table just behind us. I turned to find the rest of the Mahjong Society nodding excitedly. "And Bernie'll do her thing with her ambrosia! And Sosie makes a punch so strong you'll be giving us ladies a second look, Beale!" She lowered her voice and added as an aside, "Not really, Sosie. Sexuality doesn't work like that, so don't get all excited." In her loud voice, she said, "D'you know if they're registered anywhere, boys? Or maybe I'll just make them a condom wreath! Those are always a hit. But get back to me, okay?"

I gave her a taut smile and raised an eyebrow at Rafe, who grimaced.

There was no such thing as a small, intimate gathering on Whispering Key. If there was a party, the whole circus showed up.

"Silvio!" Dale called. "You down for Beale's party?"

I widened my eyes and shook my head vehemently at Rafe, demanding that he do something about it, but he shrugged.

"Party?" Silvio asked. He looked up from the drinks he was

prepping and gave me a quick smile before disappearing to the other end of the bar. "I'd love to."

"I'll make sure you're added to the Facebook group," Dale told him with a nod. "Hey, Mac, you boys got a Facebook?" He hopped off his stool to go plan a nonexistent party with a bunch of bikers, and I ran a hand over my face with a groan.

"You need to make this stop, Rafe."

"Or maybe you need to go with the flow," he countered.

I peered at him. "Who are you, and what have you done with my control-freak brother?"

"Come on. Isn't your whole Universe-thing about being open to possibilities? To finding your *soul mate*?"

I shook my head. "Don't joke about that."

My soul mate, when he found me, was going to be sweet and, I imagined, a little shy. Possibly, but not necessarily, a virgin like me. Almost definitely a Capricorn, to be compatible with my Virgo traits. The sort of person more interested in waking up early to take the boat out and watch the sunrise than in catching it on his way to bed after a night of dancing. In short, the patient, careful, thoughtful lover I'd been waiting for.

And I wouldn't have to go way outside my comfort zone to find him, because that was the antithesis of what a soul mate was.

"I'm very open to finding my soul mate, Rafael. I— ah, *crap*," I muttered, pushing off the stool. "My bracelet!"

I'd been worrying my fingers over the beads, when suddenly the bracelet was gone and my wrist was naked. I must have flicked the clasp open somehow, but that had literally never happened in the four years I'd worn it.

I dropped to my hands and knees to search for it in the dim light.

"Hey, Rafe!" Dale called. "Take a gander at the television. Don't that look like—?"

"No one," Rafe said firmly a short while later. "It looks like no one. I have no idea who that is." Which was funny since he prided himself on knowing every freakin' answer to every freakin' question Alex Trebek asked.

"Silvio, turn up the volume? I'm tellin' ya, the guy looks an awful lot like—" Dale sounded bewildered.

"I think I'd know if that looked like someone I knew," Rafe insisted, a little louder and a lot more strained than usual.

"Beale!" Dale yelled. "Get up here and look at this CelebTV Breaking News thing. I can't hear who it's s'posed to be, but this guy's the spittin' image of Rafe's brother-in-law."

Oh, jeez. No wonder Rafe sounded annoyed. Aimee's brother ranked slightly above Aimee herself on Rafe's List of Shit That Would Not Be Discussed.

"Busy," I called.

I patted around the very sticky floor but couldn't feel anything, and it was way too dark to see. What I did find was that, although my standards of cleanliness might be low, Blu Smoke's were lower.

I pulled my phone from my pocket and turned on the flashlight.

"Jayd Rollins is *not* my brother-in-law anymore, Dale. And that's not him, anyway."

"But Rafe—"

"Leather pants look the same on everyone!"

I ran my flashlight beam over the wood floor, even patting under Rafe's stool, but my bracelet was nowhere to be found. It was like it had just... disappeared.

I blew out a breath.

"Beale!" Dale insisted again.

"Fuck," I muttered. I nearly brained myself on the underside of the bar, and I had bigger fish to fry than spotting some lookalike of Rafe's ex-wife's brother. "Still kinda busy here, Dale. Rafe, come help me look for my bracelet?"

But even with Rafe using his phone flashlight, too, and crawling around on the floor alongside me, my bracelet was nowhere to be found.

"Cheer up," Rafe said distractedly as we left the bar a little while later. "Silvio said he'd keep an eye out for it. And maybe it'll shake out of your clothes when you get home."

I glanced down at my T-shirt, cargo pants, and boots and patted my pants pockets just in case. *Nada.*

I didn't have a lot of possessions I cared about—a few books, a couple of bigger crystals, some photo albums— but this bracelet was special. It was more than just a bracelet of protective stones; it felt like a connection to my future. And while I wasn't foolish enough to think I was cursed without it or anything, not having it made me feel sort of lost.

I didn't like it.

When I pulled into the driveway outside Mason and Fenn's place up in the Heights, I was in a full-on mope, which was totally unlike me. I sat in the Jeep in the driveway, staring up at the house for a long minute.

Outside, the house looked the same as it had a couple weeks ago when they bought it—two stories of buttery stucco with a tower in front that glowed in the moonlight like an Italian building that had survived a renaissance or two.

Rafe and our dad, Big Rafe, had given Fenn a generous helping of shit over the giant fountain burbling in the center of the semicircular driveway, since Fenn was not generally a fountain-owning sort of person. But Mason's entire being had been so purely happy, I was pretty sure even Fenn had felt it, and he hadn't found one single fuck to give over their teasing.

Honestly, I wouldn't have either. From the second floor of the tower, you could see east, past the waters of the intra-coastal waterway to the mainland, and west over the Gulf to the horizon. Around back, a bougainvillea arbor led to a giant pool and guesthouse. Let people tease if they wanted to, but Mason and Fenn had invested part of their treasure windfall into buying themselves a *castle*. They were living the dream here.

Or they would be, once the inside of the house was as beautiful as the outside.

I took a quick peek in the windows from the porch and verified that the contractors had left everything in good shape for the weekend, and then I wandered under the bougainvillea to their huge backyard. I threw myself down on a lounge chair near the pool and stared at the underwater lights, thinking.

Earlier, when I'd gotten the house keys from Mason, he'd been stressed out about the renovations—understandable, since every floor in his precious house had been stripped down to the subfloor, with the remains thrown in a dumpster in the side yard—stressed about leaving his practice so soon after moving the clinic to a new building, and stressed about having Fenn meet his family.

I'd tried to talk him down, but it was like he couldn't hear a word I said. I'd told him, "I've got the house under control. Taffy's running the clinic. Everything's gonna be fine!" But he'd paced up and down the echoing, empty front hall and stared at me like I was speaking Klingon. I could almost see the intensity of his brain waves spiraling up a notch.

Then Fenn had come downstairs with their suitcase, dressed nicer than I'd ever seen him. He'd taken one look at Mason's anxious face, grabbed him around the waist with no preamble, and twirled him in a half circle, ignoring Mason's protests.

"Remind me, Loafers. Is tonight the night we visit your old high school and recreate your swan dive into history, or is that tomorrow?"

I'd had no clue what he was talking about, but it was clear Mason did, because he'd gotten that super-severe look he got when he was trying not to laugh at Fenn's bullshit. He'd pushed half-heartedly at Fenn's chest. "That's never. Tonight we meet my sisters. And my nephew." He blew out a nervous breath. "You have the things for the girls, right?"

"Packed in the suitcase," he'd confirmed. "It's like a unicorn threw up in there. Competition for best bonus uncle will be fierce, but Constantine's no match for my shock-and-awe campaign. He's going down."

Mason had burst out laughing, burying his face in Fenn's collarbone, and when he'd emerged a minute later, he'd looked more like his usual calm, level self.

"Love you," Mason had said looking Fenn dead in the eyes, casual but not.

"Love *you*," Fenn had replied, and if you'd known the man even half as long as I had, you'd understand why I almost felt like I wanted to cry, I was so genuinely happy for him. Fenn and Mason were halves of a single unit, consciously vibrating at the same frequency. No one, except maybe Rafe, could look at them and not believe that a benevolent Universe had meant for them to be together. No one could believe there wasn't a soul mate, a perfect complement, out there for each of us.

Even if sometimes we got impatient, waiting for it.

Even if sometimes we sort of worried that the Universe had forgotten us.

I clasped my hand over my wrist where my bracelet used to rest and felt that pang of emptiness I'd felt earlier at the bar. "Please make it soon," I whispered.

The only reply was the gurgle of the water in the pool and the chattering of the night insects in the trees, so I sighed and made my way to my temporary home for the next week.

I'd accidentally left the kitchen light on earlier, but the living room was cool and tidy, apart from a couple of boxes tucked in the corner. It even smelled like expensive air freshener I didn't recall smelling earlier, and just inhaling that sweet, spicy fragrance, I felt my whole mood shift back into the right alignment.

How fucking lucky was I? To be here on this island, the most beautiful place in the world, with a roof over my head?

Somewhere in this room or in the little bedroom beyond, the only female in my life was hiding—probably under the sofa or under the bed, or maybe directly on top of the pillows and blankets I'd left stacked on the bed—ready to pee and hiss and claw the world to shit if I turned on the light, 'cause Marjorie was amusingly vampirish like that. Tomorrow, I'd get to wake up and do the volunteer work I loved—work that was important, and at some point I'd see my brothers or my dad, since it was impossible not to when you all lived on an island as small as Whispering Key.

The truth was, there were a billion people in the world who'd trade places with me right now. I was young and healthy, and my bank balance was a beautiful thing. I had important volunteer work I was doing at the Nature Center, even if Rafe believed that wasn't real or important. I was *grateful*. And I believed the rest would come in time.

I made my way into the bedroom, stripped out of my boots and clothes in the darkness, and ran my hand over the bed before I lay on it to be sure I wasn't squashing Marjorie. I left the rest of my bedding in the center of the mattress and curled up with just a pillow and blanket on top of the covers, and then I let myself drift.

In the perfect future I visualized, I walked along the beach with the wind whipping around me, hand in hand with the man I loved. I couldn't see his face, but I didn't need to, because I knew everything about him that I needed to know. He was incredibly kind. He loved me unreservedly. He adored animals, peace and quiet, and simplicity. He never pushed me to talk. He never rushed me. He was patient when it came to sex and let things develop really slowly.

And he was out there waiting for me, I thought as my brain finally wound down and I fell asleep, somewhere just beyond my reach.

3

TOBY

Help Me Hagatha (Issue #2399)

Dear Aunt Hagatha:

My sweet little girl is a senior in high school, and she insists on applying to colleges that are way above her league academically. She's done pretty well in our small-town school, but maybe my wife and I have expressed our pride a little too strongly. Sending her off to the Ivy League would be like sending a Chihuahua to live with wolves. How can we rein in her ambition just enough to prevent her from getting hurt?

Protective in Palmyra

Dear Protective,

Life hurts. What hurts worse is a parent who tries to hold you back because of their own fears.

Also, Auntie's not an animal expert by any means, but a quick google shows that Chihuahuas and wolves share 99.9% of their DNA, so if she tells you she's fierce, believe her.

Best of luck,
Auntie H.

———

I was having that dream—you know, the one where you're in the middle of the Roman Colosseum in a fight to the death, except the fight is more of a *RuPaul's Drag Race* Lip-sync for Your Life, and you arrive like Britney Spears doing "*Slave 4U*" at the VMAs, with the tiger in the cage and a giant snake around your neck, but you've somehow, impossibly, forgotten the words to the chorus? Yeah, that one—and I was so disoriented that when I woke up to a weight on my stomach and bright yellow eyes glinting at me through the darkness, I had a moment where I said to myself, "Oh, it's just the tiger," and closed my eyes again.

A second later, my entire body locked down and my heart raced. Holy shit. A *tiger*?

I was no stranger to waking up bewildered in strange beds, and I was pretty good at getting calm, assessing my surroundings, and then extricating myself silently, but I had to admit, the possibility of being mauled added a whole new level of danger to the proceedings, not least because I was lying on my back, buck naked except for a sheet, and the animal was perched directly on top of my cock and balls.

I looked left, and in the very dim moonlight filtering through some wooden blinds, I saw a nightstand but no phone.

I looked right and saw nothing but pillows and blankets.

I looked up and saw a ceiling fan… and that's when I remembered: Whispering Key, Mason, the Zamboni that ate my phone, Littlejohn Jennings "getting me sorted."

Damn it all.

"Dear Lord, I'm being murdered by a tiger," I whisper-prayed, squeezing my eyes shut. "While I appreciate the Carole Baskin homage and the inherent drama of the scene, honestly haven't I been through enough?"

The feline on my crotch did not think so, if the multiple needle-sharp jabs into my hips were anything to go by.

"Hey," I hissed, pissed off. "Enough. This is unacceptable."

I opened my eyes and stared down the animal, who was still watching me without blinking. It was not a tiger, it was a cat. A tiny, domesticated animal that was more scared of me than I was of it.

I mean, probably. It didn't look particularly afraid.

"Shoo!" I hissed, but it did not shoo.

"Go away!" I insisted, waving a hand, but it did not go, and in fact, it looked at my hand the way I looked at muffins—like something forbidden and delicious.

Aunt Hagatha would probably tell me to befriend the beast, but Aunt Hagatha had never been the innocent victim of a nocturnal feline home invasion.

Until now.

"Get *off*." I attempted to move my leg, but at my first twitch, the creature emitted a long, high-pitched growl like a chainsaw revving, and my hindbrain curled up in the fetal position.

I hid my hand under the sheet and mentally riffled through everything I ever knew about cats, which took one second, since I'd never had one. Were you supposed to make eye contact or avoid it? Should I show my dominance by just pushing him off me? How bad could it be?

The cat sank its claws deeper into the flesh on my hips and thighs like it could read my mind.

I fucking *hated* Florida.

"Unacceptablllllle!" I screeched.

I hated Florida even more when a loud crash on the other side of the room shook the bed and a giant human shape materialized in the shadows at my feet.

"Go away! I have no money! I have no credit cards! I don't even have a phone!"

A second later, a flashlight beam pierced the darkness and illuminated my crotch and the enormous ginger floof perched there with murder in her eyes.

"Gah!" I shouted as the cat hissed and swiped just below my belly button, and my dick shrank in on itself like a turtle—like a very large, virile, but startled turtle. "Get away!"

"Marjorie!" a deep, bewildered voice said. The light swung to my face. "Wait, who're you?"

"I'm not Marjorie! Don't kill me!"

"I'm not gonna kill you," he said, which was exactly what he would say if he were going to kill me. And holy shit, how had I avoided being murdered at the hand of Littlejohn Jennings—a man who might make a mean can of Spaghet-tiOs but was irredeemably hopeless at *Wheel of Fortune*, judging by the letters he kept screaming at Pat Sajak—only to be slaughtered by Paul Bunyan hours later?

"Marjorie is the cat," the giant continued in a deep, soothing voice. "My cat."

But his voice seemed to upset the creature, who was kneading her claws into my abs like they were dough—by which I mean rock-hard, muscular dough, obviously—and that reminded me I had no reason to trust this intruder and every reason not to.

"Do you always bring your cat when you break in to murder people? Is she trained for this? Have you trained a murder cat? Oh my God, Florida, why?"

The giant snorted—fucking *snorted*, like this was at all, in any way, *amusing.* "Murder cat," he repeated. "Rafe will appreciate that."

"Oh, goody. Glad I could amuse someone as I shuffle off my mortal coil. I won't have died in vain." I huffed. "Get it off me! Get it off, get it off!"

The cat made a noise like a cross between a hiss and a smok-er's cough. It was bizarrely terrifying, and I shut my eyes again.

"Oh, God. When they talk about my murder on the true crime podcasts, they'll mention that I haven't had a really good fuck in months. Everyone will pity me. Unacceptable."

"Hush! You're agitating her," the giant chided.

My eyes popped open, and I glared through the darkness. "*She* is agitating *me*! Do penis wounds bleed out quickly? I'd think they would. Lots of blood flow."

"Thank the Universe, I wouldn't know." Gigantor shuddered. "You're being really dramatic. Would you like my help or not?"

I wanted very badly to say *not*, and tell this intruder, whoever the hell he was, to fuck off with his help, but I owed it to myself and the single gay male population of New York to remain dick-us intactus even more. Still, relying on someone else made me tetchy, as my grandma used to say.

"Is *not* an option to you? Really? You'd just walk back out the door and pretend your cat's not devouring my naked flesh?" I could sense him watching me steadily, and it pissed me off that he could see me, but all I could see of him was a huge shape in the darkness. I finally blew out a breath. "Fine. Yes. I would appreciate your assistance in getting your murder cat off my dick."

"Still not a murder cat," he said easily, which was not the point at all.

He moved around the foot of the bed to stand near my hip, blocking out even the weak light from the window, and focused the flashlight on the cat.

"Can you turn the light on?" My voice sounded quavery, and I hated it. Hated just waiting to be rescued. I cleared my throat. "Please. I can't see anything."

"She hates when I turn the light on. She really *would* be a murder cat, then." The giant hesitated, then held out the hand with the flashlight—which turned out to be his cell phone. "Just hold this so I can see what I'm doing, 'kay? And don't shine it in her eyes."

I nodded silently, and I wasn't sure he could see, but he seemed to understand.

I could not think of a single life experience more lowering than this. Hunted by paparazzi to the wilds of Florida, abandoned and alone, attacked by a house cat, forced to accept help from an intruder... though, yeah, an intruder who'd given me his cell phone, so maybe not even a very *good* intruder. I wondered where my life had gone wrong.

"No more VIP parties," I swore. "No more parties at all."

"Wanna play fetch, Marjorie?" The guy reached out a hand and petted the cat, who batted his hand away. "Let's go for a walk?"

She pointedly ignored him and clawed me.

"*Eeep.*" I cleared my throat. "Um. Not to tell you how to do your job, but fetch is for dogs. Are you sure she's yours?"

"Know a lot about murder cats, do you?" he asked in that same mild voice.

He reached for the edge of the sheet, and the cat hiss-coughed again. I shuddered.

"I'm just saying—" My voice was mortifyingly high. "If you could maybe find her a mouse to chase or a bowl of cream to eat before she de-peni-fies me, that would be great."

The guy gave me a stern glare I could sense more than see. "I'm tryna make sure she doesn't de-peni-fy either of us. Now, hush and let me do this."

"Excuse me? I am not your servant. I will not hush. I will continue to—" I moved the flashlight to get a better look at the guy and shut my mouth with a clack because *holy shit*, it seemed the rescue-intruder was naked also.

What the hell? Did he run around naked with his cat, invading people's homes? Was that a *thing* in Florida? Or had Mason left out important details about life on this little island?

First things first, I reminded myself sternly. When the bomb squad rolled up to defuse your bomb, you didn't ogle them or wonder why they were in the neighborhood. To be fair, I was pretty sure they didn't generally show up naked, though, and they sure as fuck never looked like this guy did.

He was tall—and not just tall, honey, I mean *taaaalllll*—and beefy, but not like those gym rat muscle daddies who were so swole one wondered how they could bend their arms far enough to brush their own teeth. Maybe it was because this guy's shoulders were wide enough to accommodate his pectoral muscles. Maybe it was because his thighs were so tree-trunky. Who cared? Everything about him was perfectly, wonderfully... proportional.

Which naturally made a person—*me*—wonder how proportional his other... proportions were. Right? If I were about to bleed out from a dick wound, I figured I deserved one last glimpse of a cock besides my own, especially since it was the intruder's fault I was about to be a murder victim anyway. I casually nudged the beam of light closer to his waist, just in case this might be my last chance on earth to catch a glimpse, and—

"... your penis," the guy concluded in that same deep voice.

I fumbled the phone and caught it again. "Sorry, what?"

"I said, stop looking at me and put the light on the cat if you want me to move her before she claws off your penis." He sounded annoyed now. No longer mild. "Or mine."

Ooops. Busted.

"But remember not to shine it in her eyes."

"I was just trying to get a good look at you so I could identify you," I sniffed as I obeyed. "When I report this incident to the police."

"Me? I'm not the one who... Wait. How would that even work? You're going to put my dick in a lineup?"

"Hardly," I said haughtily, but I was momentarily caught by the idea of me saying, "I just don't know for sure, Officer. Can you make them all turn for me again?" and I snickered.

"Is this funny?" the guy demanded.

"No! And I didn't even see anything." I sounded pouty. I *was* pouty. But in my defense, these were trying circumstances, and I was not at my best.

The giant sighed. "Okay. On the count of three, I'm going to reach my hands under the sheet and lift her off you, to minimize damage. You ready?"

"Under the sheet."

"Yes."

"Where my junk is."

"Yes."

"So it's okay for you to touch my junk, but I can't even see yours?"

"That—" The guy broke off and ran a hand through his hair, and a blush stained his high cheekbones. "It's not like I want to—Jesus Christ. Not everything in the universe revolves around your... your... junk!"

"Pardon you? Everything in *my* universe does!" I huffed right back.

"If you're feeling uncomfortable—"

"Of course I'm uncomfortable! Each of her claws is creating a separate and uniquely painful incision mere inches from my very best feature, and I'm relying on *you,* a perfect stranger, to save me."

"If you'd rather take care of this yourself, feel free, as long as you don't hurt her. Or you could wait. She'll be hungry soon."

"Hungry?" I gasped, and the bastard intruder snort-laughed. Somehow, even that sounded sexy.

"I meant hungry for her food, which she'd have to leave to eat." He shook his head. "You're really funny, you know?"

"Obviously. Men are dying to get me naked just so they can compliment my sense of humor." I squeezed my eyes shut. I'd have been so much better off in the Maldives. "I'll just lie here, then. And trust you. To handle me gently." I gripped the phone tightly.

The guy shook his head again. "Count of three. One—"

"Just to say, you wouldn't have such sangfroid if it were *your* pleasure sword on the line," I sniffed.

"Two—" His hands were large and rough where they slid over my stomach and leg, and I shivered.

"If asked, please tell the true crime podcast people I died bravely!" I squeaked. "And don't give the tabloids any details!"

"Three."

He lifted the cat and the sheet in one smooth motion, and I curled my legs up to my chest and screeched. The cat exploded into movement, screaming like something out of a nightmare, before she jumped out of his arms like *she* was the victim in this scenario and disappeared.

"Is she gone?" I whispered, moving the flashlight around the room.

"Yes. And not happy about it." He flipped on the light in the corner by the window and peered over the far side of the bed near the door. "Poor baby. She's probably petrified."

"Poor baby? *Her*? What about *me*?"

"Yes, what about you?" The guy's voice hardened, and he folded his arms over his chest to stare down at me. "Who the hell are you, and why are you here?"

I wish I could say I was immediately restored to sanity by his tone and used the phone he'd handed me to do something intelligent like call the police, but that would be a lie, because adrenaline was flooding my system and... did I mention he was tall? And fucking hot? Because he really, really was.

He had floppy gold-brown hair in need of a haircut, bristle on his jaw that was halfway between scruff and full-on-mountain-man, and freckles. His eyes were deep cerulean blue, and the happiest happy trail I'd ever encountered—and it must be said, I'd followed a lot of trails—led down to a cock that was...

"Holy Mary, mother of God," I breathed. Every size-queen fantasy I'd ever had suddenly seemed tame in light of what I now knew was humanly possible.

I licked my lips.

"Excuse me!" The giant said, reaching down a hand—and forearm—to protect his modesty. "Eyes up here! And could you..." He waved his other hand at me. "Cover yourself?" I'd swear he was—oh my God, he actually *was!*—blushing as he said it.

What kind of unicorn home invader was hung like a horse and blushed like a schoolgirl?

Not the point, Toby. *Jesus*.

The man was probably straight. And more importantly, he'd broken in here. People didn't just come into other people's houses unannounced unless they were there for nefarious purposes.

Or unless they were me.

"Forget about me! Who are *you* and what do you want?" I demanded, belatedly scrambling back and clutching the guy's cell phone like a weapon. "Talk."

The giant strode to the far side of the bed, blocking the exit, and I jumped up to face him, standing on the balls of my feet. "What are you doing?" I demanded. "Don't you dare—"

"I'm getting my pants on, since you seem to be distracted by my... my *junk*, as you call it." He grabbed some shorts off the floor and turned away as he pulled them on over a very firm ass. Then, he turned to face me and crossed his arms over his chest again. "Fine. I'll start. I'm Beale—"

Oh, damn. Damnity damn.

I was even more of an idiot than I'd thought.

"Goodman," I whispered. "Fenn's cousin. The gay one. Who believes in crystals and magical woo-woo."

He frowned. "I suppose that's me. Yeah." He shook his head. "And you are?"

"Mason's friend Toby," I said. Then I winced, remembering too late that I was supposed to be incognito.

"Oh. I've heard of you." Beale's posture relaxed just slightly, his eyes unwrinkled... and if this guy thought that putting his shorts on was gonna be enough to tone down the sex vibe in this room, he had another think coming.

I wasn't the only junk-checker-outer in the room.

"And now that we have that out of the way, what in the name of fuckity fuck are you doing in Mason and Fenn's guest-house?" I demanded.

"Sleeping." He nodded at the side of the bed closest to him, where I was shocked to notice a dented pillow and a discarded throw blanket that hadn't been there when I came in earlier. "I'm house-sitting while Fenn and Mason are out of town."

Oh. Oh, shit. "You're staying here?"

He nodded.

I ran a hand over my forehead. Littlejohn had made it sound like Mason's house-sitting friend would be swinging by to check on the contractors, not staying in the guesthouse. Of course, he also believed I was the house-sitting friend, so he clearly wasn't an accurate source of information.

Now I'd blown my cover to Beale, and I'd possibly have to find new sleeping arrangements, and I still didn't have any money or a phone.

"Fuck." I sank down on the bed and bent over to bury my face in my hands. To my absolute shock, tears of frustration filled my eyes. "Fuck this day." I sniffed. "Fuck cameras. And dumbass, shitty *users* who betray your trust. And fuck Florida. And fuck rental car computer systems. And vomit. And fuck me for being a sucker for SpaghettiOs, especially when I'm hungover."

The bed dipped as Beale sat beside me, and then his warm hand patted my shoulder with surprising gentleness for a guy his size.

He whistled low. "That's a comprehensive list of fuckery right there," he said, his deep voice dry and sympathetic at once.

This wry humor was so wildly unexpected, I snorted against my will and lifted my head. Beale watched me with blue eyes full of sympathy.

"Long day?"

I snorted again. "You might say that. There was a whole *thing* going on back in New York." I waved a hand, because no way was I explaining it. "Mase said I had a standing invitation to visit, so I came here. Then I lost my phone and my credit card at the airport. I couldn't get a rental car. A toddler puked on my sandal." I glanced up at him. "Armani. Last season, but still."

"Still." Beale nodded solemnly.

"I called Mason a billion times, before the phone incident, but he didn't pick up—"

"Ah. He was probably on the plane to New York—"

"To visit his sister," I finished glumly. "Yeah. I knocked on the door across the street, and Littlejohn Jennings filled me in. Then the cat incident." I sniffed morosely. "Not sure how much Mase has told you about me, but suffice it to say, my dick hasn't been that close to a pussy in my life, so I'm extra traumatized. And... actually, I think that's all." Aside from the paparazzi hunting me down, which I still would not be sharing. "More or less."

His lips twitched. "You skipped the part where you got in here."

"Oh! Well, that was the only easy bit of the whole night." I shrugged. "Littlejohn has a spare key, so he let me in after dinner."

"Of course he did." Beale snorted. "Having *Dale* Jennings messing with my life wasn't bad enough, his cousin had to take a turn."

"Excuse you?" I pushed to my feet and threw my shoulders back. I could do the arm-foldy chest-thing, too, even if my biceps weren't quite as bulgy and impressive as his had been. "'Messing'? I am not 'messing.' I'm a motherfucking *delight*."

Almost like he couldn't help it, Beale's avid gaze slid down my smooth chest and torso, as hot as a physical touch. "You're something, alright."

My cock stirred to life again, still on a hair trigger from all the adrenaline flooding my system—though, let's be honest, with a guy who looked like Beale, I was never gonna be a tough sell—and my breath hitched.

Didn't they say an adrenaline rush made for phenomenal sex? I didn't know, since I tried to avoid adventure. What I did know was that I hadn't had a decent fuck in weeks, and Beale's enormous cock would be the perfect magic wand to bibbity-bobbity-boo all my troubles away for the moment.

"I could show you how delightful—" I purred.

But Beale glanced away quickly and—God, why was this somehow erotic?—blushed beet red again.

"No, thank you." His voice was strained. "Would you, um, put your clothes on now, please?"

Well, damn. No magic for me.

"Could you, *um*, stop acting like seeing me naked is the most traumatizing part of this evening?" I rolled my eyes and grabbed a throw pillow from the bed to dangle in front of my dick, like I wasn't genuinely disappointed by his rejection. "There. Your delicate sensibilities are protected. You know, a true gentleman would offer me *comfort* in my time of need. Just sayin'."

His eyes flew to mine, and I could almost hear his heartbeat. "Comfort?" He swallowed. "I could make you some tea if you want? Maybe Sleepytime?"

Tea? I arched an eyebrow. For half a second, I had to wonder if I was losing my touch. The dude was definitely gay—he'd confirmed it—so was he just not into me?

But no. The way his eyes were now staying very firmly above my waist, I would bet my entire shoe collection that Beale Goodman was very, very interested. Maybe he had a boyfriend or something? Was monogamy contagious down here?

Why did I even care? Since when did I give a fuck what some random dude thought of me, when I had way bigger fish to fry?

I suddenly realized that I didn't.

"You know what? I'm done with this conversation for now. As I mentioned, it's been a shit day, so if you're not gonna fuck me, I'm going back to sleep," I announced. "*Are* you going to fuck me?"

Beale's already red face turned forty shades of heart-attack puce. "N-no!"

"Figures." I handed him his phone, threw my dick-covering pillow on the bed, and twisted to put my feet up. "Anyway, you're welcome to sleep here or else find your own place to crash."

"But... there's nowhere else. All the floors in the main house are being redone while Mason and Fenn are away. There's all kinds of nails and stuff."

"Wow. Sounds dangerous." I plumped my pillow.

"And I've been living with my dad, but his house is torn up now, also, and he and his fiancée are staying with my brother, so there's no room there either." He sounded panicked.

"Everybody's renovating! How special." I yawned. "Didn't you help your cousin Fenn, and Mason, and your brothers find that... treasure thing—" I waved a hand airily. "—that's worth a kajillion dollars or something?"

"The Whispering Key Treasure," Beale supplied a little brusquely. Looked like I'd hit a nerve. "Yeah. So?"

"So, get yourself a hotel room, buddy. Or buy an entire hotel. Or book a trip. Might I suggest the Maldives? Heck, go knock on Littlejohn's door and buy his house—he'd probably sell it to you for a case of SpaghettiOs. Or go sleep in your Lamborghini. Or sleep on the beach. Or find someone whose dick you *do* want to look at and sleep with him. I'll be here sleeping."

"I don't *have* a Lamborghini. And the motel is full—I know because my dad owns it—and it's the only hotel on the island."

"Too bad, so sad." I yawned. "Two seconds 'til I'm asleep. You in, or you out?"

"I guess I could sleep on the sofa." He looked toward the living room. I'd noticed a pink floral rattan thing that looked like it was salvaged from the *Golden Girls* set out there when

I came in, along with a coffee table, and a single easy chair that I doubted would fit Beale's ass let alone his entire body.

But if he thought that was preferable to sleeping with me, whatevs.

"M'kay, then. One second."

"Look, it's not that I... it's just that you...and we would..." He rubbed at the back of his neck, then blurted, "I don't want to have sex with you."

Well, ouch.

But annoying as it was that he kept treating me like a vile case of hemorrhoids, I'd also never seen a big guy blush that hard, and I couldn't help finding him adorable. His eyes were earnest and sweet as a puppy's.

"Then don't have sex with me." I yawned again, loud enough to make my jaw crack. "Jesus. Didn't you have a college roommate? It's possible to sleep without fucking."

He looked dubious. "I didn't go to college."

I rolled my eyes, then shut them firmly. "You're missing the point. You know what? Just go. Please shut off the light and close the door on your way out so your murder cat can't get back in. One attempted castration is enough for an evening." I pulled the blanket to my chin. "*Castration*. More like cat-stration, am I right?" I snort-giggled tiredly at my own joke.

Beale sighed, and I heard him move toward the door, and that was all for the best. I didn't know him, and I sure as fuck didn't need him, and hadn't I just promised myself earlier that I wasn't gonna make a fool of myself for a hot, muscle-bound guy ever again?

In the whole sea of my troubles, this one idiot acting like I had simultaneous leprosy and pink eye wasn't even the tiniest drop of—

The door shut with a click, and only a second later did the light switch off.

I held my breath as Beale got into the far side of the bed, and the relief I felt was a sign of how very tired I was.

"I'm sorry if I seemed rude," he said as he settled in. "I've never done this before."

"Slept?"

"In a bed. With someone else." He hesitated. "Except the summer I spent off island at Adventure Camp. But that... wasn't like this. Platonic."

My eyes popped open. I wanted very much to ask what his experience at Adventure Camp *had* been, because that might be the kind of adventure I could actually get behind, damn my overwhelming natural curiosity.

Instead, I sniffed and admitted to the ceiling, "I don't have experience with it either."

"Really?" Beale sounded bizarrely eager. "I sort of figured you would."

I shrugged, though he couldn't see me. "When I sleep with men, I don't *sleep*-sleep with them."

"Oh."

I waited for him to say more, but he didn't. Yet I somehow knew he wasn't sleeping, either.

"So... do you have a boyfriend?" I demanded. I cursed myself for an idiot the second the words were out of my mouth. "I only ask because if someone's going to show up tomorrow demanding a duel to restore your honor, advanced warning would be nice."

"No boyfriend," he said softly. "No duel." He sounded like the most innocent of innocents, which should have been grossly unappealing.

It was *not*.

"Excellent—"

"But I'd still like to keep things platonic. I don't... know you."

Part of me wanted to laugh at the very idea of knowing someone before fucking them, but then who the hell knew what life for a gay man was like on an island where people were so old-fashioned they had keys to each other's houses and let random strangers inside?

Besides, this big dude could have thrown me out to sleep in the yard, and instead he'd offered me... tea.

"Fine. I'll stay on my side if you stay on yours," I promised, holding up my pinkie finger over the mound of blankets in the center of the bed. "Pinkie swear."

He huffed out a breath, and a second later, his hand rose, too. The moonlight through the blinds turned our skin the exact same shade of silvery white. He wrapped his enormous pinkie around mine, and the contact made me shiver.

"Pinkie swear."

4

————

BEALE

————

I woke up to bright sunshine streaming in the window on my closed eyelids and the smell of warm sunshine, salt water, sweet lime, and spicy pepper in my nose. I took a deep breath and sighed sleepily. I'd never found one of Gloria's scented candles so intoxicating before, but apparently this one triggered something in my brain, because my morning wood was particularly woody. I buried my face in the pillow and pressed my aching dick against the mattress.

"Mmm," the mattress moaned. "Go 'way Zamboni."

My eyes flew open in a panic as several impressions flipped through my brain one after the other like one of those old silent movies—Toby's yell in the darkness, Toby's cock, Toby's intelligent brown eyes, Toby's naked cock, Toby's smooth chest, Toby's impressive cock, Toby's flirty smile, and once again Toby's cock—which had been naked and impressive and right the heck there, when I hadn't seen any but my own up close and personal in ages—before finally processing the fact that I was clinging to Toby like a life preserver in a flood.

Worse than that, the two of us were surrounded by a puddle of tangled blankets that suggested we'd each fought our way to the center of the bed over the course of the night so we could... cuddle.

Oh, shit.

I'd never cuddled anyone in my adult life, and certainly not a naked someone. It felt so good, I could almost convince myself to just enjoy the sensation of having someone warm and comfortable in my arms... but I couldn't quite get there.

This was not supposed to happen. Not like this. Not with Toby, a man who casually propositioned a perfect stranger because he couldn't stop staring at my dick and—oh my God, stop thinking about that, Beale!

My heart stuttered and the only thing that kept me from going into full-on panic mode was the fact that Toby's breathing was still soft and steady and his eyes were fully shut. I needed to extricate myself before he woke up so I wouldn't have to try to explain our actions to Toby... mostly because I had no excuse for mine. He'd made it pretty damn clear what he wanted from me, but I'd made it clear what I didn't want. And still, here we were.

Removing myself from the bed without waking him was torture. I guess I'd wrapped myself around him at some point before deciding to lie on top of him, because both my arms were stuck between him and the mattress in a way that could not have been comfortable for him. But when I started to pull my bottom arm free, he frowned and muttered something like, "Jebediah, no!" and clung to me more tightly—which was thrilling and also wrong—so I had to take extra care to move away super slowly. Whoever Jebediah was, Toby sure seemed passionate about him.

When I finally managed to roll myself off the bed, I took a second to stare down at him, just to check that he was still deeply asleep, of course. His smooth, tanned skin—and there was a lot of it, since he was fully naked—flowed like honey against the white of the sheets. His dark hair stuck out from his head like he'd been electrocuted. His forehead was puckered in a concentrated frown, and his full lips pursed in displeasure.

He was really, ridiculously good-looking, even asleep. Heck, especially asleep, when he was all warm and soft, with the sheet hanging on the curve of his—wow. I really, really needed to stop thinking about this.

I wasn't even sure that I liked the man. There was zero excuse for me noticing him this way.

I headed out of the room, closing the door gently behind me. As fast as I could in case Toby woke up, I grabbed one of my boxes from the closet, exchanged my cargo shorts for gym shorts, and slid my feet into my sneakers. I took a quick look at my horoscope, which seemed annoyingly obscure today, then set out food for Marjorie, who hadn't appeared yet, and headed out for a nice, excruciating run that would punish my body and hopefully reset my mind.

At the last minute, I hesitated. Toby was alone with no transportation, no money, and no phone. I had to assume since Mason and Fenn weren't here, he'd want to catch the next flight back home or... wherever else he might go. I didn't want him to think that I'd run out on him—even though I was literally running out on him—so I grabbed a scrap of paper from the kitchen drawer and left him a note that said I'd be back in an hour if he needed a ride to the airport, and then I escaped into the early morning.

My body was amped up to an unreasonable degree. The air felt muggier than usual against my skin, the early morning sun felt hotter, and even my vision felt sharper. For the first time in maybe my whole life, I felt a kind of arousal I couldn't shake off or ignore. I didn't like it one bit.

It wasn't like I'd never been attracted to someone before, because I had. Plenty. Like the actor Tom Welling from *Smallville* with his kind eyes. Oh, or my adorably dorky roommate Martin, the summer my grandmother had paid for me to go to Adventure Camp. And the guys I'd hooked up with in my early twenties, who'd all seemed so exciting. Heck, even Silvio with his cute smile and fine ass. Good-looking guys were everywhere.

But I'd figured out years ago that a few minutes of happy release was not worth the major letdown I'd feel when I realized the person I'd shared an amazing, mind-blowing experience with had no feelings for me at all. I knew most people didn't feel like I did—they were able to separate the physical from the emotional, and that was cool. Sometimes I even envied it—but I wanted more than an uncomplicated orgasm, I wanted connection. Someone who understood me, maybe better than I understood myself. I wanted the first time I fell for someone to be the only time I fell for someone. I wanted a soul mate.

And even after twenty minutes' acquaintance, I could not imagine anyone less like my future soul mate than Toby. He was hot and he knew it. His snarky humor and aggressive flirtation were annoying, and the opposite of my soul mate's soothing, patient spirit. He was quicksilver fast in all things —his retorts, the play of emotions over his face, in amping up drama from zero to a billion. All in all, Toby was like a candle flame—pretty to look at but dangerous, and impossible to hold without harming yourself.

So why was I still thinking about him, two miles into a four-mile run?

I forced myself to run faster and headed down toward the beach, where the horizon was still tinged pink. I pushed myself until I was breathless and dripping with sweat, and only when I was pleasantly exhausted did I allow myself to run back to Mason and my cousin's place, where I dropped to the ground beside the pool house and forced myself to do three sets of sit-ups and push-ups for good measure.

I was nearly done my second set of push-ups when I heard the clink of china through the open kitchen window, and then a voice muttering, "Who the hell, in actual America, has a cabinet filled with twelve kinds of herbal tea and no coffee?"

I told myself Toby's outrage was not amusing and spread my hands wider, increasing the burn on my muscles.

"Oh ho! So we meet again, nemesis."

I paused with my chest in the air and my hands still flat on the ground.

"Don't you look at me like that, hussy! How dare you just sit there grooming yourself after what you put me through."

Oh, God. Marjorie. I started to scramble to my feet to rescue one of them—I wasn't sure which—but a second later, Toby hmphed.

"Nothing to say for yourself, then? You're just going to try to stare me down? Fine. Fine. You won't win this round, I assure you. I can out-stubborn the stubbornest human, so I can sure as heck out-stubborn you. In fact, I hardly notice your existence."

Oh, God. Was he using reverse psychology on my cat?

"Also, I adore cats. I am thrilled that you're sitting there on the floor watching me with your freaky eyes. I am in no way put off by your presence or—motherfucker!—by the way you've jumped on the counter to stalk me. I am perfectly sanguine. Sanguine, I tell you!"

I lowered myself to the ground and just lay there for a second, chest to the concrete, breathing deeply. Toby was talking to my cat like she'd know what sanguine meant when I wasn't entirely sure what sanguine meant, and shit, I really, really, really needed to stop thinking about him.

Clearly, the run had done jack shit. I was just glad he'd be leaving the island soon. And once he was safely on a flight back north, with his weird visit to the island just a blip in my memory banks, I'd spend some serious time meditating and cleansing my chakras, reminding myself of exactly what I wanted.

My energy must have gotten blocked by loneliness or anxiety or something. I'd been trying so hard to manifest my soul mate that I'd manifested this crazy attraction... to the wrong guy. I hadn't even known a person could do that, but trust me to be the first idiot to manage it. I looked down at my naked wrist and wished, for the first time in a long time, that I had someone who could actually guide me in these things.

I thought about staying outside and avoiding Toby for the rest of the morning, or until he left Whispering Key, which-ever took longer. But then I heard the fridge door slam, the crinkle of a wrapper, and more muttering.

"Wrap burrito in paper towel and microwave two minutes? Hmm. Don't paper towels catch fire in the microwave? Oh, well! Instructions are instructions, right?"

I was a tiny bit concerned that he was asking the cat, and I was even more concerned that Marjorie would somehow answer him.

Preventing Toby from burning down the pool house prob-ably fell under the heading of "Responsible House-sitting," didn't it? I groaned. So much for avoiding him.

Still, after I stood, I took a second to lift my arms up to the sky in a Sun Salutation before folding into a forward bend, letting each of the vertebrae in my back obediently pop back into alignment. I breathed deeply into the stretch and tried to let go of my frustrations, expanding my conscious-ness. I was profoundly grateful to—

"Holy Christina Aguilera. Could you just turn, like, forty-five degrees to your left and repeat that move?"

I spun around so fast I almost fell over.

Toby peered out the window at me, his gaze focused unapologetically on the rear of my shorts, and the air temperature on Whispering Key immediately shot up twenty degrees.

"Uh, hey. Good morning." I ran a hand through my hair.

"Great morning, and even better now," Toby said with a leer that made me blush. "My, don't you look all hot and sweaty."

I cleared my throat and fought the urge to cover my damp, naked chest. "I... I ran."

Toby grinned like I was being adorable. "So your note said," he agreed. "Your breakfast will be ready in a minute and forty-five seconds. Come on in."

"My breakfast?" I blinked, but Toby's face was gone from the window, and I heard the teakettle whistle, so I headed for the door because I couldn't think of a single excuse not to.

I toed my shoes off inside the door and turned toward the little kitchen area separated from the living room by a bar and three barstools. In the kitchen, Toby did a little dance and sang a song I couldn't hear under his breath as he got out the tea, shaking his ass from side to side.

I wasn't sure how a person could look sexier in clothes than they did naked, but something about the way his cropped jean shorts that showed off his sleek, toned thighs and his sleeveless, cropped, black Calvin Klein T-shirt showed off leanly muscled arms and abs just highlighted everything I knew he was hiding. His dark hair was tousled and shower damp, begging to be touched.

I curled my hands into fists.

Then I headed for the back hall closet where my shit was stacked and grabbed the box labeled "Crystals."

"Hey! Where'd you go?" Toby demanded as I carried the box back to the kitchen.

I didn't answer. I rummaged through the box of carefully wrapped stones, found the one I wanted immediately, unwrapped the soft cotton cloth around it, and set it on the counter. The rock was a large chunk of deep green and amber variscite I'd gotten at a flea market a few years back and hardly ever used except to cleanse it and charge it and make sure it was attuned to me.

"Pretty," Toby remarked as I shifted the rest of the box onto an empty stool and took a seat. "What's it do?"

"Every living and nonliving thing in the universe has energy. The things you draw into yourself can change your energy for better or worse. This stone calms the mind and helps you think logically," I said gruffly.

I'd actually tried to talk myself out of buying the stone, since I was almost always calm, and logical thought wasn't really my go-to, but some impulse had made me buy it, and now I knew why. If there were ever a time for some rational thought, it was today.

"Oh, cool. I need some fucking calm," Toby said, unconsciously echoing my thoughts. He grabbed the stone off the counter before I could stop him and examined it closely. "What are these brown—? Uh, Beale? Why are you looking at me like I just boiled your bunny? Oh! Oh, shit." Toby set the rock down carefully and held his hands up, big brown eyes wide. "My bad. Is it bad manners to handle another guy's stones without permission? Did I just fuck up your juju?"

I exhaled a shaky breath and fought the urge to visualize him handling my stones.

"No," I lied. "No, of course not. Don't be silly. It's fine. You're fine. The whole thing is just... fine."

"Fine." Toby's brow creased. "Did you sleep okay?"

"Yes. Yes! Great." I felt my cheeks flush, which was apparently their default state when Toby was around. If he didn't leave soon, I'd probably have a stroke. Then a horrible thought occurred to me. "Why do you ask? Did you sleep well? Did anything... disturb you?" Like me, lying on you like you were my personal mattress topper, please say no?

"What?" Toby's face went carefully blank in a guilty-ish sort of way. "No. I slept perfectly! Wonderfully. Deeply. Platonically." He cleared his throat. "Definitely at no time did I wake up to find I'd crossed the middle of the bed and curled around your half-naked person like you were the only source of heat in a cold and unforgiving universe, with my naked dick lying on your thigh like a lizard sunning itself on a rock, so you can get that thought right out of your head, mister."

"Oh." I blinked at the visual and squirmed slightly on my seat as my own naked dick pressed against my shorts. I debated the benefit of more push-ups. "Okay. Good."

"Because if I had done such a thing, which I obviously didn't, I'd have scurried back to my own side of the bed immediately. Immediately."

"Right," I choked out. "Same."

"Good. Great. So that settles that." Toby turned around and busied himself pouring water into mugs while the microwave continued to hum. "But, I'm glad you slept well, because I did want to talk to you about—"

Oh, shit. Was this the part where he called me on the cuddling?

Before he could finish his sentence—and honestly, that was probably for the best—a sound like machine-gun fire emitted from the microwave.

Toby screamed, spun, and ducked. "Oh my God! The microwave is shooting at us!"

I ran into the kitchen and pulled open the microwave door. Inside, a burrito-shaped log sat on a decorative plate, covered by a scorched paper towel. I grabbed the plate gingerly and set it on the counter.

"That appliance attacked us in cold blood!" Toby exclaimed, so close I could feel his breath against my damp shoulder blade and smell his spicy, clean cologne. "It murdered that vegan burrito! Unacceptable."

"A murder microwave to match the murder cat?" I snorted. "Why is it always murder with you?"

"Excuse you—"

"How long did you put it on for?"

"Two minutes! As instructed."

"Toby, I've been in here way longer than two minutes."

His mouth opened and closed like a fish. "Are you... are you insinuating that I cannot program a microwave for two minutes? Because... because that's crazy talk. I have a job. I have a-a-a degree. I am a very capable person!"

I could feel emotions streaming off him—annoyance, injured pride, embarrassment, curious vulnerability—and it was the last one that jabbed me in the solar plexus. I remembered something I'd been blocking out all morning —Toby stretching his arm across the Great Wall of Blankets to link pinkies with me. And I realized, with that same instinct that had made me buy the variscite years ago and told me never to settle, that Toby really hated feeling vulnerable.

He was a lot like Marjorie that way.

"No," I said solemnly. "I'd never think such a thing. I'm saying that clearly this microwave has been plotting its attack for more than two minutes. It was deliberate. And cold-blooded."

Toby jabbed the burrito lump angrily with his finger. "Much like this burrito, which is smoking but somehow still frozen inside."

"Even worse." I took the plate to the trash and dumped the burrito in. "This burrito was innocent. A whatjamacallit? Casualty of war."

"And there goes your home-cooked breakfast," he sighed.

"You didn't need to make me breakfast anyway."

"I was attempting to pay you back for rescuing me last night. I'll have you know, I'm a fucking amazing cook. I make a steak au poivre that is to die for. I make a cheese-and-bacon soufflé that has made men drop to their knees."

Yet another helpful visual. "I believe you," I croaked. "But did I mention I'm vegetarian?"

Toby's eyes shot to mine, and his full lips twitched in a smile that made me take a step back.

"So, what time's your flight?" I moved around the counter and slid back onto the stool, just as Toby set a steaming mug of water and a few boxes of tea in front of me. "I'm assuming you're leaving today, and I'm happy to drive you to the airport! I can be ready anytime. Even now, if you wanted. And I technically have plans this afternoon, volunteering for the Nature Center, but I'll postpone them if you need me to!" The sooner I got this confusing man off the island, the better.

Toby pressed his lips together. "Actually, that's what I wanted to talk to you about, before the murder microwave. I don't have a flight... as such. For one thing, I don't have a phone, and I had to cancel my credit card—"

Oh, right. "Well, then I'll lend you the money!" I interrupted. "Heck, I'd gift it to you!"

"Absolutely not." He shook his head. "I would never accept money from anyone, and I don't borrow money from anyone either... except maybe Mason," he said reluctantly. "Maybe."

"Then let's call Mason! You can borrow my phone!" I grabbed it out of the inside pocket of my shorts. "Easy as that."

"I considered that. But, um..." He blew out a breath and cast his eyes to the ceiling. "That's not the only consideration. I left New York under less than auspicious circumstances."

I narrowed my eyes. He was holding himself upright, his shoulders locked tight, but those same emotions I'd caught earlier were still bleeding through—wounded pride over-laying desperation.

"These circumstances... are we talking a bad breakup? Or like the FBI might be assembling on the lawn?"

Toby rolled his eyes and leaned his elbows on the counter. "Nothing that exciting, no. More like, circumstances involving a man and... well... another man, and... you know what? The details are unimportant here."

I huffed out a laugh. If I'd needed further confirmation Toby wasn't the guy for me—and I did not—this would have been it. Wounded and vulnerable he might be, but he was also a freestanding drama generator.

"Suffice it to say, going back to the city right now would be sort of problematic," he continued. "Because I'd really rather that none of my acquaintances knew where to find me. So I'd rather stay here."

"Here," I repeated.

"Yes, here."

"On Whispering Key."

"Yup."

"In... in this house."

"Uh-huh."

"With, um... with me. And Marjorie."

Toby sighed and set a hand on his hip. "Yes. Until Mason comes home. Once I explain the situation to him, he might have some advice." He snorted. "Oh, who am I kidding? He'll have all kinds of thoughts and opinions, and he'll express them forcefully." He rolled his eyes. "But I don't want him to know until he gets here, otherwise he'll feel like he has to come home early. I don't want him to ruin his trip just because I made some choices."

I caught myself on the verge of smiling, because this sounded so much like me and Rafe, but then the penny dropped.

Mason wouldn't be home until Friday. Almost a week from now.

A week of sleeping next to Toby. A week of having him share this small space. A week of smelling whatever sexy cologne he wore and knowing exactly how he was built under his clothes.

"That, um... things could be tight?"

Toby's eyebrows flew up. "Things?"

Fuck.

"I meant... space. With you and me. And—" I waved toward the single bedroom with its one bed.

"True," Toby agreed. "We'd be re-enacting that age-old story of two incredibly attractive men in one teeny-tiny bed."

"You make it sound like the setup for some cheap porn," I croaked, my voice gone all rusty.

"Precious, any porn involving me would be the highest-quality porn."

I lifted one eyebrow.

"But that is, indeed, how all the stories end." He gave me a sinner's grin that made my palms sweat. "We could cut to the chase now and get it out of the way if you want? I'd be happy to mitigate any... inconvenience...my presence might cause you? Tit for tat?" He came around the counter to walk his fingers up my bicep.

I shook my head

"No, thank you," I said primly, moving his hand away. "You can keep your tits and tats right where they are."

"Fine, fine." Toby rolled his eyes and resumed his spot on the other side of the counter. "I'm not going to coerce you. I shall resign myself to starring in the most boring, platonic non-porn of all time. But is it alright, then?" He raised his chin, clearly hating every moment of having to ask this favor. "For me to stay?"

I shrugged. "It's not my house, Toby. Mason would kick my ass if I threw you out, and..."

Toby shook his head. "No, no. Don't do that. Say yes or no, Beale. If you say no, I will leave." He frowned. "It's not ideal, but I'll figure something out. I'm not entirely without means." He set his jaw, which was a surprisingly sexy look. "What do you think?"

I folded my arms across my chest. What I thought was that Toby Elford reeked of desperation... and it smelled an awful lot like an over-nuked vegan burrito. I also thought the holes in his story were big enough to drive a truck through.

But there was something about Toby's combination of nerves and defiance that got to me, even more than any of the physical things about him, and even though part of me needed him to be on the other side of the planet from me, a larger part of me felt like maybe he needed me.

I was a sucker for a wounded stray, and it turned out sexy, overly dramatic New Yorkers were no exception.

"I think you'll stay," I confirmed.

He closed his eyes for a brief second in relief, and when he popped them open, he gave me a brilliant smile. "My knight in shining armor!"

My heart galloped at that smile, and I vowed to build a wall of blankets so high it could be seen from outer space. So high, I couldn't fight my way through it.

"I'll repay you for the inconvenience somehow." Toby sank his teeth into his firm lower lip thoughtfully. "Otherwise I'd owe you."

"You really wouldn't. At all."

"I'd feel like I did, which is the same thing. So, sex is off the table, and my best cooking involves meat. Don't suppose you need anything written?"

I shook my head, bewildered and amused. "Nope."

"And you're not in need of any... advice?"

"From you? No." I winced the second the words came out. "I didn't mean—"

Toby's mouth twisted. "Yes, you did. And fair enough. So far you've saved me from imminent demise twice, and I've thrown myself on your mercy for the next week. I wouldn't take advice from me either." He muttered something about professional liability.

"Are you okay—?"

Toby rolled his shoulders, which looked tight. "I'm fine. No worries. I'll think of something I can do."

I shook my head, deciding not to fight this battle right then, and pushed up to standing. "Alright. So I'm gonna grab a shower and head out. I've got some stuff to do for the Nature Center. The contractors might be coming by for a bit to work on the floors up at the main house, but they shouldn't bother you if you wanna use the pool. Oh, and I can have Jim Pickles run up some groceries, if you make me a list of what you want."

Toby's eyes widened at the mention of contractors and widened further when I mentioned Jim. "Or I could just lock the door and not talk to anyone! Ha! I'll be fine, don't worry about me. I have my laptop. I... oh, shit! I have my laptop!" Toby was nearly buzzing with nervous energy, and I didn't get it, but it was hella distracting. "What's the Wi-Fi password?"

I bit my lip. "There kinda isn't one."

"What?"

I shrugged. "Fenn and Mase don't have it hooked up yet."

"Fuck." Toby pushed both hands through his hair and shook his head at the ceiling. "So close and yet so far. If anyone ever asks you, baby puke is not lucky."

"Sure." I folded my arms over my chest and watched him pace the kitchen for a minute. "Look, I want you to do something for me. Stand up straight and take a deep breath."

"What?" One side of his lip came up in a grimace. "No."

"Seriously," I insisted. "I want you to do a yoga pose that will open up your solar plexus chakra."

"My who now?"

"This right here." I touched a hand to my own bare chest, halfway between my ribs and navel. "Your solar plexus chakra. It corresponds to your feelings of self-esteem and control over your life. If it's blocked, you're gonna feel out of control and unable to tap into your own power. Doing this stretch and focusing on your breathing can really help unblock you and remind you that you're in the driver's seat."

Toby lifted a skeptical eyebrow. "Is this the time to mention I was born without chakras? It's tragic but true. I blame my mother. She didn't have them either."

I tilted my head to one side. "Doing this would repay any debt you might feel you owed me." I blinked innocently.

He narrowed his eyes like he might protest, but in the end he threw up his hands. "Fine, then. What do I do?"

"Stand up straight, feet hip width apart." I demonstrated. "Good posture is crucial for any yoga pose. Sometimes just standing straight makes all the difference in making you feel powerful."

"Sure," he grumbled, getting into position facing me. "When you're a seven-foot-tall monolith."

"Six and a half," I said mildly. "Not quite Stonehenge." I usually rolled my eyes at height comments, because I'd heard every single one of them a billion times, but I couldn't deny Toby noticing my size felt different somehow, and I liked it.

And didn't like that I liked it.

I was so screwed.

"So now what?" he demanded.

"Huh? Oh, right." I refocused my attention on the situation at hand. "Now you close your eyes and breathe deeply, in through your nose and out through your mouth. Extend your arms out to the sides. Then slowly, hinge at your right hip like this." I sank into triangle pose with ease.

Toby twisted his lower back and leaned so far right, he nearly fell over. "M'kay, sorry, but that's a big N-O. My hip doesn't hinge in that direction."

I rolled my eyes and stood up. "Of course it does. Everyone's does."

He shook his head sadly. "Born with no chakras and an unhinged hip."

I chuckled helplessly and came around behind him, setting my hands on his waist. "Okay, start small. Just focus on your breathing for now," I instructed, forcing myself not to notice how it felt to have my hands on him. "Inhale and let your stomach expand, exhale and suck your stomach in. Yeah! That's it. Good job."

Toby snorted. "Thanks. Been breathing on my own for nearly thirty-five years, but I'm glad I'm doing it right."

I shook my head in amusement, though he couldn't see me. "Arms out like an airplane—yes, good. Now, keep your legs and arms in alignment, and stretch your hand down like this." Gripping his wrist, I guided him into position. "Let your hand rest on your leg and... yeah! That's it. Now breathe deeply into the stretch. Awesome! Count to ten slowly, then straighten up, and do the same thing on the other side. Perfect! Focus on your breaths again. Feel yourself loosening right here."

I reached around to slide my palm up his stomach, forgetting for a second that he was wearing a cropped shirt and that his warm skin would be directly under the heel of my hand. A hard jolt of electricity ran through me that had nothing whatsoever to do with my chakras and everything to do with my suddenly plumping dick, and I snatched my hand back like I'd been burned.

Of course my sudden movement meant Toby, whose legs were still spread and whose body was still tilted to one side, was thrown off balance just slightly. He windmilled his arms and grabbed the counter in front of him to brace himself while I belatedly grabbed his hips back against me to keep him upright.

"Shit. I've gotcha," I told him firmly. "You're good."

"Damn." He rested his cheek against the counter, leaning his head on his arm, and panted a little. "I told you I didn't bend like that."

"You bend perfectly," I soothed, running a hand down his back. "I just moved too fast. You weren't ready for it."

He lifted his head to look at me over his shoulder, and his voice was shaky with nervous laughter. "I almost splattered on the floor, loose chakras and all."

"Fuck," I groaned, remorseful. "I'm so—"

"Sweet Jesus, what am I seeing?" a voice demanded from the doorway. "Gage? Gage, am I seeing what I think I'm seeing?"

I looked up so fast I nearly got whiplash and found both of my brothers standing by the open door to the pool house. Rafe had both hands clasped over his eyes, while Gage watched me and Toby with a mischievous little smile playing on his lips.

"I dunno, Rafe. Do you think you're seeing our brother fuck a hot dude against Mason's pool house counter?" Gage asked, rocking back and forth on his feet.

"What?" I glanced down at my position, one hand grasping Toby's hip while he was bent over, the other hand braced on his back. Fuck.

"'Cause if so," Gage continued gleefully, "I'm definitely seeing what you're seeing."

5

TOBY

Help Me Hagatha (Issue #2411)

Dear Aunt Hagatha:

I've been dating a girl for a while now, and I'm totally into her. I want to take things to the next level, but only if I know for sure she's into me, too. What should I do?

Terrified in Tarpon Springs

Dear Terrified,

This reminds me of when I was a tiny Hag-let who desperately wanted to learn to swim like the other youngsters but feared getting my hair wet. Alas, to this day, I won't venture into anything deeper than my own bathtub.

Don't be like Aunt Hagatha, darling. No risk, no reward. The only way to know is to ask her... so *ask her*.

Best of luck,
Auntie H.

"No!" Beale jumped away from me. "No. No, no. No. You're... it's not... we're... I was opening his chakras," he finally managed to choke out.

I rolled my eyes and looked back at him. "Really? *That's* what you're going with?"

"I'm *not* looking at some guy's open chakras," Rafe, the older, stockier guy at the door, insisted. "It's bad enough that Dad and Gloria moved into my place, and I woke up this morning to Gloria screaming, 'Oh, yes, Mr. Mayor!' in a way that made me never want to have sex again. Do you *know* how scarring that is?"

"Yes," Beale said with feeling. He seemed to regain his ability to speak as he walked around the counter. "Welcome to my life. And I'm not having sex, dumbass, so you can open your eyes. We were stretching, that's all. What the heck are you doing here?"

"*Me?*" Rafe finally uncovered his eyes. "What's *he* doing here?"

By *he*, of course, he meant me, and I... Well, I had no fucking clue what to say. The truth was not an option. It was bad enough that Beale knew who I really was. The more people who knew, the more people could potentially sell me out to the media, when the media finally figured out my name, if they hadn't already.

"Littlejohn Jennings was down at the Bean telling the whole island about a dude named Trey who's a *Wheel of Fortune* prodigy and who's house-sitting for Mason and Fenn. Littlejohn said he let him in to the pool house." The shorter guy —Gage?—grinned. "Rafe, here, said that was impossible—"

"Because it was *supposed* to be impossible! Beale is staying here."

"Uh-huh. Except here he is. Here you *both* are," Gage concluded happily. He dodged around Beale, holding out his hand for me to shake. "I'm Gage Goodman. You must be Trey?"

"Er." I looked past Gage to Beale, hoping for some insight on how best to handle this, but Beale looked a little nauseous and a whole lot confused, so clearly he wasn't going to be any help. "Yes, indeedy. Trey. That's me." I shook his hand.

Beale turned and raised one eyebrow, which I interpreted as *Trey? Really? You needed an alias?*

I narrowed my eyes and projected the words, *Yes, really, and shut up. It was a difficult evening.*

Gage grinned and gripped my hand harder. "Oh my gosh, so many things make sense suddenly. It is great to meet you, man. Welcome to Whispering Key!"

"I..." I cleared my throat, surprised by this enthusiastic welcome, and again looked at Beale, but he shrugged, as mystified as I was. "Thanks?"

"Not a damn thing about this makes sense to me." Rafe folded his arms over his chest. "Who are you, Trey? Why are you house-sitting with Beale?"

"Well," Beale began, but he stopped and rubbed at his left wrist like he'd forgotten his watch or something.

Entirely unhelpful.

"The thing is..." I started, but no new inspiration had struck regarding which way to spin this best. Aunt Hagatha would have said to be honest and blah blah, but Hagatha had never had to lie to her temporary, mostly-but-not-entirely-platonic roommate's busybody brothers while on the run from the paparazzi.

Until now.

"Rafe, don't be an idiot," Gage said. "It's obvious who he is."

"It is?" Rafe, Beale, and I demanded in a weird chorus.

"Yes!" Gage cast his eyes heavenward. "He's here to see *Beale*. They clearly arranged this."

Beale blinked at Gage. So did Rafe. For that matter, so did I, but I was the first to recover.

"Yes. Yes, exactly that. Shoot. And here we thought we were being sneaky, huh, Beale?" I poked him in the side, and he gave me a narrow-eyed look. "It was a, um... a hookup."

"A hookup?" Rafe narrowed his eyes. "I call bullshit. Beale doesn't do hookups."

Beale didn't do hookups?

I side-eyed Beale, who widened his eyes in a way that meant, *Yeah, so?*

And I gave him a return look that clearly stated, *No tea no shade, but could you not have spelled that out last night, instead of making me think I was putting out subpar sex pheromones? Jesus.*

I smiled brightly. "Oh, no, I didn't mean we were *hooking up-* hooking up. No, that would be silly. I meant, we agreed we'd hook up in the larger sense of, um… two people who already know each other arranging a meeting. Which happened to be here. At this location," I finished, super smoothly.

Beale closed his eyes and shook his head, patently unimpressed by my smoothness, which was annoying. He could jump in anytime now.

"So, you knew each other before?" Rafe wrinkled his nose. "How? You're not from around here."

Did the designer sandals give it away?

"Oh, the usual way that people meet other people." I waved a hand airily. "Beale and I have known each other for ages. We've been through a lot together."

Not a lie, really. Cats. Cuddling. Murder microwave. Death-defying yoga. We were basically married in some cultures.

"But, Beale, the only time you've been off island for more than a night was the summer Grandma Goodman sent you to camp a billion years ago." Rafe huffed out a laugh.

"Hey!" I snapped. "Don't knock Adventure Camp, okay?"

Rafe stared at Beale, who stared at me, probably trying to remember when he'd mentioned Adventure Camp.

I gave him a look that said, *In bed. Last night.* And I knew he'd gotten the message when his cheeks went red.

I had no idea why Beale's blushes were such a turn-on... but then again, I didn't really know a lot of men who blushed, period. Maybe any of them would affect me this way.

Maybe.

"You mean to tell me you met at Adventure Camp?" Rafe demanded, drawing our attention back to him. "Really?"

"God," Gage breathed. "Just look at them, Rafe! Seriously, this explains *so* much."

"I still don't get what it explains," Rafe complained. "You went to that camp when you were what, Beale? Sixteen?" He side-eyed me. "Were *you* sixteen when he was sixteen?"

I had no idea how old Beale was, but I was guessing he was a good bit younger than my thirty-five, so it was a fair assumption that when I was sixteen, Beale would have been... illegal. *Still.* I resented the implication that I looked like the oldest person in the room, even if I was.

"Are you calling me old?" I demanded. "Beale, is he calling me old? Because I'm not old. I'm in prime physical form."

Beale's mouth opened and shut again, and I made a note to self to kill him for his hesitation.

"Of course you are," Gage soothed.

I gently skimmed my under-eye area with my fingertips, checking for any bags that might have formed since I last looked in the mirror. "It's not my fault my sleep last night was interrupted because I was callously awoken for hijinks involving Beale and, er—" I stopped myself before I referenced the cat. "Beale."

"Hijinks," Gage said avidly. "Do tell."

"Please do not," Beale said firmly.

I huffed. "My point is that age is just a number."

"And what's *your* number?" Rafe demanded.

Beale made a sound halfway between laughter and vomiting, which I did not appreciate, so I did what came naturally. I kept talking.

"Imagine, if you will, that I was a handsome lad of nineteen summers." I decided I was willing to be three years older than Beale in this story, no more. "Charged with guiding virile young men on their adventures, as one does at Adventure Camp."

"Ooookay, then. I'm gonna stop you right there, *Trey*." Beale laid a hand on my shoulder and squeezed... rather hard. "Before you make this already weird story into a *Dateline*-NBC-weird story. Yes, Trey and I know each other from camp," he told his brothers. "It's not a big deal."

"We bonded over shared interests." I sighed happily, settling into the lie. "It was magical."

Rafe looked at me in my crop top and then at Beale, who was still damp with sweat from his run. "Which interests would those be?"

"Er..." Shit. Like Icarus, I had flown too close to the sun, and I was about to get caught. "Like..."

"Animal rescue," Beale said smoothly.

"Animal rescue." Rafe's frown deepened. "Really?"

"Totes." I nodded. "We save people from animals at all hours of the day or night. Especially murder cats. We live for it."

"You mean we save *animals*," Beale corrected.

Shit. "Isn't that what I said? Ha. Silly me. *Again.* Yes. Obviously that's what I meant. Beneath this current-season Calvin Klein top beats the heart of an animal lover."

Beale shot me a look that said, *You'd better not be thinking of steak au poivre when you say that,* and I pursed my lips because maybe I had been and maybe I hadn't, and that was none of his beeswax.

"God, it's so perfect." Gage pressed his palms together in front of his mouth. "You two fell in love because of animals."

A giant noise like a record scratch filled the little pool house —or maybe just my brain—but all three of us stared at Gage simultaneously.

Love? Really? I felt like Gage had missed a couple crucial steps there. In fact, entire staircases.

"Are you high?" Beale scowled. "How the hell did you hear that story and think *perfect* and *love*?"

"Well, not perfect," Gage agreed. "You've been estranged for over a decade, knowing the world wouldn't be kind about your age difference, but—"

"What? No. It's a minuscule age difference," I felt the need to reiterate. "Hardly anything, really. I'm quite young."

Beale shot me a look. "Focus, To—*Trey.* Our age difference is not the point here."

"Because it's so small," I told Gage in a low voice. "Negligible."

"But it's obvious you've carried a torch for one another all along, because you finally got back in touch!" Gage concluded. He bit his lip. "It's maybe the most romantic thing I've ever heard."

Rafe *hmm'd* thoughtfully.

"Who are you right now?" Beale demanded. "Since when are you a closet romantic, Gage Spence Goodman? Where's Mr. Algorithms and Science?"

"Since *now*." Gage's brown eyes were soulful. "Jesus Christ, Beale, I'm not heartless! Algorithms and science are beautiful, but love conquers all, and your story is like a fairy tale."

"You know... it really kind of is," I agreed, getting into the spirit of the thing. "Two men, torn apart by the whims of fate and the vagaries of life, finally reunited last night—"

"Yes! Only to find your connection is still there!" Gage pressed a hand to his chest. "Just like the first time you met."

"Yes," Beale said sourly. "Last night felt very much like the first time we met."

"I can honestly say, I've never felt closer to Beale than I do right now." I sighed and clasped Beale's arm. "We're like... whajamacallit? Soul mates."

Beale's muscles locked down beneath my fingers. Gage's eyes widened. Rafe's mouth dropped open.

"Ohhhh," Rafe breathed. "*Now* I get it. You're right, Gage, this *does* explain so much."

"No!" Beale began, shaking his head wildly. "No, no, no. It explains nothing. It's not—"

"All these years," Rafe went on, "you've been saying you're not interested in casual hookups because you were holding out for your soul mate, blah blah, and I thought you were being hypothetical, but you were actually holding out for *Trey*! For this guy here!"

The look that Beale shot me could have stripped off more layers of skin than a chemical peel, but in my defense, how was I supposed to know he actually believed in this shit? Crystals and yoga and chakras were one thing, but soul mates? That was a bridge too far.

Fuck, that was a *continent* too far.

"Well. I-it's still early days yet," Beale stammered.

"But when you know, you know. Right?" Gage demanded. "Isn't that what you told me? The Universe will show you the one true path? The signs will be unmistakable?"

Beale's mouth opened, and then he closed it again. He nodded reluctantly. "I... had no idea you were actually paying attention when I said those things. Who knew?"

Rafe shook his head in disbelief, looking almost angry. He took a step forward, and I was positive he was going to hit one of us, probably me. But in the end, he threw his arms around Beale's waist and hugged him hard.

"Shit, man," Rafe muttered into Beale's chest. "I'm so sorry. I wish you'd said something!"

"Oh. Oh, wow. Okay." Beale patted his brother's back and grimaced at me over his shoulder. "So this is happening."

"And you!" Rafe said, pulling back and wagging a playful

finger at me. "Get over here!" He pulled me into a firm embrace. "Welcome to the family!"

The family? *Fuckity fuck.*

Rafe gave a loud sniff and clapped Beale on the shoulder. "I get that you're probably trying to be careful because of what happened with Aimee and me, but I hate that you couldn't tell me about this. I guess what's important is that you've told me now. But no wonder you didn't want to flirt with Silvio last night or throw that party to get to know him better, huh? I mean, Silvio might have an ass for *days*, but you're already all set."

An ass for days, hmm? I gave Beale a look that said, *For a guy who doesn't hook up, you sure get around,* and sure enough, Beale blushed again.

"Yes. Yeah. I'm set." Beale cleared his throat. "Which means there's no need for a party anymore. Best to cancel it."

"Are you kidding?" Rafe shook Beale's shoulder, but he looked at me. "Can you believe this guy? Cancel the party? Not fucking likely! Now we've got even more to celebrate. You two need to come down to the Bean—that's Bean Me Up, our breakfast spot," he explained for my benefit. "Everyone will want to meet you."

"Golly gosh darn it all to heck, I would *love* to, but we can't." I spread my hands helplessly. "Beale has plans for us today with, um... nature." I was pretty sure he'd said something like that.

"Oh, that," Rafe scoffed. "Beale's volunteering can wait while he introduces his soul mate to the town." He draped an arm over my shoulder. "And Scotty's coffee is incredible."

"Coffee?" I repeated, looking from Rafe to Beale. I was about a quart and a half low on caffeine, and herbal tea was not cutting it, especially in light of recent developments.

I had no desire to show my face to "everyone" at the Bean… but judging from the looks Beale was giving me, sticking around here wouldn't be a picnic either. Plus, with no phone, no internet, and no television, it would be impossible to know whether anyone was looking for me by name unless I got out of the house. "Yeah," I told Rafe. "I could do coffee."

***

"I'm not sure why you're mad at *me*," I huffed as Beale and I flew down the road in his doorless, roofless Jeep at a speed entirely incompatible with a decent hair day.

Beale had a blue bandanna tied around his head with his messy golden-brown hair hanging over top, which *should* have made him look like he was about to go all Karate Kid and sweep the leg, Johnny, but instead just made him look hot as fuck.

Because of course it did.

Because this was my life now, being fake soul mates with Florida's only hookup-hating gay *giant*, doomed not only to phone-lessness and penury, but to unending sexual frustration.

Yay, me.

"Really?" Beale shot back as he slowed down to make a turn. "Not a single clue why I'd be annoyed, *Trey*?"

I would like to say that I totally did *not* notice the way his thigh muscles bunched and flexed beneath his cargo shorts as he worked the clutch or the way his biceps flexed to enormous proportions when he shifted gears... but that would be a lie.

"Hey! If anyone else talked to Mason and told them *Toby* showed up, he'd come home, right? And I didn't come up with the idea of being your soul mate. I just..." I paused. "Ran with it."

"And you couldn't have run in another direction?" Beale demanded. "Literally any other direction?"

"How was I supposed to know you didn't do hookups and whatnot?" I demanded right back. "Not that asexuality isn't perfectly valid, obviously, or that being sexual should be the default, just that it would've been nice to know."

"I'm not asexual."

"Fine, then. A serial monogamist."

"I'm not a serial monogamist either," he mumbled. "I'm just a monogamist. Period."

"A monogamist," I scoffed. "That would mean having sex with one person ever in your whole entire life, and since you don't currently have a... a..." I trailed off and stared at Beale's gorgeous blushing face, and his enormous body, which was curled in on itself slightly like he was waiting for my judgment. Puzzle pieces finally connected in my brain.

Beale Goodman was a virgin.

An actual, real live virgin.

Holy hot damn.

If you asked Aunt Hagatha, she'd probably stress how important it was, after a person has admitted something like this, to express your support and validation. To be encouraging. But Aunt Hagatha had never been riding shotgun while her fake soul mate revealed himself to be not just a gay unicorn with an enormous cock, but a big gay *virginal* unicorn with an enormous cock that no one had test-driven *ever*.

So what came out of my mouth was something slightly shittier and less supportive, like "Sweet, slow-fucking Shawn Mendes, are you serious?"

Beale gave me a look. "Do you ever shut up?" he demanded. "Like, *ever* ever?"

No lie, this stung just a little, even if I maybe deserved it.

"Fine," I said sitting up as straight as I could and folding my arms over my chest. "Then I won't speak."

"Great! Starting now? Or..."

"But for the record—"

"Okay, so *not* now."

"*For the record*, I waited to see how you wanted to handle the situation, and you didn't do anything, so I did. If you wanted to have a say in how things went down, you should've stepped up."

"You didn't give me a chance! Besides, was I supposed to announce that you were Mason's friend Toby, and that you'd randomly shown up because you had to flee New York under... circumstances?"

No. No, I was very glad he hadn't said that. I rolled my lips together and didn't reply.

"Right. Didn't think so. So, what the heck is going on?" Beale pulled the Jeep to a stop in a parking space next to the curb and looked at me across the center console.

I blew out a breath. "I told you, it was a misunderstanding with a guy…"

"Yeah, that doesn't explain why you're using a fake name. I mean, unless the guy is hunting you. Is he Liam Neeson? Did you take his daughter?"

Not Liam Neeson, but someone approximately as famous and slightly hotter. I picked at a fray on my shorts and said nothing, which apparently spoke volumes.

"Whoa whoa whoa. Be serious for a minute. *Is* someone looking for you, Toby? Are you in trouble? Do you need a safe place to stay?"

I glanced up and found Beale's blue eyes watching me, competent and steadfast, like he was ready to throw down and fight if I needed him to. It was kind of thrilling, even if I figured it had nothing to do with me personally and everything to do with Beale's personality. I wished for a second that I could bring myself to just lie and say yes… but I couldn't.

"Not trouble like that. Not, like, domestic violence trouble."

"Beale! Trey! Come on!" Gage called from the sidewalk.

"Give us a minute," Beale said, waving them on. "So what kind of trouble, then? And *is* someone looking for you?"

I raked my fingers through my hair, which probably looked like a frizzy, brown pompom on top of my head after the drive down. "Sort of? Look, your brothers are waiting for us, and I don't want to discuss it right now." Or, ideally, ever. "Just... tell me how you want to play this. Do you want me to go in there and say I was kidding about the soul mate thing? Because I will."

"And say what instead?"

I shrugged. "I don't know exactly, but I'll figure something out on the fly." I gave him a half-smile. "I generally do."

Beale's jaw worked for half a minute, and his nostrils flared. "No," he said finally. "Just stick with what we have. It's easier."

I didn't like the feeling of owing him *again* or of making myself his problem, but I also couldn't think of a better alternative, so I nodded once, unbuckled myself from the Jeep, and waited on the sidewalk in the baking-hot sun for Beale to take my hand and usher me inside the little restaurant.

The inside was really cute, if you were into kitschy sci-fi stuff, which it turned out I was. The walls were painted a cheerful yellow and hung with old movie posters of *The Blob* and *Attack of the Killer Tomatoes*. A sign on the wall behind the counter in the shape of a *Star Trek* logo read "Bean Me Up" in classic *Star Trek* font. But I was the only one in the place checking out the decor. Everyone else—literally two dozen people—were staring at *me*.

"Beale?" I asked without moving my lips. "Why is everyone staring?" For a heart-stopping moment, I wondered if my picture had made it to TMZ already.

Beale tightened his fingers around mine and lifted our joined hands. A hushed "Awww" filled the restaurant, like every patron had sighed at the sight.

"They're staring because they've never seen me holding hands with someone, and because my brothers got in here before us and spread the word about who you are."

"Oh," I said dumbly.

"Not that that'll stop all of them from coming over and wanting to welcome you." He sighed.

"And that man over by your brothers." I tilted my head casually in that direction. "Is he practicing to be a flag-waver in a marching band, or is he three decades too late to wave his Zippo for Guns N' Roses?"

Beale chuckled. "That's my dad, Big Rafe. He's the mayor of Whispering Key, if you couldn't tell by the shirt."

I darted a glance back, and sure enough, the man was wearing a purple shirt with the word MAYOR written across the front in iridescent letters.

Well. Alrighty, then.

"He's not-so-subtly suggesting we come over," Beale continued, "but I'm getting food fir—"

"Heya, Beale!" A middle-aged lady with a bright white smile and long, straight dark hair bounced to a stop beside us as we took our place in line.

"Whoa. Uh. Hey, Juju. How's it—?"

"And this must be Trey!" She folded her hands and nearly squealed. "Welcome to Whispering Key!"

Beale shot me a look that said *Told you,* and I tried not to smile.

"Thanks," I agreed. "Nice to meet you."

"Oh, same. *Same!* And is it true you two are..." She made a back-and-forth motion between us and glanced pointedly at our joined hands.

"Hungry?" Beale suggested blandly.

"Gay?" I whispered.

"Together?" she said brightly.

I very pointedly studied the menu board on the back wall and pretended not to hear her, leaving it up to Beale to explain shit. He sighed and squeezed my hand.

"Yeah," Beale said, earning bonus points for succinctness.

Juju beamed like she'd engineered the whole thing. "You guys are so adorable! Meeting at summer camp, writing love letters to each other for years."

Love letters? I blinked at Beale, and he shrugged.

"Beale!" An overly tanned older guy wearing a half-unbuttoned tropical print shirt came over and slung an arm over each of our necks. "Congrats on your new beau, honey. You turned me down so many times, I was wondering if you were really gay at all!"

Beale removed the guy's arm from my shoulder with force and shifted me to his other side. "Appreciate the concern, Gerry."

Juju covered her mouth and giggled softly. "I was kinda worried the crystals had affected your brain, Beale."

Gerry snickered. "That, too. But I guess you weren't crazy after all, huh?" He elbowed Beale in the ribs and waggled his eyebrows at me.

I not-so-secretly hoped Beale would elbow him back, but instead Beale rolled his eyes and stepped up to the counter.

I frowned, annoyed. Not crazy after all? If I were Beale, I'd have laid that asshole out flat.

"What was that about?" I demanded.

Beale shrugged, apparently used to this. "You know what you want yet?"

"Yeah. Um... Venti ristretto cinnamon dolce macchiato with almond milk, please," I told the barista, whose name tag said Scotty.

I dug out the folded-up twenty I'd put in my pocket before we'd left the house and set it on the counter, only belatedly noticing that Scotty was staring at me like I'd been speaking Klingon. Actually, no, he probably would have understood Klingon. "On second thought, maybe just an iced coffee?"

"You got it." Scotty grinned. "Your usual, Beale? Green tea and oat milk?"

"Please."

When Scotty disappeared to make our drinks, Beale bumped his arm into mine. "I had no idea you spoke fluent Italian, Trey. It's so..."

"Sexy?"

"I was thinking pretentious, but I guess it depends what turns your crank."

I laughed and firmly told myself not to ask him what turned *his* crank. He'd made it clear he wasn't interested, and deflowering virgins was hardly my thing anyway.

Probably.

"You'd think you'd know me better after the decade or so of letter writing. How long have we been pen pals?"

Beale thought for a moment. "I'm twenty-eight, so... a dozen years I guess?"

I winced.

"Problem?"

Only that I'd been twenty-three when he was sixteen. "Not at all," I lied. Because, really, what was one more lie, at this point?

Scotty brought our coffees over, and I ended up sucking down half my cup before we even left the counter—Rafe was right, it really *was* good—to fortify myself for the next step.

"You okay?"

"Sure." I wiped my damp palm on my shorts. "I've never met anyone's parents before, but how bad could it be?"

Beale frowned. "Never?"

"Nope. I don't do boyfriends any more than you do."

"Huh." Beale hesitated, then put a hand at the small of my back to guide me to the table where his dad sat. It felt weird. Nice-weird. Or maybe just nice. "Look, please don't invent any more details about our summer camp love affair."

"I won't!"

"Or promise that we'll get married on the beach in the fall or whatever."

"I wouldn't!"

"Or let Dad rope you into doing anything for the Whispering Key Extravaganza."

"What extravaganza?"

But it was too late for Beale to explain, because we were already standing by a table in the back of the restaurant.

"Morning, everyone. Um. Trey, this is my dad, Big Rafe. His fiancée, Gloria. Ms. Pepper, my kindergarten teacher. And you know Young Rafe and Gage." He pointed to each person at the table in turn, but as he spoke, more people crowded around. "Uh. And this is Mike Hooper, who does real estate on the island. And Viv Mickell, who runs the arcade with her brother Jeremy. And... oh hey, Jeremy, didn't see you there. And Jaya Kaur, and Christine Miele, and Oswaldo Lopez, and Maddie McKetcham, and..." He kept going, but my brain reached critical mass at that point.

I was used to working alone. I went out plenty, and I wasn't agoraphobic in the slightest, but I wasn't used to having so many people look at me with open curiosity either.

And this is what your whole life will be like if the story gets out, my brain reminded me helpfully. *On a global scale.*

Except at least the Whispering Key folks were generally smiling at me right then. I was pretty sure the rest of the world would not be.

"And everyone, this is To... Trey," Beale concluded, which seemed to be permission for every single person to start babbling at me all at once.

Beale looked down at me, amused, and I tried to smile back, but whatever he saw on my face had his hand moving from my back to wrap around my side. "Chill, guys. One at a time," he admonished, taking charge with his usual competence.

"Yes, everyone, get in line! I'm first." Gloria got up from the table and wrapped her arms around me so her curly red hair tickled my cheek and her Shalimar perfume filled my nostrils. "It's not right to play favorites, but you've got the best of the bunch," she whispered in my ear. She pulled back and gave me a tremulous smile. "And now you get to be here for the party!"

I nodded, then shook my head. "Party?"

"The one Beale's throwing Friday," someone piped up. "In Mason and Fenn's backyard."

"A surprise housewarming for them," Maddie explained.

"They'll love it," Big Rafe said firmly.

I wasn't so sure about that, and from the way Beale's teeth squeaked together, it sounded like he wasn't either.

"Wait," I frowned. "Is this the party Rafe mentioned earlier? With Silvio?" And his ass for days?

"Him and a bunch of other guys I know," Rafe said with a shrug. "I texted them all last night, so it's too late to cancel, but don't worry about that. I'll let them know Beale's off the market, but I can introduce them to Gagie-poo here." He ruffled Gage's brown hair, and Gage shoved him away. "In fact, if you'll still be around Friday, Trey, maybe you can help Beale with the party arrangements. Party planning is *not* Beale's thing."

"Not unless the stars align for it," an older lady tittered.

"Maybe the Universe will tell him what to serve," the Christine person teased with a gentle smile.

Beale's hand tightened on my hip, and without thinking, I patted his abs with my free hand in a soothing sort of way... until everyone around us did that weird sigh thing again, and I snatched my hand back.

I really didn't understand the vibe happening in this cafe. Everyone clearly liked Beale a lot, but they also gave him shit in a way that didn't feel entirely like a joke. It was confusing, because crystals or not, Beale Goodman was the smartest and most capable person I'd met in a long time. In fact...

I held my breath for a second as I realized that *Beale* might be just the perfect person to help me brainstorm the best way out of the mess I was in.

Trusting him would be a huge risk, since the information I'd be sharing wouldn't just be *my* secret, but Jayd's secret, too. Still, Beale had already saved me repeatedly, and remembering his serious expression as he'd asked if I was safe made my cold, black heart flutter harder than I cared to admit. Some part of me trusted him already.

"I'll be here," I agreed staunchly. "And I'm happy to help Beale out, if he needs anything." In fact, that might be one way I could pay Beale back for all the shit I'd inadvertently stirred up.

Beale exhaled impatiently. I gave him a look under my lashes that said, *Excuse* you*! I'm trying to be a good fake soul mate here,* and he squeezed my hip again in what seemed like acknowledgement.

"I'll add you both to the party group chat!" Gloria said. "We're thinking potluck."

"Lovely." I summoned a smile.

All the while, I noticed Big Rafe watching me with his head tilted at an angle, like a curious dog. He wasn't *unfriendly*, precisely, but he wasn't friendly either.

"Beale, why don't you and Trey come over to Rafe's house this afternoon for a little family thing?" Big Rafe said abruptly, interrupting the party chatter. "We can all get to know each other better."

He seemed pleasant enough, but I felt like he was the Godfather, making us an offer we couldn't refuse.

"I'm afraid we can't today." Beale pulled me more closely against him.

"I think around five thirty?" Big Rafe looked at Gloria, who nodded. "We'll grill out."

"I'll grab brats," Gage said. "Rafe can get beer."

"We're heading out to Menucha," Beale said in clear and concise English. "Tracking snowy plovers."

"I'll make a butter cake," Gloria offered. "And some potato salad."

I frowned up at Beale, and he gave me a half-smile like this was something he expected, but I was kinda tired of this bullshit after only ten minutes.

Aunt Hagatha would probably tell me to follow Beale's lead, especially after getting us into a mess earlier, but then again Aunt Hagatha had never stood by while her fake soul mate was ignored by his boisterous family members... and she wasn't gonna start today. If he wasn't going to stand up for himself, I'd do it.

"You all have fun!" I said brightly. "We won't be there, but you can text Beale some pictures."

Young Rafe frowned at Beale. "What? Why won't you be there?"

"He just *told* you why." I set my hand on my hip. "Weren't you listening?"

Beale's hand tightened on my hip again, but in a restraining sort of way this time. "I signed up to track plovers on Menucha for the Nature Center," he repeated easily. "As I told you earlier today. And yesterday. And now."

Rafe's frown deepened. "Oh, shoot. That's right. I—"

"Rafe! Rafe, lookie here." A man who looked remarkably like Littlejohn Jennings rushed over with a newspaper and waved it in Young Rafe's face triumphantly. "I told you! Didn't I tell you?"

Rafe blinked down at the paper, attention caught.

"Well, for God's sake, don't make Trey go to Menucha with you." Big Rafe leaned back in his seat and rolled his eyes at

Beale. "He'll be bored to tears. He can come hang out with us at the house. Go for a swim."

I shot Beale a look that said, *I would literally rather hang out with your murder cat*, and his lips twitched.

"I don't think—" he said.

But Gage interjected, "Dad, come on. Beale and Trey have been reunited for like ten nanoseconds. They wanna spend time together. And they can swim at Fenn's place."

Or not swim. Ideally not.

"Besides which," I said solemnly, "I love plovers. Adore them! In fact, they're my favorite type of um..."

"Bird?" Beale supplied. I figured everyone could hear the thread of laughter in his voice, too, but no one else seemed to notice.

"Yes! Yup. Bird. Also, I love being out in the... air? And, like... under the sky and whatnot? I'm basically Outdoorsy Barbie."

Big Rafe started to object, but Gloria cut him off.

"Another time, then," she said. "Rafe and Gage, maybe you boys can... Rafe, honey? You okay?"

Young Rafe stared down at the newspaper in his hand like he'd seen a ghost.

"See? It's your brother-in-law!" Littlejohn's doppelgänger jabbed a finger at the paper.

"I told you, he's not my damn brother-in-law, Dale." Rafe set the newspaper facedown on the table and covered it with his hand. "He can do whatever he likes with whomever he likes. It's all media speculation, anyway."

"What speculation?" Gage demanded, trying to grab the paper from under Rafe's hand.

"What's happening?" I whispered softly, so only Beale could hear. "What's up with his brother-in-law?"

"Boys! Stop this instant!" Big Rafe yelled, as Rafe and Gage played tug-of-war with the paper like a pair of toddlers, knocking over a sugar canister.

Beale took the opportunity to quietly back away from the table and out the door. He let out a huge sigh when we reached the sidewalk.

"Not sure what's going on exactly." He rolled his eyes. "Probably not a big deal, but for Rafe, everything with Jay is a big deal."

"M'kay, I'm gonna need you to spill all the tea," I demanded as we got to the Jeep, proving that maybe Aunt Hagatha and I were more alike than I cared to admit. We both liked to be up in other people's business.

"Well... up until a year and a bit ago, Rafe was married, right? He and Aimee started out as childhood friends, kinda—her family summered on the Key back when *no one* summered here, so we all became close. Aimee's brother Jay was only a couple years younger than Rafe, so they'd go off adventuring, or sometimes Jay would try to teach Rafe guitar. Whatever they were doing, Gage would trail after them like a puppy. And meanwhile my mom taught Aimee and me about crystals and tarot cards and stuff. Rafe and Aimee weren't romantically involved until after college, but then all of a sudden, they were in love and getting married, and they seemed happy more or less?" Beale shrugged. "I dunno. They lasted for seven years or so. But I guess Aimee couldn't have been all that happy in the end, 'cause one night she just up and left."

"Left Rafe?" The idea made me hurt for the guy.

"Left the Key. Left Florida, for all I know. She was just... gone. *Poof.* Rafe looked for her, but Jay wouldn't tell him anything except that she was safe and she didn't wanna see him." Beale winced. "Personally, I get it. I'm loyal to my siblings above anyone, even if they're assholes. I think Rafe was more hurt by Jay's behavior than Aimee's, though." He paused. "Don't tell him I said that."

"I won't," I promised solemnly, and Beale's face went red again. I was pretty sure making him blush could become a legit hobby of mine, it was that appealing. He was so damn *likable*. And smart, too. It was no surprise I found myself trusting him the way I did.

He started the engine and shifted the Jeep into gear. "Anyway, so now anytime anyone says Jay's name, Rafe looks like he's been sucking a lemon. That's the whole story."

"Well, who could blame him?" I sipped at my coffee, then leaned back against the seat and turned my face up to the sunshine, happier than I'd been in a week... or possibly longer. I felt *hopeful*. Less panicked. Like maybe this shit situation wouldn't be so bad after all.

"Yeah, but it's pretty inconvenient. I mean, if you're gonna pick a guy to hate on, it's best if you can pick someone who doesn't have a million Instagram followers, you know?" He grinned.

I frowned.

"Or whose hit song hasn't been on the radio all summer."

"What?" I demanded, sitting upright. My heart beat rapidly, and my blood ran cold, like my body knew what was coming before I did.

"Or who isn't coming to play a concert for the Whispering Key Extravaganza over Labor Day in a month." He gave me a side-eyed look. "That was my dad's idea, by the way, and Rafe was *not* happy."

"Beale? I think you missed a crucial piece of information. Who, um... who is Jay?"

"Oh." He laughed. "Jay is Jayd Rollins. You know, the singer?"

I nodded woodenly. Oh, I knew him alright, and the paparazzi had the pictures to prove it. And my plan to tell Beale everything evaporated before my very eyes.

"Toby? You okay? You sure you're up to volunteering today? If you're not ready..."

I swallowed hard and did my best to summon a flirtatious smile despite my churning stomach. "Nonsense! I was born ready."

6

BEALE

"I am absolutely not ready."

Toby stood with his arms folded and tapped one sandal on the wooden dock as he watched me load my gear bag into the bottom of the tender. He'd done something to his hair before we left the guesthouse that made it look artfully tousled, unlike my own unruly mop, and his skin glowed gold in the sun, maybe partly from the sunscreen I'd forced him to coat himself with... but I wasn't going to tell him that.

"I was not informed that this would be an aquatic expedition," he continued. "Birds, last I checked, were creatures of the air. The *air*, Beale, which is not wet." He swiped a wrist over his forehead. "Except here in Florida, where I suppose it rather *is*. Still."

I found my lips twitching, wanting to smile, even though I had only the smallest clue what he was ranting about, and I was pretty sure he didn't know either. I wasn't sure how his rants had gone from massively annoying to mostly funny in the span of half a morning, but here we were.

I still wasn't a hundred percent sure I liked him as a person, but I definitely liked looking at him. I liked watching the way emotions shifted over his face like sunlight on water. I liked hearing him talk...

Or at least I had, back when he'd actually been speaking, back before I'd told him that story about Aimee and Rafe and he'd clammed up for the rest of the car ride.

I resettled my bandanna on my head. "I take it you don't like boats?"

"Of course I like boats! I love boats. Boats are delightful. Boats are a feat of human engineering. Riverboats, ferryboats, yachts, cruise ships? Beautiful. I'm fond of all vessels that don't require me to actually become one with the ocean."

"Well." I scratched the back of my head. "The goal is to not become one with the ocean today either, otherwise we'd be swimming out to Menucha." I hefted the cooler full of water bottles, ice, and snacks we'd just picked up at Pickles' grocery store into the tender also. "Instead, we'll both be wearing life jackets." I nodded at the yellow vest in his hand, which I'd gotten out of Fenn's cubby at the Goodmen Outfitters office. My dad made fun of me for still wearing a life jacket every time I went out, but I'd lived on the water too long not to take safety seriously. "And we'll stay inside the boat, on top of the water."

"This is not a boat," Toby informed me, a thread of uneasiness in his voice. "That is a boat." He pointed at the *Mary Anna*, Goodmen Outfitters' fifty-foot tour boat. "This is... this is an overgrown pool float! I saw Taylor Swift and her girl squad on something like this in her backyard over Memorial Day."

"Taylor Swift and her girl squad had a twelve-and-a-half-foot aluminum frame PVC dinghy with an outboard motor? In her pool?" I gave him an exaggerated frown. "Badass."

Toby huffed and rolled his eyes.

"I told you before," I added more gently. "You don't have to come if you'd rather not. You can take the Jeep and go back to the guesthouse. Sit by the pool. Or you could hang with my dad."

Toby set his shoulders and shrugged into the life vest. "Yeah, right. I said I was coming, so I'm coming." He lifted his chin like a queen. "But if we die, I am *so* blaming you."

"I'd expect nothing less," I said solemnly.

"You ready to come aboard?" I held out a hand since it was a bit of a step down from the platform. "Be careful in those sandals—"

Toby clasped my hand and stepped, but his hand was slippery from the sunscreen, and he stumbled. I caught him around the waist and held him firmly against me as the little boat rocked against the dock. The scent of his cologne along with the ocean air and my coconut-lime sunscreen was basically the best scent in the entire universe, and I nearly groaned at the feel of his skin under my hands for the second… no, *third* time that morning. This was worse than either time before, though, because his mouth was mere inches from mine, and—

"Sweet Benedict Cumberbatch! I've defied death three times this day!" Toby pushed weakly at my arms.

"Whoa," I said softly, gripping the shoulder of his life jacket with my other hand. "Settle for just a second. I've got you. You're alright. You're fine."

"Yeah." Toby took one deep breath and another, and then he pushed me away again and cleared his throat. "Yes. Of course I'm alright." His voice still had a slight quaver to it. "I'm confident that Rose felt just this way whilst boarding the *Titanic*." He sat primly on the seat in the middle facing aft with his hands folded in his lap. "Like she was boarding the vessel that would ultimately seal her doom."

I couldn't help smiling a little. "Doesn't Rose survive?"

Toby sniffed. "Beside the point."

"Sure." I took a minute to cast off and coil the ropes, then sat in back where I could work the tiller. I took up a lot of the space between the seats, and my knees ended up just a few inches from Toby's, close enough that the movement of the boat was going to make our legs touch as soon as we got out on the water.

I attached the safety switch to my own life jacket and pulled the cord to start the motor.

The morning was strangely quiet on the water, especially for a summer weekend. Once we cleared the small dock near the center of town, the only sounds were the hum of the engine and the call of startled gulls.

Toby took in the waves and the sunshine without saying a word, and that was fine—I wasn't a person who needed to talk or be talked to—but it was different from the way he'd been all morning. Back at the Bean and later in the Jeep, when he tilted back against the seat and grinned at me, he'd seemed open and relaxed. I wasn't sure what had happened to get his back up, but it reminded me a little of Marjorie when I first found her.

"I hate Florida. Only *Florida* could turn something like beautiful sunshine into a thing that's abusive and rude and hurtful. I can feel myself crisping like bacon."

I dug a hat out of my gear bag and plopped it on his head. It looked kinda cute on him.

"Hey!" He pulled the hat off and looked at it. "I am not wearing a hat that says Bubba's Bait."

"Why not? No one will see you but me, *Trey*, and we're already madly in love, remember?"

Toby blinked like I'd startled him somehow, but he replaced the hat on his head without a comment and went back to staring out at the water, which seemed unlike him.

Unlike him. Because you know him so well, Beale? I rolled my eyes at myself but couldn't help asking, "Everything okay?"

"You mean, aside from the obvious? No phone, no credit card? Having survived near-death experiences with cats and kitchen appliances and yoga stretches? Out in the middle of the great, wide ocean with only the thinnest rubber membrane between me and the briny deep? No, other than that I'm peachy."

"I meant more like, did I do something to upset you? 'Cause for a minute there, you almost seemed like you were having fun, and then…" I shrugged. "You didn't."

Toby shot me a look—another of those curiously vulnerable looks—before his face blanked. "I'm fine. Perfectly fine. Are *you* okay?"

"Me?" As we passed out of the little harbor, I nudged the throttle a little and sent the boat skipping on the waves. "Why wouldn't I be?"

Toby clutched the baseball hat. "Because people were rude to you back at the Bean."

"Nah."

"Yeah," he insisted. "There was a whole vibe going on about your crystals and stuff. I didn't like it."

I was honestly surprised he'd noticed. I didn't love it either, but…

"I'm used to it. I believe in things they don't." I shrugged. "It's just their way."

"Disrespecting your worldview is not 'just their way.' They don't have to believe what you believe, but they don't get to give you shit for it. If you were Buddhist or Wiccan or Catholic, would it be okay for them to make snide remarks?"

"No. Of course not." I frowned. I'd never thought of it that way before—as something that people ought to take seriously, simply because it was important to me.

"You need to stand up for yourself and—eeep!" The boat hit a swell, and Toby shrieked. One of his hands grabbed the edge of his seat, and the other grasped my hand where it rested on my knee. "Is it supposed to do that?" he demanded.

"Yes," I reassured him over the hum of the motor. "Just a little chop. You really don't like little boats, huh?"

"You might say." He gripped tighter, but his tone was firmly casual as he raised his voice and said, "My point was, don't let them get to you."

He was so unfairly cute, half hunched over my lap and braced for us to capsize, though I hadn't opened the throttle hardly at all.

"I won't." I patted his shoulder gently. "Thanks."

"Being serious," he insisted, looking up at me from under his lashes. "You're smart, Beale. No one has the right to make you feel less than."

I frowned at him quickly before looking back at the water.

"The thing is, I'm a Virgo."

"Right." Toby nodded. "Yeah. You kinda indicated that in the car earlier. I, um… I support you. I should have said that earlier." He reached out a hand and patted my arm. "Thank you for coming out to me."

"What? No! I'm not… I mean, I *am*, but that's not…" I pulled away and felt my cheeks go fire-hot. "I'm a *Virgo*. As in, my astrological sign. Because I was born in September?"

"Ohhhh. Of course. Duh. I knew that."

"Also, thanks for the support, but I don't think people need to come out as virgins. Or Virgos."

Toby's brow furrowed. "Fair enough. So, you're a Virgo. What does that have to do with anything?"

"Virgos generally don't waste time convincing other people of things. I accept that folks have opinions just like I do— like about how I should live my life, and what kind of a career I want, and what I should do with my share of the treasure money we found…" I looked at Toby, pretty confident Mason had filled him in about all that, and he nodded in confirmation. "But I don't argue. I just let them talk. I know they worry because they care. And also, they can talk as much as they like, but I'm not letting them change my mind once it's made up. I'm stubborn that way."

"'Cause you're a Virgo."

"No, 'cause I'm a Goodman." I grinned. "I refuse to settle for any old career or any old guy. I'm waiting for the things that feel right. The things that feel like they're meant to be mine." I shrugged. "But I don't enjoy the tussle of an argument the way my dad and brothers do, which is probably why there aren't a lot of things I have nonnegotiable opinions on."

Toby sat back in his seat. "Only important stuff."

"Yup."

"Like… holding out for the one right path and the one right person."

"Right. Yes."

"Hmm." He nodded thoughtfully.

I shrugged again. "It's fine if you disagree—"

"I don't know if I do or don't. I don't believe in absolutes. There are lots of right answers to most questions, including this one."

I swiped at my forehead under my bandanna. That was a nonanswer if I'd ever heard one. For all that he liked to make *me* talk, Toby was shit at opening up about himself.

"So, when you meet your soul mate, what will this paragon of virtue be like?" he prompted.

I darted a glance at him, expecting to find him scoffing, but he seemed genuinely curious. I lifted a shoulder. "I'm not entirely sure."

"But surely you must have some idea."

"Well, I mean, he's the person who's supposed to fit perfectly with me, so I'm guessing we'd share the same interests—"

He nodded. "Birds. Boats. Vegan burritos. That's reasonable."

"Yep. And yoga. Maybe crystals. Reading. Beach walks. Nature Center."

"Beach walks are good," Toby approved. He reached for a reusable water bottle in the cooler and uncapped it.

"He'd probably be a Capricorn—that means born in January—"

"Ah, and here I am, a May baby." Toby pouted, and I smiled a little.

"And we'd talk, I guess. I'd be able to talk to him about

anything—my day, the meaning of life. We'd watch movies and discuss 'em. Basic stuff, really."

"Movie discussion sounds good, too." He sipped the water. "Like what movies? What was the last movie you saw you wished you could discuss?"

"Hmm. *Saw*, I guess."

Toby choked on his water, then glared at me while he thumped his own chest. "*Saw*? Are you fucking kidding me? I was thinking *Shawshank Redemption* or *Sophie's Choice* or something. What is there to discuss about *Saw*? 'Which sequel made *you* pee your pants most, soul mate? Wow, me too! We have so much in common!'"

I laughed out loud. "Come on. *Saw* wasn't that scary! The bad guy wasn't even really *bad*. Most of the people he hurt were genuinely terrible, and the goal was to teach them a lesson, so in a way—"

"Lemme stop you right there, Beale, my sweetie pie, my honey bunch. You said yourself, he's the bad guy. The. Bad. Guy. Not the morally ambiguous gent. Not the misunderstood dude. He's the villain, so by his very nature, he is bad. And this bad guy is, like, the baddest of the bad."

"So says the man who doesn't believe in absolutes."

Toby gaped at me for a minute. "In real life I generally don't," he finally said snottily. "But fictional bad guys are fictional. And *bad*. You cannot argue with them or rationalize them. When people are mean to you, your only choice is to get away from them and save yourself." He sounded like he was speaking to a toddler. "That's a free life lesson for you, right there."

"Nope. I disagree. Take your *Titanic* movie, there. Rose—"

"Oh my God, no! Don't even try it. Billy Zane is soulless and corrupt, and represents capitalist greed and profligate—"

"Toby, listen to yourself! The man's girlfriend, who was only marrying him for his money, had car sex with another dude. Wouldn't *you* be cranky? He just has a passionate nature."

"He chases them with a gun while the boat is sinking! No, no, go back to your Virgo 'I'm not gonna try to convince you' schtick, because you'll never win me over! You're probably one of those people who'd try to redeem Darth fucking Vader—"

"You mean poor Anakin, who only joined the Dark Side to protect his wife and babies?"

Toby laughed so hard his eyes crinkled at the corners, which was... really damn attractive.

"Motive matters, that's all I'm saying!" I laughed, too. "That's what Aunt Hagatha would tell you."

Toby's smile evaporated, and he blinked at me like he could think of no comeback to something this stupid. I felt my face go red. Again.

At least out here I could blame the sun.

"Aaaand I guess now you see why people tend to give me shit about my weird opinions, whether it's about crystals or horoscopes or whatever, huh?" I tried to smile.

Toby didn't respond except to rock with the motion of the boat, but when I darted a glance down, he swallowed hard. "You know, you missed the most important thing about your soul mate."

"Did I?"

"You have to be sexually compatible."

"Oh. Well, yeah. Obviously." I frowned. "I mean, how could we not be?"

"Beale, angel." Toby shook his head sadly. "There are lots and lots of ways to be sexually incompatible. As in *lots*. But like, most obviously... what if you don't find him attractive?"

I scowled. "I will. He'll be attractive because he's my soul mate, not the other way around. I don't have a lot of preconceived ideas about whether he's tall or short, dark or fair, or any of that. "

Toby scowled. "How lovely, my precious unicorn. But here in reality land... I dare you to convince me you don't want someone like that bartender with the nice ass everyone keeps mentioning."

That was the second time he'd brought Silvio up since Rafe had mentioned him that morning, and I had to bite my lip to keep myself from pointing it out. Some people always wanted to be the center of attention. "Silvio *does* have a very nice ass," I admitted.

"Better than mine?" He gave me an arch look and twisted in his seat to give me a visual, like I might have forgotten what his ass looked like or where he kept it.

I fixed my eyes on the water, a little turned on by his flirtation, but mostly amused. Somewhere in the course of the morning, I'd figured out that his forceful flirtation was more like a distraction—a deflection—when he felt vulnerable, so now it didn't make me feel pressured, it almost made me feel... protective.

For all his world-weary attitude, Toby was naive enough to miss that the biggest part of what made him attractive had nothing to do with his ass and everything to do with the way he'd stuck up for me earlier, and the way he tried to listen when people talked, and the hilarious, dry-as-dust comebacks to almost everything.

I found myself saying, "You have a very nice ass also…"

I darted a glance at Toby, who seemed shocked for a second but decided to play it off. "Why thank you, dearest—"

"Just not quite as nice as his."

Toby gasped and clasped a hand to the base of his throat. "Excuse you? What a thing for a man to say to his soul mate."

I rolled my eyes. "You're not my soul mate."

"Not if you talk about this ass with such casual disregard, that's for damn sure." He slapped it lightly.

"So, now that you know way, way more than I'd rather have you know about me, what's *your* deal? When you're not getting into 'circumstances' and jetting down to Florida, what do you do?"

"Oh, the usual." He waved a hand. "Work. Exercise. Skincare."

"Right. Same. My skincare routine is intense. Do you have family?"

"Sure. Everyone comes from somewhere."

"I guess you're not close, then?" I persisted.

"I came out to my mom after a bad breakup freshman year of college, and she suggested my problem was in dating guys instead of girls. When she offered me religious pamphlets, I left town immediately and never came back, and they sure as hell didn't come after me. So, no, you might say we're not close."

"Gotcha. So, what do you do for work?"

"Boring. Better topic: did you know Mase and I met back in college? Freshman year. He was my roommate."

I ran my tongue over my teeth. Was he being deliberately evasive? Had he missed the part where I said I was stubborn?

"Cool. So where do you work?"

"New York. Ever been?"

I shook my head. "Never been out of Florida. What kind of work?"

"This and that. Writing mostly. Never out of Florida! Wow. You know, I was gonna be in the Maldives this week? You'd like it there. Plenty of water. Birds, too."

He almost, almost got me. But not quite. "Writing! That's an interesting job. What do you write? Novels? Grants? Musicals?"

"Nothing you've ever read." He snorted. "*You're* not exactly my target audience."

"Oh." Well, then.

That put me in my place, didn't it? Whatever he wrote was clearly way above my pay grade.

It felt like the sun had gone behind a cloud, and even the breeze off the water felt cold, which was silly, really—more than silly—when I thought about it. This was a guy I'd known for less than half a day. He'd said nice things, but in the end, was it really a shock that he'd established the same opinion about my intellect after spending a few hours with me that the rest of Whispering Key had after knowing me for decades?

"So how long until we reach this island?"

"A few minutes." I pointed ahead of us. "That bit of land is Menucha."

He turned to look at it, then glanced back at me. "It looks delightfully dry." He grinned.

I gave him a clipped nod. "There's actually a small dock on the northwest of the island where we can tie up, so you won't have to get wet at all. If you grab the binoculars from my bag, you can probably see it."

Toby frowned, probably because my jokey-ness had evaporated, but he opened my bag and removed my binoculars, looped the strap behind his neck, and set his sights on the island.

"The east side is..." I frowned as I noticed a boat in the distance getting steadily closer, and adjusted our course to make sure we passed them to starboard.

"Is?" Toby prompted.

"Full of mangroves," I finished, watching the other craft. "What the hell is that guy doing?"

Toby lifted the binoculars. "Dancing. I'm guessing TikTok is involved. And there are a bunch of people in bikinis and board shorts. T-shirts suggest Sigma Alpha... something." He grimaced. "It's five o'clock somewhere."

Great. Once again, I adjusted the tiller and steered wide to avoid them.

"You know, I wasn't kidding."

I shifted my gaze back to Toby. "Yes, I know. It's definitely five o'clock somewhere. Probably France. I understand how time zones work." How dumb did he think I was?

He laughed shortly. "Not that. I mean, that you probably haven't read anything I've written. It wasn't a slam. Not to you, anyway. I don't talk about work, Beale." He hesitated. "I can't, even if I wanted to, which I do *not*. I signed a nondisclosure agreement years ago."

This was unexpected. "What do you write, man? Hateful political tirades?"

"No, darling. Nothing *that* terrible."

"Is this the reason you had to leave New York?"

"No, I... No. That was a whole different—" He broke off as the thumping bass of the *Venga bus* song floated across the water, along with high-pitched squeals.

It seemed like no one on the party boat was paying attention to their heading or the location of any other boats in the water, because their current course and speed meant they'd collide with us in about a minute.

I cut the tiller sharply, setting us on a westerly course that would put us nearly parallel to the wake of the other boat, which was going to suck but would be infinitely better than a collision.

"Hang on," I told Toby sharply. I twisted the tiller to slow us a bit as the other vessel passed, but we still hit the trough of their wake at the worst possible angle. The boat dipped and rose like a roller coaster.

Toby hunched over and grabbed onto my right leg with both hands, throwing me off balance. In a panicked voice, he asked, "Would now be a good time to mention that I can't swim?"

"Wait, what? Are you serious?"

"The murder cats and the yoga weren't enough!" he wailed. "Now the sea will claim me!" He buried his face in my thigh.

I resisted the urge to laugh. Instead, I grabbed the back of his neck with my free hand and stroked the skin there gently, feeling way more protective than the moment called for.

"Hey, it's alright. Look, Toby. Toby, it's *fine*. They're gone. We're back on course. It was just a blip." I tugged gently on the hair at the nape of his neck. "Shhh. We weren't in any danger, okay? And I wouldn't've let anything happen to you, even if we were. Your life jacket would've kept you afloat, and I'd've taken care of everything else," I soothed. "If you'd told me you couldn't swim, I'd've explained that before. It's all good."

"Just a blip?" Toby lifted his head enough to look around.

"Just a blip," I confirmed. "It happens."

He peered at the asshole boat speeding off into the distance, and my gaze followed his.

"*Sea Me Beachin.*" I read in disgust, my hand still stroking his neck. "That's maybe the douchiest boat name I've ever heard. Don't worry, Toby, I'm gonna talk to a guy I know at the Fish and Wildlife Commission as soon as we get back and make sure—*mmmph!*"

I broke off as Toby launched himself almost into my lap, whacking my forehead with the bill of his hat—*my* hat—as he pressed his mouth to mine. If my hand hadn't been braced on the tiller, I might have toppled off the back of the boat out of sheer surprise... and then out of pure, unadulterated want.

Toby's kiss was sweet, crystal perfection, more invigorating than cold water on a hot day. Without conscious thought, my hand slid up into his hair, knocking the hat off his head, his mouth opened over mine, and every one of my brain cells powered down in a chain reaction, like a video I once saw of a power outage rolling through a city.

Then, as suddenly as it began, it was over. Toby scrambled backward into his seat and grabbed his hair with two hands.

"Sorry! Fuck. *Sorry.* I specifically told you I wasn't going to jump you and I did, and just *fuck.* But that was so... and you were so... and I'm really not cut out for adventure." He stared at me and panted for a second. "Which is not an excuse, I know it's not an excuse, but it's an explanation. Because I have a low tolerance for adrenaline?" He stared down at his fingers, which he knit together and pulled apart. "And now I'm babbling when I never babble. I blame Florida. At least partly. I'm really not at my best here."

He peered up at me, gauging my reaction. Trouble was, I had no idea how to react. I knew what I *should* feel, but I couldn't deny the deep coil of need that unfurled in my belly, stronger than anything I'd felt last night, or this morning, or ever before.

"Say something," Toby insisted worriedly. "Call me out or throw me overboard. I mean, don't *actually* throw me overboard, please, just—"

I grabbed him by his T-shirt and hauled him toward me to kiss him again.

Our lips slotted together perfectly, and Toby groaned. Those smooth, soft hands kneaded the muscles of my thighs over my shorts, and I gasped against his mouth. I cradled his jaw in both palms so I could hold him still and settle in to savor the shocking rightness of our tongues gliding together.

Toby made a breathless, encouraging noise and fit himself against me as much as possible while balancing his ass on his seat. One of his cool hands reached up to cover mine on his face, and the other reached under my shirt to splay against my lower back. For once I was enjoying myself too much to care about what came next or worry about what I ought to be doing. I was all in.

Which of course was when we hit something in the water that launched the tender half a foot in the air. I grabbed Toby around the waist and pulled him down to the bottom of the boat, covering him with my body and pulling the safety key from the motor. The engine stalled.

We lay there for a second, staring at each other in the sudden quiet, legs tangled as the boat rode the swells. Toby looked every bit as stunned as I felt, and I couldn't tell if it was adrenaline, or the kiss, or both, but my cock was suddenly hard as a rock, and if either of us moved an inch, Toby would know it.

I immediately rolled off him and sat up, bracing myself on the stern of the boat and looking out into the turquoise water to see if I could spot what we'd hit. It looked like a giant piece of driftwood bobbing nearby.

"Was it another boat?" Toby croaked, crowding in beside me. "Or a giant fish?"

I couldn't meet his eyes as I reattached the safety chain and restarted the motor. "Fish are smart enough to get out of the way. It was debris in the water. Pieces of shipwrecks and old docks get shaken loose by storms and tides and float to the surface. Which is why you have to be watching for it."

And I hadn't been.

I sucked in a huge lungful of air and blew it out, forcing my muscles to loosen. In my entire life, I'd never not paid attention while I was manning the tiller of the boat. That was Safety 101. Inviolable. The very thing I'd just cursed at the people on the party boat for doing. But then, I'd also never, *ever* had a kiss that took me apart and left me craving more the way this one had.

It seemed a little bit like a cosmic joke that the guy who made me feel so uninhibited, so comfortable, was the last guy on earth I should want. He was so wrong for me in every possible way.

I ran a hand over my wrist, over the place where my bracelet should have been and wasn't. Everything had started going so wrong the minute I'd lost it.

"Is your wrist okay?"

"It's fine."

"Should we talk about—?"

"You should hold on," I instructed. "Maybe grab the hat again. Sun's a killer today."

"But what—"

"We'll need to check the boat for leaks when we get there," I continued, and only felt a little guilty when Toby gave a gasp and hurried to take his seat. "Better safe than sorry."

Which applied to so much more than boating, and I really needed to remember that.

7

TOBY

Help Me Hagatha (Issue #2427)

Dear Aunt Hagatha:

My boyfriend Tom is gorgeous, funny, hardworking, and kind. He's twenty-five, I'm twenty-eight, and we've been in love nearly four years, so we've recently begun talking about marriage, but his family have never liked me much and I can tell their lack of enthusiasm is giving Tom doubts. How can I convince Tom *and* his folks that I'm the right one for him?

Above Rubies in Aberdeen

Dear Ruby,

Lord, honey, why would you? You say he loves you, and that's a beautiful thing, but love is a lot like the Loch Ness Monster—everyone describes it a little differently, and it's tough to know when you've found it, even if you squint. I think it looks a lot like someone who'll stand up for you and your relationship, someone you'll be able to count on in sickness and health for as long as you both shall live.

In general, precious, if you have to convince someone you're worth their time, they're not worth yours.

Best of luck,
Your favorite Auntie

Let it be stated for the record that my feelings were not hurt.

To be hurt, I would have to care what the giant with the blue eyes thought about me—a guy I'd met only the night before, who'd turned me down repeatedly for sex, who kept denying I was his soul mate like a broken record, and who went from kissing the shit out of me in the boat one minute, to treating me like a leper at a beauty pageant the second we reached the little dock on Menucha.

Yes, I'd kissed him.

Yes, that was inadvisable for many reasons.

But *he'd* kissed *me* the second time, damn it. He didn't have to act like I was the devious rake in one of those historical romances—which I read *only* to get in character as Aunt Hagatha, obviously—bent on seducing him at a ball and destroying his innocence.

"I don't even waltz!" I grumbled aloud.

I'd been lying in the sunshine like turkey bacon under the broiler for the last hour. My tan lines were going to be ridiculous, and I didn't want to contemplate what my hair was doing, but I'd been in Florida twenty-four hours and was basically Tom Hanks in *Castaway* by now, so I figured there was nothing for it but to acquire a volleyball and live like the locals.

"Uh, Toby? Do you want your water bottle or something?" Beale asked from farther down the dock, concern in his voice. "If you're talking to yourself, you might be getting dehydr—"

"I'm fine," I bit out. "Perfectly fine."

This was the reason I did not attempt to have adventures. All the adrenaline made me feel quite, quite fragile. It was also the reason why I kept to guys who knew exactly what they wanted—delightfully casual, amusing, mutually beneficial encounters—and I didn't go around kissing hot guys in tiny blow-up raft-things that were susceptible to a "slow leak in one of the tubes," whatever the fuck that meant, when they hit debris in the water.

Honestly, Beale wasn't even that good-looking! He was tall, sure. With an enormous cock I couldn't stop thinking about, yes. And beautifully muscular, certainly. But besides that...

I turned my head against the rough wood dock and regarded him through my sunglasses. He sat ten feet down the dock facing me with his gear bag open and a bunch of tools laid out around him, the inflatable upside down on the wooden planks between us.

That silly blue bandanna was still tied around his head, and his hair glinted gold in the sun. He'd taken off his T-shirt to dry the boat, for reasons I couldn't fathom, and the sun gleamed off his freckled shoulders as his muscles bunched and rippled. His legs were folded up pretzel-style, like his limbs had never been told that someone so big shouldn't be that bendy. A little frown played between his eyebrows, and he'd tucked his tongue between his teeth in concentration as he smoothed his hand over the boat, which should have looked dorky but didn't. As he worked, he hummed a tune.

Okay, so I was lying. He was fucking gorgeous. He was also insanely capable—the kind of guy who could do anything, from animal removal, to yoga, to small watercraft repair, to calming me down with a whispered "you're alright, you're fine, I've got you" that was almost enough to make me wish that someone did *have* me. All in all, he was the total package...

If a person were interested in a total package.

Which I wasn't.

And meanwhile, I'd reacted to this open friendliness by sharing... absolutely nothing at all, because that was my way. No man was an island, except me.

Even when I thought I owed someone.

Even when they'd asked very, very little of me except some minor details of my life and what circumstances had led me to co-opt half the space in the guest room bed.

I bit my lip and shifted the baseball hat lower on my head. I was pretty sure I was allergic to guilt; I fucking hated it.

There were very compelling reasons why I couldn't share things even if I wanted to, of course. If I spilled my guts to Beale about what had happened at Dive the way I'd been tempted to earlier, I'd be outing Jayd... and somehow this seemed like a way bigger deal now that I knew Beale didn't just know Jayd Rollins the pop-folk singer, the way most people did, he actually knew Jay Don Rollins the human being behind the persona. He was among the people Jayd should be able to come out to in his own time.

Plus, Beale's brother had a huge grudge against him, and I didn't know Rafe well enough to know how he'd use that information when Beale told him, because of course Beale would tell him. Beale might be a mythical unicorn in many ways, but there was no chance he'd keep a secret for me, a total stranger, when he'd specifically said earlier he was loyal to his brothers above anyone.

As for my other secret, my Hagatha secret…

I winced, remembering how Beale's face had gone weirdly blank when he'd thought I was insulting him.

I wanted to clear the air, but I really couldn't. Shouldn't. In ten years, I'd never shared my secret with a soul. Doing so would be like directly handing someone the power to destroy my career, and that was not me being quirkily over-dramatic. I had responsibilities. I knew better.

Or maybe I didn't, because just then, Beale's tune reached a crescendo, and I realized with a stomach-twisting lurch that he was humming "*My Heart Will Go On*" from *Titanic* like an off-key Celine, probably without even realizing it, and it was so sickeningly sweet I started chirping like a fucking canary.

"I write an advice column," I blurted, apropos of nothing.

Beale's humming cut off, and I could feel the weight of his stare, even though I closed my eyes and turned my face back to the sky.

"Like Aunt Hagatha? That kind of advice column?"

"Yes. Yes, very much exactly like that."

"No way! Really?"

"Would I lie about that, precious?" I demanded hotly. "Ask yourself. Is that the kind of sexy, impressive career someone invents?" My face burned from something besides the sun, and I sat up quickly. "Good Lord, is there no shade whatsoever on this island? I'll be *seared*. I can feel my organs literally boiling inside my body."

"You could always get in the water," Beale said reasonably. "It's cooler, at least. Or you could hike back into the trees. Just be careful where you step."

"My choices are drowning or being savaged by some manner of forest beast?" I sniffed and lay back down. "A Hobson's choice if ever there was one." I pulled the hat down more firmly.

Beale ignored my whining. "So when you say you write a column very much like Hagatha..."

I swallowed, body tense, and waited for him to ask me outright, not sure whether I could make myself confirm it in so many words. But Beale looked at me for a long moment, hesitated, scraped his bottom teeth over his top lip, and deftly changed tack, focusing back on the boat.

He knew I was Hagatha, and I knew he knew it, but he also knew I didn't want him to acknowledge it, so he didn't. He just... accepted it.

I didn't understand why the people of Whispering Key didn't build shrines to the wonder of Beale Goodman, I truly didn't.

"There was this letter maybe two years back in Hagatha's column from a person called Stranded in Paducah," Beale began.

"Oh?" I'd answered over two thousand letters over the years. I didn't remember most of them.

"I remember it so well because my mom had died almost exactly a year before."

My head swiveled toward him instinctively.

"Cancer," he added shortly. "And I was feeling low and kinda looking for a sign from the Universe that things would be okay."

Ah, damn. I was *nobody's* sign from the mother-freakin' Universe.

Beale cleared his throat and rubbed at his wrist again, which I was starting to think was a nervous tic of his.

"Anyway, Stranded said he wasn't smart enough for college and not capable of learning the stuff he needed to know to get a job he wanted…"

A thrill ran up my spine. I did remember this. Shit.

"I remember thinking I'd've told Stranded to go into business with his family, since that's what I'd done in his shoes, and I was happy enough, more or less." Beale bent his knees up and wrapped his forearms loosely around them, totally folded in on himself and perfectly comfortable that way. "But Hagatha's answer was way better." His eyes were a steady blue, as infinite as the ocean. "She talked about learning difficulties and work-arounds, and how tons of successful people had the same issues, like Richard Branson and Tommy..." He wiggled his fingers. "Whatever his name is. Some clothing guy."

"Hilfiger," I supplied, though it came out all raspy. "I changed my mind. Can I have my water bottle, please?"

"Yeah." Beale stared at me hard for half a minute before he twisted, dug my bottle out of the cooler behind him, and tossed it over the boat to me.

It missed my outstretched hand by inches, and I squeaked just a little—in a very buff and outdoorsy sort of way, obviously—but Beale didn't seem to care.

"Hagatha said not to let your difficulties define you," Beale continued softly. "She said, 'It won't be easy, Stranded, but the only wrong choice would be thinking you don't deserve better.'"

"Ah. Well that's... I mean... it's not bad advice, is it?" I uncapped the water bottle and sipped gratefully. "As advice goes?"

"I cried." Beale's lips pulled up in a ghost of a smile. "First time I'd cried since my mom died. Don't think I've cried since, really?" He paused with his head cocked to one side like he was pondering it, but he gave up with a shrug. "The answer was just so no-bullshit, you know? Not fake sympathy, just real, genuine empathy, and I felt that connection to the soles of my boots. I knew that was why the Universe had sent me there that day. *That* was the connection I'd been meant to establish. And it's okay if you don't believe in any of the energy stuff, but I did—do—and that helped me. A lot." He shrugged. "Just throwing that out, in case you needed to hear it."

I gaped at him.

He stood and dusted his ass off, took his binoculars out of his Mary Poppins bag, then somehow managed to leap the boat in a single bound like a cat... or a superhero.

"Wanna go look for the plovers while this patch sets up?" he asked, like he hadn't just turned me upside down and shaken me hard. He held out a hand to pull me to my feet and then led the way down the dock while I trailed after him.

"So... so then what?" I asked. "After you read that column?"

"Hmm? Oh. Then I started thinking about what I liked to do." Beale paused as he stepped onto the rocky shore. "And there wasn't any *one* thing I was passionate about, but I like rescuing animals, and I like crystals and holistic medicine, and I like nutrition. So I started listening to audiobooks a good bit, while I was running or working out, or even sometimes out on the water. Did you know they even have poetry collections on audio?"

I shook my head.

"Wild, right? And after I learned a bit and got a little confidence, I started volunteering with the Nature Center, and I got to have this whole other thing in my life that I loved. And it's all thanks to Hagatha." He winked. "Whoever she might be."

"Oh."

Look, it's not like I'd never considered that I helped people. I was sure I helped the actual people who wrote in—at least helped them to feel heard and seen, even if they never took my advice. But the idea that people who read this weren't just entertained by it but *touched* by it?

No, I could honestly say I'd never considered that.

Beale cleared his throat. "So, okay. Our goal here is to count plovers."

"Which are birds."

"Still birds, Toby, yes." He rolled his eyes, as I'd expected, and the mood lightened. "We can't really walk the whole perimeter of the island because the mangroves grow so thick on the far side, so we're just going to walk the beach. We'll start in this direction." He nodded right.

"And then back the other way." I nodded confidently, as though plover-spotting was a thing I did regularly.

"See? And you made it sound like this was your first rodeo."

I snorted.

"We'll try to get a count of birds and eggs, and I'll upload the information to the website when we get home. Okay?"

Home was a very weird concept as pertained to the little guesthouse, but I nodded. "It occurs to me that it would be helpful if you were to give me a brief primer on what, precisely, a plover looks like."

Beale's mouth twitched. "I was wondering if you were going to ask." He pulled up a picture on his phone and handed it to me.

"It's not bad-looking, as sky vermin go," I approved, looking at the short, pudgy, brown-and-white creature.

"The black stripe on their foreheads indicates that they're ready for mating."

"Handy. Probably saves them a lot of time hanging out at bird bars, chatting up other birds who just want to be friends. Enables them to find their feathered soul mates that much faster."

Beale's lips quirked and he shook his head.

We set off, and for a few seconds, the only sounds were the squeaking of fine sand under our feet, the crash of waves, and the cawing of birds overhead.

"You know, I almost sent a letter to Aunt Hagatha once."

I nearly tripped over my sandals. "*You?*"

He shot me a glance. "Surprised?"

"Maybe." I shrugged. "You seem to have things so very under control."

"Me? After everything I've told you?" Beale adjusted the bandanna on his unfairly un-sweaty face and gave me his "you're insane, but I enjoy it" look. "No."

"Let's recap, shall we? Last night, you kept Marjorie from attacking me, this morning you saved me from a vigilante microwave—" I counted off on my fingers.

He laughed.

"And you saved me from drowning when our boat sank." I threw an arm out in the direction of the water.

"It didn't come close to sinking. Those rafts are nearly unsinkable. And do *not* say that's what they said about the *Titanic*," he added.

"Pretty sure *you* just said it," I singsonged.

"You were in no danger of drowning, Toby, I promise. I told you I wouldn't have let that happen." His voice was low and serious, solemn even, and it made my palms prickle. I couldn't make myself look up at him.

"Which is exactly my point," I continued breezily. "You know how to calm homicidal cats and patch boats and hunt for plovers, sweetness. What advice could you need from m—er, from Hagatha?"

Beale paused to type something in his phone, and I realized belatedly that there were quite a few birds hopping along the shore and I hadn't noticed. *Oops.* Add "terrible plover hunter" to the list of reasons why Florida and I would not suit.

"I maybe wanted advice on finding a soul mate," Beale admitted.

I felt my eyes go round. "What?"

"But then I realized the whole point of a soul mate is that you don't have to find them," Beale rushed on. He rubbed at the back of his neck. "They find you. The Universe sends them to you. Obviously. So I changed my mind and didn't send the letter. Anyway, back to the plovers!" He pointed to a sign someone had staked into the ground that read Protected Area. "I spotted a nest over that way last time I was here. We need to be really quiet and stealthy while approaching. We don't want to startle the adults."

"Yeah, yeah." I could not care less about the mating habits of birds when I was busy thinking about the mating habits—or lack thereof—of the man beside me. "So you're looking for your dream guy—"

"I'm not looking. I'm *waiting*. Big difference. Very big. Just forget it, okay?" He made a slashing gesture with his hand. "We're here for plovers. Look closely, just by that tall tuft of grass." He jabbed the binoculars at me and pointed.

"Yes, fine." I sniffed, holding them obediently.

I lifted the binoculars and aimed them where he pointed, and... "Oh! Oh, hey!" I turned to Beale with a shocked smile. "There's a bird there." I looked again. "Definitely a plover looking for action." I drew a line across my forehead where the plover's markings were. "And I think there's a couple eggs under her. Or him. How can you tell?"

"It's usually females during the day." Beale's voice was a low rumble by my ear that made my stomach flip. "Can you see how many eggs?"

I looked closer. "Two... no, three. Definitely three. Ha! Mark that down, Goodman. Who's a fucking eggs-pert plover hunter?" I grinned at him again, triumphantly this time.

"It's you, Toby," he deadpanned.

"Damn straight." I handed him back his binoculars and wiggled my hips. "I'm not just a pretty face."

"No, you're not," he said with a hungry look in his eyes that made me want to kiss him again.

I looked away and rubbed my palms against my hips.

This was dangerous. Really, really dangerous. If any other guy on the planet had given me that look, I'd already have him backed against the nearest flat surface and gotten on my knees, but Beale was kind of a special case. A virgin-shaped special case.

And yet...

"Why is it that you have to wait to have sex until you meet your soul mate?" I held up both hands innocently when he opened his mouth to protest. "Genuine, honest question."

"Because sex is a waste of time otherwise."

"Mmmm. Maybe in a cosmic sense? But it's a really *fun* and useful waste of time. Like, in the hierarchy of time-wasters, it's more like counting plovers than crushing candy on your phone."

He rolled his eyes. "Toby—"

"No, no, hear me out, okay? What if the Universe wants to see that you're putting in an effort to find your soul mate? If you were destined to win the lottery, Beale, it would only happen if you played. You can't be destined to have a sandwich for dinner if you don't buy bread. There has to be some way that humans make shit happen. You said that all living and nonliving things have energy, right? So where's your energy going?"

"You sound like Rafe."

I winced. "Great. Well, in this case maybe he's right. I mean, I'm looking out for your future soul mate here, Beale. Don't you think it would be good if you learned a little bit about having sex? What you like and don't like, what *he* might like and not like?"

"It's not something you have to learn!"

"You're just going to, what? Know how to find his prostate instantly and psychically, because your soul-matey-ness will make it so?"

His face turned red, and his nostrils flared.

"Oh, my poor Beale. I assure you, precious, that is not how it works. If you think it's all jump, jab, and jiggle… well, you're not too far different from most of the men I had sex with in my twenties." I shuddered delicately. "Aspire for better."

He frowned.

"Besides which, you have this idea that your soul mate is fated, right? Like, every step you take is another step on the path to finding him? So why isn't this a step?" I motioned between us. "Unless I have gone utterly blind and insensate, you are attracted to me. You kissed me. Quite thoroughly. So maybe *that* was fate. Maybe I'm the final stepping-stone before you meet your one true person."

"That's not how it works!"

I threw my hands up in the air. "How do you *know* how it works when you haven't experienced it? Half an hour ago, you thought Hagatha was a middle-aged woman from Lebanon, Kansas, who likes Shasta daisies and romance novels, just like it says in her bio, and right now I'm telling you, I picked Lebanon off a map because it's the geographical center of the lower 48 United States and the concept *amused me,* so recognize that there are mysteries in the Universe that you haven't solved."

"Are you yelling at me because I don't want to have sex with you?" he demanded.

"No!" *Or was I?* Shit.

I cleared my throat and moderated my volume. "No. I'm just recognizing that you are, indeed, quite stubborn." I blew out a breath and turned resolutely toward the far side of the island. "Okay. More plovers. Onward."

I marched insistently toward the birds on the far side of the dock.

"I like you, Toby." Beale hurried up behind me. "You seem like a great guy."

I whirled to face him. "You'd better not say 'but' unless it's to compliment the perfection of mine." And not fucking *Silvio's*.

"However," Beale said instead with a little quirk of his lips that made his blue eyes flash. "I don't really know you. And you don't know me. True?"

Weirdly, this did *not* feel true. I felt like we'd been through several wars together. I figured this was just because I was overwrought and needy, though, so I nodded.

"I've tried hooking up with guys I don't know a couple of times, and it didn't work. I mean, it *worked*," Beale added quickly with an impatient gesture at the front of his cargo shorts that made me snicker. "It just didn't feel right or easy. It made me feel bad after. Disconnected and anxious, like when you're super hungry and you eat a candy bar, and then your body starts to feel gross and jittery. That's why I've been waiting until I meet the right person to have sex. You with me?"

I shook my head sadly. "Not even a little, sweetness. Candy is delicious. If I didn't have to be ruthless about my carb intake, I'd eat it every day. If I looked like you, I'd eat it twice a day. I think you're going about this wrong."

"I am?"

"You definitely are." I tapped my lips thoughtfully. Poor Beale lacked all the confidence a man as smart and funny and hot as him should have. He'd also saved me from grievous injury multiple times in twenty-four hours, and I felt that debt keenly. Now I knew exactly how I could repay him. It might not be the *smartest* thing to do, given the real reason I'd come to Whispering Key, and the whole thing might end in tragedy, but it still felt like the *right* thing to do. Not coincidentally, it was also the thing I *wanted* to do.

"Now, here we go. Ahem. Dear Virgo the Virgin." I batted my eyelashes at him.

"Oh, no."

"Not every person you have sex with will be your soul mate, Virgo."

He gave me another "you're ridiculous but enjoyable" glance, this one slightly lighter on the "enjoyable," but it still warmed me from the inside in ways I didn't want to think about too much. "I know, Hagatha."

"But you'd be foolish to turn down a fake soul mate you're attracted to who's gonna be sharing your bed for a week anyway. Love, Auntie H."

"And that's your professional advice, huh?"

I blinked. In truth, my professional advice would probably be more like, "run away from the man trying to peer pressure you into sex." But we'd already established that Hagatha was totes incompetent.

"I don't think I can make an unbiased judgment since I have a vested interest in the outcome. But weren't you the one who said learning new skills made you more confident?" I fluttered my eyelashes.

"I was talking about audiobooks!" he said a little desperately.

"Sex is better than audiobooks."

"Maybe you need better audiobooks."

"Beale, honey, maybe you need better sex."

He opened his mouth to retort, but I held up my hands.

"Fine," I said in defeat. "The truth is, I've wanted to climb you like a tree since thirty seconds after we met. You're gorgeous and you're funny, and I apparently have a kink for guys who are really capable or something. Also, abstinence makes me twitchy, and you're my only option for the next week, fake soul mate." I blinked my eyes in my very best starving orphan impression, though I wasn't looking for gruel so much as one particular enormously hot male.

"And you're not suggesting this because you feel like you owe me, are you?"

I hesitated, running my tongue over my top lip and studying him like a puzzle. "Which answer would make you more likely to agree?"

"Ah, fuck it."

He bit his lip and pulled me nearer, his eyes fixed on my mouth, and I'd have sworn I could feel his heartbeat pulsing in the air between us. Or maybe it was mine.

He wrapped a hand around the back of my neck, lowered his head... and sank his teeth into my bottom lip. It was so arousing and so fucking unexpected I gasped and shivered.

I saw the flash of Beale's grin a second before he captured my mouth more fully, and I realized too late that, virgin or not, if the man could take me apart with a kiss, sex with him was going to be about as safe as riding a roller coaster in an earthquake.

But given that I was so very, very screwed, what was there to do but hang on and enjoy the ride while it lasted?

8

BEALE

Czarina's StarCharts for Today
Delayed gratification isn't always the best policy, Virgo. Dissolve
your inhibitions; grab what you want.

"Wawasthat?" Toby mumbled against my mouth as I steered us around the fountain in Mason and Fenn's front yard and headed for the backyard without breaking the kiss we'd started in the driveway, which was really just a continuation of the kiss we'd started back on Menucha.

"Fountain," I said shortly.

"Mmm," he agreed before plunging his tongue back into my mouth. He groaned like a starving man who'd finally been given a meal, like it had been years instead of milliseconds since he'd tasted me, and fuck if my dick didn't perk up at the sound.

I swept my hands up his back under his crop top, soaking in the feel of his smooth skin under my fingertips. He was so much smaller than me, but firm and solid, too.

We crashed through the gate, and Toby pushed me away with two hands, his brown eyes alight with mischief. I stumbled back into the column of the pergola that shaded one corner of the backyard.

"Are we alone?" Toby's chest heaved. "No remodeling dudes around? Not that it's a deal breaker for me, but I'd rather not be interrupted."

"Oh. Um." There was no space in my brain for thoughts about this, but I tried to make some. "Yeah. Yes. No trucks in the driveway. They only work a half day on Saturdays. We're alone."

"My God, you're gorgeous when you're thinking," Toby breathed before stepping back into my space and lifting up on his toes to lick a path up the side of my neck. "And you taste delicious. *Fuck.* Salty and sweet. I want to put my mouth on you. *All* over you. Okay?"

Was that an actual question? Did he expect an actual answer? Just in case, I said, "Good. Yes. Do that."

Any further response I might have made evaporated when he clamped my earlobe between his teeth, and my goddamn knees actually quaked.

"Holy Jesus," I breathed, like I was experiencing a religious conversion, because I kind of was. "I've never... Do that again!"

"Wait." Toby pushed me away again and kept both hands

braced on my shoulders. His breath came in rough pants. "Wait. Wait, wait. You've never had someone kiss your ear?"

I shook my head. "Not that I remember." And I would definitely have remembered something that felt this good.

He tilted his head to one side. "How virgin is virgin, Beale?"

"Uh." I shook my head, momentarily unable to form a sentence since all the blood in my body had rushed to my cock and it was literally *thrumming*. "Not entirely virgin?"

"Oh, okay." Toby pressed a hand to his stomach and sounded a little relieved. "I was worried I was moving too fast—"

"Too fast? No way." Once I'd given in and said yes, it was like twenty-eight years of want had suddenly been unleashed, and things couldn't happen fast enough. And it felt good.

Really good.

Fated, even.

It wasn't that I thought Toby knew what he was talking about when it came to understanding how the Universe worked—I was pretty sure he would've told me the sky was on fire in his attempt to convince me to have sex—but that didn't mean he was entirely wrong, either. Maybe this *was* a necessary stepping stone. Weirder things happened every day, right? And the part about me having a say in how my future manifested had the unmistakable ring of truth to it. Like I'd known that, once upon a time, and I'd let myself forget it.

I shook my head again. "I told you I hooked up with guys a few times. It was a few years back now, but it happened."

"You did say that." He went up on his tiptoes and bit at the edge of my jaw. "Silly me."

My breath juddered out in a rush. "Yeah, like four times? Five, even," I reassured him.

Toby pulled back again and did not look reassured. "Wait. Five *times*?" he repeated. "Or five guys?"

"Uh... both?" I gripped the back of my neck. "Maybe a couple extra times if you include Martin, my bunkmate from Adventure Camp."

"Martin from Adventure Camp?" he scoffed. "My erstwhile rival? No. He doesn't count. Ever. For anything."

I snorted.

Toby's expression turned sly as his fingertips danced up my arms. "But in the interest of total honesty between us as soul mates, what did you two get up to in that bunk?"

I licked my lips and pretended to hesitate. "I'd tell you... but I don't wanna get him in trouble, what with you being a counselor and all."

Toby's mouth opened in an excited little O.

"For the love of Chris Evans and every single one of his abs," he breathed. He cleared his throat. "I'm thinking you should tell me right away, Beale. No one will get in trouble as long as you give me *all* the details."

I bit my lip to keep from smiling. "Well, he snuck into my bed the first time maybe a week before camp ended? It was the middle of the night, but it was a billion degrees outside —way too warm to sleep—so I was still awake."

"Uh-huh. You were naked and sweaty."

"Um... no. I was wearing shorts and—"

"Shhh." Toby shut his eyes. "You were *naked*."

"Right. Sure. Well, I'd noticed Martin before, obviously. He was cute, but kinda geeky. Small. Way, way smaller than me. Which was hot."

"Yeah, it is." Toby squeezed his eyes shut and sagged against me, his face mashed against my chest while his fingertips caressed the sides of my neck. "Keep going."

I let myself touch Toby's skin, let my fingertips trail over that smooth swath of skin just below the waist of his shorts, which felt so forbidden and erotic I could hardly remember what I'd been saying.

"I guess he'd seen me checking him out, because he stuck his hands down my shorts without saying a word, and then he kinda climbed on top of me?"

Toby whimpered, and the sound sent a bolt of lust straight down my spine.

I was glad someone was getting something out of the story because, to be honest, it hadn't been all that great in the moment. I mean, it *had*, because orgasms were nearly always good, but it hadn't been some earth-shattering experience or even anything hot enough to jerk to after the fact. I couldn't remember Martin's last name, and I was pretty sure we'd exchanged a total of two dozen words if you didn't count unimportant stuff like "fuck" and "yeah" and "oh," which I didn't.

"He rubbed off on me, really fast and quiet, so we didn't wake anyone else, and then he snuck back to his own bunk. But the next night, it happened again."

"Christ." Toby shivered. "Gonna think about *that* some more later, but with me in the starring role."

I grinned. I liked that idea better, too.

"Then after that?" Toby prompted.

"Oh. Um. I used to go to this dive on the mainland called the SandBar." I shrugged, starting to get uncomfortable.

"Ah ha. And let me guess... you didn't leave alone?"

"No, actually I did. There's a back hall, and..." I winced, remembering the last time I was there. "It's kinda dark."

"Why, Beale Goodman, as I live and breathe!" Toby grinned. "Clandestine, semi-public hookups?"

"Yeah, I guess," I said tightly. "It sounds better when you say it than I remember it." Like a success instead of a catastrophic failure.

Toby stroked my chest with gentle pressure. "What's going on in your brain, Virgo?" he whispered.

I ran a hand over my face. "Those experiences were super awkward. I kept trying, thinking it would be less awkward eventually, but it wasn't."

"Because they weren't your soul mate."

"No! I mean... yeah, probably," I allowed. "But also because... Look, you might have noticed last night that I'm, you know." I waved a hand down toward my erection, which was still jutting insistently against the front of my shorts, proving that my dick had no ability to read the room.

"You're...?" Toby shook his head, confused. "More effective than Viagra? Mouthwatering? Perfectly formed? A testament to the existence of a higher power? Paul Bunyan with a great big axe?" Toby palmed his own erection and gave a little *mmmph* that made me wish it was my hand there instead. "Help me out here, Goodman."

"Big! Really big. Possibly too big." I swallowed. "And before you say I'm crazy, be aware that these other guys *thought* the size thing would be great, but it turned out to be too much work." I clenched my hands into fists and struggled to speak around the vise that gripped my chest. "So, I don't want you to... you know."

"To blow you?" Toby looked almost tragically disappointed, and somehow I found myself huffing out a chuckle. "But my blow jobs change *lives*."

"No!" I scrubbed a hand through my hair. "I mean, yes. I mean... If it's uncomfortable for you, please don't feel obligated to—"

Toby laughed out loud. "Beale, I don't know who these philistines were that they could not appreciate the utter work of *art* they had a chance to see up close, but I promise you, obligation is the very last thing I feel when I look at you."

He pushed me against the column again, pretty forcefully for a guy his size, and I was so startled I let him. He looked up at me with brown eyes gone liquid hot. "You're at my mercy now, Beale Goodman."

I swallowed. "I am?"

Toby nodded. "Oh, yes. And hear me now: I did not survive a half-dozen near-death experiences and at least two painfully awkward conversations only to have this body withheld from me because you're getting in your head over this."

He whipped his shirt off and threw it on the ground, and... *oh*. Just oh.

My brain turned to soup at all that golden skin laid out before me like a feast, and I couldn't think of words that had more than two letters.

He licked his lips and ran his fingers just behind the waistband of my shorts, trapping my shirt against my stomach. His thumb teased over the button.

"I wasn't asking you about this stuff because I wanted a resumé of your sexual experiences, Beale. I was asking because I want this to be good for you. I wanted to know what you liked, and I didn't want to rush you. Okay?"

He glanced up at me through his eyelashes, and any resistance I had faded away. He was so damn beautiful, and I could see how badly he wanted me. It made me feel powerful.

I cupped his jaw in one hand, committing the feel of his skin to memory. "Okay."

"Okay." Toby grabbed the hem of my shirt and tugged, and I bent to help him. He dropped my shirt on the ground next to his, and something about the sight captivated me—the way the fabric pooled together in the sunshine, the symbolism of the thing, the—

"Fuck, look at you," he breathed, pulling my attention firmly back to him. He slid both hands up my stomach slowly with open palms, exploring each ridge and bump, and then he pinched my nipples lightly.

I hissed, and he did it again. Then slowly, deliberately, holding my gaze the whole time, he leaned in and captured one between his teeth.

My head thunked back against the pole, and I groaned. My cock was hard as iron, and I couldn't help the way my hips shifted up, seeking attention with each brush of his thumbs.

"Later on, I'm going to spread you out on the bed," Toby said conversationally, tilting his head toward the guesthouse. He licked a stripe over my left nipple while his fingers toyed with my right, and I gasped as the breeze blew over the damp skin. "I'm going to straddle you and tell you not to move."

"Hmmphokay," I managed.

"It's gonna be better than okay, baby," he purred, and my mind tried to catch hold of the *baby*, but it slipped away like ripples in the pool. He brushed kisses over my collarbone and up my neck to my ear. He tugged my hair to one side, to give him more room. "I'm going to lick and suck every square inch of this chest, and mark you up, and do all kinds of things. I'm gonna make you tell me every single thing you've dreamed up for the last decade but never got to do, and then we're going to do them."

"*Hnghhhkay.*"

He chuckled against my skin, which was a special kind of pleasure. "I think I broke you, and I think I like it. I haven't even touched your cock yet, and my capable, competent Beale is already a boneless puddle of 'okays,' which—*eep!*"

I reversed our positions in the blink of an eye, grabbed both his hands, and pinned them to the column above his head. He stared up at me, eyes wide and excited, and I couldn't *not* kiss him... so I did, taking my time and savoring the feeling of his body melting against mine.

"Toby?" I said hoarsely when I pulled back.

Those pretty brown eyes blinked open, not quite focused.

"Quit fucking around."

"Hmmkay," he breathed, and I grinned.

"Okay."

He tugged at my grip, so I let him go and was rewarded when he leaned up to kiss me again. His hands smoothed down my back to cup my ass, pulling me against him, and I sucked in a breath because the heat of his skin on my skin and the glide of my cock against his stomach felt so fucking good it was nearly painful.

Then he sank to his knees on the cement and reached for my fly, and my brain nearly short-circuited at the sight. He shifted slightly to undo the button and winced a little... and I blinked out of my haze.

"Wait." I slid sideways, grabbed the cushion off the lounge chair, and dropped it on the ground. "Here. Continue."

He stared up at me.

"It's for your knees," I explained. Then, when he still looked completely perplexed, I explained further, "Put the cushion under your knees so you won't get hurt on the concrete."

"Yes, yes, I understand the concept," Toby huffed. "I just can't believe you, at this moment, were thinking... Actually, never mind, yes I can." He snorted something that sounded like *unicorn*, but after he put the cushion under his knees, he pressed a kiss to my belly button that made my abs contract, so I figured he wasn't really upset.

"Anything else, Goodman? We done being polite?" Toby moved lower, mouthing my erection through my shorts, and my hips punched forward of their own volition.

Toby carefully slid the zipper down over my erection. My shorts and underwear dropped to the ground with a soft noise, and my thick cock sprang free, bobbing against my stomach in the afternoon sunshine.

"Oh, wow." Toby's voice literally trembled with excitement that made it impossible for me not to believe he was totally into this.

He grasped the base of my cock. His fingers and thumb came nowhere near touching, which was the point where I'd seen some guys go from excited to wary, but not Toby. He tugged lightly, and when a bead of precum gathered at the tip, he made a sound of raw appreciation. Without even a second for me to brace, he leaned forward, sucked my tip into his mouth, and ran his tongue over the slit.

For exactly one second, I was grateful for the high fencing around the yards, the nearly empty neighborhood, and the fact that the contractors weren't working today, because I yelled so loud it bounced off the trees.

"Oh, shit. You taste fucking amazing. I knew it. I *so* knew it." Toby pumped my dick a couple of times and licked me again, humming happily like he was savoring it. Then he turned those big eyes up at me. "I want every drop."

Then he opened his mouth even wider and sank down on my cock, holding my gaze the whole time. He couldn't take the whole thing, not even half, but his hand jerked me in counterpoint to the sucking of his mouth, and it was so damn good, sweat ran down my back and my legs wanted to give out. My slick hands clenched and unclenched around the column in front of me, and I had to spread my legs wider to brace myself so I could stay upright as pleasure wracked me.

He pulled back a little while later so he could tear at his own shorts and push them down his thighs, baring his erection.

"Don't you move," he said severely, voice wrecked. "This was poor planning, in retrospect. I just need... a little... Fuck, yeah." He wrapped a hand around his own shiny, swollen length, and both of us groaned.

Toby looked up at me as he jacked himself, and his eyes burned. "In a minute, I'm gonna have you on your knees for me, too. You want that?"

Shit, yes, I wanted it.

But he didn't wait for my reply before he drew my tip back into his mouth with a contented little noise, like there was nowhere on earth he'd rather be.

His lips and jaw were stretched fully around me, but he worked his tongue over the underside of my dick in ways I hadn't known were possible, sucking and slurping with no inhibitions whatsoever, like this moment—this pleasure—was so much more important than appearances.

His hair had fallen across his forehead, his brown eyes watered, and he looked real and raw—*nothing* like the put-together guy he'd been earlier. It made the whole experience feel like a fantasy come to life, and I gave myself over to it.

My hips shot forward slightly, and Toby choked, but when I went to move back, he made a noise of protest and moved his hand away from my dick so he could grab my ass and hold me in place.

"*Fuck*," I bit out and Toby hummed around me in agreement.

The visual of him staring up at me, cock out and face wrecked, did me in. My balls tightened and I gripped the column tighter, fingers digging into the wood as I tried to hold back. I tried to commit every detail to memory—the lap of the water against the pool, the warm breeze cooling my sweaty skin, the flush of arousal on Toby's cheeks, the blissed-out look in his eyes, the *slick, slick, slick* of his hand as he worked himself, but it felt too good.

"I'm close." The deep growl didn't sound like my usual voice. "Shit, Toby, I'm really close. Stop for a minute—"

But he didn't stop. In fact, he brought the hand he'd been using to jerk himself up to tug my sac, and *holy mother of fuck*, I had no idea how good it would feel for someone else to do that to me until he did it.

"*Fuck*, Toby. Fuck, yeah. Oh, God."

That was the last straw. The entire world contracted for a second—every muscle in my body locked down, even my hearing cut out—and then exploded the next as I yelled Toby's name again and came down his throat.

He choked a little, dribbling cum and saliva, and my spent dick gave another half-hearted twitch inside his mouth because it was so fucking messy and hot, and I loved it.

Twenty-eight years, and I hadn't known I liked messy and hot.

I reached out a trembling hand to Toby's hair—it was soft, *fuck* it was so soft—and pulled him off me. He panted up at me, wild-eyed and swollen-lipped, and wordlessly resumed stroking himself.

I sank to my knees, spreading my thighs on either side of his, and pressed our mouths together. Toby's lips were hot and wet with spit and cum, but he opened for me unhesitatingly. I trailed the backs of my fingers down his abs, absorbing his shudders, and wrapped my fingers around his so we could work him together.

"Show me what you like," I rasped against his mouth. "Show me how you like it. You want me to suck you?"

"No, I want your hand on me. That big, capable fucking hand. Get it wet," he instructed, his voice hoarse. I raised a hand to my mouth and licked my palm until it was dripping. His gorgeous brown eyes sank half-shut, and he whimpered when I wrapped my hand around him again.

"Fuck, yeah. Like that but tighter." Toby moved his hand away and instead clenched my shoulders tightly, trusting me to take care of him. "Harder. Like—*oh, yeah*. Yeahyeahyeah. Just like that. Shit, you're good, Beale. Don't stop."

"Not gonna stop," I promised. Even if my arm fell off. Even if an earthquake hit. Even if my heart actually exploded from all the rapid-fire thumping. Even if my leg muscles gave out, like they were threatening to do, because I could still feel the aftershocks of my orgasm in my balls.

I thought about all the shit he'd said to me and how it had amped me up unbelievably. So with no plan whatsoever, I cleared my throat and leaned in so I could whisper in his ear all the things I'd like to do to him.

"I can't wait to get my mouth on you. I can't wait to... to suck your balls. And I want to eat you out. I've never done either of those things, but you'd be my first. You could... you could show me?"

I worried I was failing epically, reminding him how inexperienced I was, but Toby let out a high-pitched wail and gripped me harder, so I kept going, moving my hand faster, grasping him more firmly.

"I want to fuck you over the counter in the guesthouse kitchen." Once I started, it was easy to just spill every fantasy I'd ever had. "Against a wall with your legs around my waist and my hands spreading you open. Maybe I'll do it when the contractors are here so you'd have to be extra quiet, since you're fucking filthy and seem to like that idea."

Toby groaned.

"And I want to fuck you in the pool, too. I'd blow you under the water, then finger you and get you ready for me. Then

I'd push inside you and—" I paused, remembering how he couldn't swim. "And I'd hold you up the entire time and keep you safe. And then I'd—"

"Oh, fuck. Oh, yeah. Fuck, Beale! *Fuck*." Toby came in giant splatters that hit my chest, my stomach, and the patch of pubic hair right above my dick, and, no lie, it felt like the greatest accomplishment of my entire life.

I'd done that. I'd *made him* do that.

We smiled at each other wildly, then fell to the ground side by side with the lounge cushion under our heads, both our chests heaving like we'd swum all the way back from the island *and* run back to the house.

Gold afternoon sunlight fell through the slats of the pergola's roof, creating rainbow fractals that burst on the inside of my eyelids—beautiful Catherine wheels of color splashing across my brain.

I couldn't move. I couldn't think. I'd never felt more at peace. And the idea drifted across my brain that I'd been so, so, *so* wrong, because it turned out "oh" and "fuck" and "yeah" were maybe the most expressive three syllables in the English language.

And I wouldn't have known that, if not for Toby.

He was right. His blow jobs really did change lives.

It was a long moment later when he finally turned his head toward me. "That was." He had to pause and swallow, still breathless. "Seriously high quality. Eight point five out of ten."

My heart, which had finally slowed down slightly, started to beat faster, not with fear but promise. "Not sure how it could get better than that."

I turned my head and found him grinning.

"Give me a few minutes and I'll show you," he promised.

And then... he did.

9

TOBY

Help Me Hagatha (Issue #2441)

Dear Aunt Hagatha:

I'm not like most of the people who usually write you. I've actually got a perfect life! My job pays well, my girlfriend is amazing, and my family loves me a lot. I remind myself each day to be grateful.

But every once in a while, I wish I could just walk away from it all and start over. That I could build something... different. How can I stop myself from feeling this way?

Roberta in Ridgemont

Dear Bobbikins,

You can't.

I mean, you could. Or you could try, anyway. But, like... what for? You get one life. So cowgirl up, get thee a therapist (no, but for reals, tho), own your feelings, and make some big changes. You just might find your perfect life gets even perfect-er.

Best of luck darling,
Your Aunt H.

"Listen, missy, what did we discuss earlier today?" I lifted one eyebrow. "I don't need you over here, rubbing yourself all up in my business, while I'm trying to cook and I've still gotta get ready for Littlejohn's Trivia Night."

Marjorie twined herself around my ankles, looking as innocent as a ginger floof the size of a small tank possibly could—which was to say, not innocent in the slightest—and I shot her a warning glare before continuing to spread the cinnamon sugar topping on the french toast casserole I was preparing for the following morning.

Yes, to reiterate, I, Toby Elford, was standing in a tiny Florida kitchen, drowning bread products in cream and covering them with enough butter and sugar to give myself a contact high, using a recipe of my mom's I somehow remembered perfectly, despite not thinking of it since leaving Ohio a billion years ago, whilst chatting with a cat and preparing to engage in a trivia night organized by a man who'd shouted at the television the other night that Europe was a country in Asia.

Who the fuck was I?

How the fuck had I gotten here?

Why the fuck wasn't I running away as fast as my shapely legs could carry me?

Excellent questions, all.

I recalled only vague glimpses of my descent into this madness. There was that blow job by the pool on Saturday, after the harrowing horror of our trip to the Island of Plovers. A decidedly non-platonic night in the guest room with Marjorie locked firmly out and Beale's arms locked firmly around me.

Breakfast at this little restaurant called the Concha on Sunday, followed by a barbecue at Rafe's house that had ended up being way too crowded for the inquisition Big Rafe had wanted to give me, and which Beale and I had left early so we could walk on the beach at sunset... holding hands, because apparently that was a thing fake soul mates did.

More coffee at the Bean yesterday, after which we'd checked on the contractors at Mason's house and attended a town meeting about the end-of-summer Whispering Key Extravaganza that, in retrospect, should not have intrigued me as much as it did.

Then, this morning, I'd been cuddling in bed with Beale—yes, *me,* cuddling—catching my breath after a very enjoyable sunrise frot session in which Beale had done 90 percent of the work because he was a quick study like that, when we'd gotten to talking about breakfast foods. Beale had mentioned missing his mom's french toast casserole, and I'd found myself promising to recreate it for him... and that was when I'd felt my first faint awareness that something strange was happening to me.

Still in that fugue state, I sort of remembered driving Beale's Jeep—yes, *me*, driving a vehicle with a manual transmission and no doors—to the little store on the island, where I'd used my precious cash resources to purchase enough white sugar and heavy cream to float a barge, just to make Beale smile... and that same feeling had come back right in Pickles' dairy aisle, but stronger.

When I'd come home with my groceries, Littlejohn had waved from across the street, and I'd spent a solid fifteen minutes chatting with him about deadheading his dahlias before they bloomed—yes, *me*, engaging in conversation about dubious methods of horticulture—then when he'd pressed a dish of his "Homemade SpaghettiO Surprise," into my hands and begged me to come to his trivia night as a member of Team Whispering Key, I'd *agreed*. Red flags had been hoisted all over my brain, but Beale had grinned and kissed me when he'd heard, so I'd found it hardly any trouble to ignore them.

I was pretty sure if you asked Aunt Hagatha, she'd say that I should examine my motives and stop living in denial posthaste, since I was building myself a house of cards on a rickety table, lying to the whole damn town and lying by omission to the guy I was sleeping with. But then, Hagatha had never found herself having Beale Goodman's luscious body and gorgeous smile at her beck and call for days on end, nor found herself inexplicably enjoying a town of wackadoo misfits... so once again, Hagatha was utterly unqualified to say what a person should do in this situation.

Marjorie jumped up on the counter just as I finished snapping the lid on the casserole dish. "Excuse you, what did I say? No counters! It's impolite and unhygienic. Recall, please, that I am the alpha in this relationship. My word is law. Also, I *might* have gotten you another rotisserie chicken at the grocery store earlier if you behave."

She butted her orange head against my arm, and I sighed as I stroked her soft fur. I had to admit, I felt a sort of kinship with the beast. Both of us were a little wary and reacted poorly when stressed. Plus, she hadn't tried to murder me in days.

"Your desperation for chicken is pathetic," I crooned, scratching her under the chin. "Deplorable. You have no self-respect whatsoever. Do you, hmm? Your weakness makes you putty in my hands, you know that?"

Marjorie made one of her weird cough-barking noises, which I took to be acknowledgement and possibly shame.

The bathroom door opened, releasing a little cloud of steam, and Marjorie and I both turned our heads to watch Beale emerge, bare-chested and rubbing at his hair with a towel in a manner guaranteed to give him split ends, not that he cared about such a thing. He wore another pair of cargo shorts—the man dressed exclusively from Badasses 'R' Us's camouflage line—but he wore it so fucking well, I couldn't complain, and in fact, I had to roll my tongue up in my mouth to prevent it from extending across the counter and the floor to lick up the little droplets of water that dotted his chest.

I sighed.

Okay, so maybe the cat wasn't the only one with a deplorable weakness.

"I was *supposed* to be in the Maldives right now," I muttered at Marjorie, but she didn't look nearly as impressed as she should have.

Beale's head emerged from the towel, and a slow grin spread across his face when he caught us watching him. "You're gonna need to stop looking at me like that if we're going to trivia night."

I thought briefly about denying that I was looking at him in any kind of way… but I figured that ship had sailed.

"Why not? The whole island thinks we're together anyway. Isn't this the way your soul mate would look at you?" I fluttered my eyelashes besottedly.

Beale came up behind me, wrapping his giant arms around my chest, and pulled me against his chest. "It's not the way someone should look at me if he wants to leave the house," he explained, sidestepping the soul mate issue neatly. "That kind of look is more 'Let's curl up in bed, watch *Lucifer* on my laptop, and fuck around,' and I know that, because it's the look you gave me last night before we curled up, watched *Lucifer* in bed, and fucked around."

"Yes, well, we can't do that every day." I sounded a little waspish because I was totes fighting the urge to give in and do exactly that. "I get weak-kneed contemplating the data charges we'd be racking up, streaming shows that way."

"You do know I have plenty of money, right?" Beale murmured the words against the join of my shoulder, making me shiver… then chased the shiver up my neck with his lips. "And other than donating to charity, buying you a phone with a hot spot is the most worthwhile thing I've done with it all month."

I bit my lip. This reminded me that, in reciting the litany of evidence that I'd fallen into a sex-induced fever dream, I might possibly have failed to account for Exhibit A, the smoking-gun: I'd allowed Beale Goodman to buy me—yes, *me*—a cell phone.

And yes, I had made him pinkie swear I could pay him back for it as soon as I got the replacement credit card that would be arriving the following morning, but still. I did not *do* gifts. I did not *do* loans. And the knowledge that getting good dick three nights in a row made me swoon like a middle schooler with his first case of puppy love and abandon all the principles I held dear was lowering in the extreme.

Aunt Hagatha would be horrified, and for once, she'd be right.

"How 'bout I make you weak-kneed in other ways," Beale continued, nudging my face toward his. "Or at least try."

Like he had to *try*. The very idea was laughable.

"You showed me your 'other ways' thirty minutes ago, and you can show me more 'other ways' when we get back ho—here," I corrected, feeling my cheeks flush. Whispering Key was not *home*. "But Littlejohn will be expecting us, so I've gotta finish getting dressed."

Beale snorted, but let me go. "Alright. But I think someone's got a crush."

I spun in place. It was bad enough that I *felt* like a teenager; he didn't have to call me on it. "Excuse you? No one is crushing around here, I regret to inform you. And if you think—"

Beale blinked, all adorably bewildered and held up his two big hands. "I was just teasing, Toby. I meant Littlejohn. You know, 'cause he brought you his SpaghettiO Surprise? And 'cause he's never invited me or Mase or Fenn to trivia night before? No harm meant. It's cute."

Ohhh. He meant *Littlejohn* had a crush. Well, I doubted that was the case either. "I think he just wants to beat the Cooter Key trivia team, and he thinks I'm a ringer." I shrugged. "I know a little bit about a lot of things."

"Yeah, you do." Half of Beale's mouth turned up in a grin. "I wish I did. It's fun watching your brain work."

I shook my head and ignored the little leap in my belly. "Nonsense. It's much better to be an expert at a few things, like you are, but alas, my brain doesn't stick on any one thing for too long. Anyway, here's breakfast for tomorrow done." I grabbed the casserole and put it in the fridge. "Now I just need to get some decent clothes on." And by decent, I meant my Thom Browne twill shorts and a white button-down, which was maybe the most casual thing I'd brought with me.

I maneuvered past Beale's outstretched hand and headed for the bedroom.

A second later, I found myself spun around and tacked to the wall by Beale's hard body.

"Just to say, I have no complaints about your ability to focus this week." Beale's voice was a rumble in my ear, and when he rubbed that body idly against mine, my cock perked up with no hesitation. "Also, have I mentioned how very glad I am that we managed to rescue you before Marjorie castrated you?"

"Shush," I said against his lips. "She'll hear you and feel bad."

And Beale laughed as he kissed me.

God, every time he touched me was better than the time before, which was amazing and scary and... really amazingly scary. I fucking *yearned* for him, even when he was standing a few paces away, and let me tell you, darling, Toby Elford did not *yearn* for any man. I'd learned early that yearning begat pining, which begat letting myself be taken for granted, which begat drowning my sorrows in copious amounts of Blue Bunny Peanut Butter Party eaten directly from the carton. I'd only had to experience it once... or, alright, fine, maybe thrice... to know that, like gas station sushi, it was a situation best avoided. Since then, I hadn't allowed myself to be the yearner, I was the yearn-ee. Or something.

Yet, here I was, breaking all the rules of an entire adult lifetime—*crackity crack crack*—just to have him kiss me in that unhurried way of his, like kissing wasn't the vehicle that got us to our destination but the destination itself.

"Definitely better to be an expert at a few things," I slurred, licking my lips when he finally pulled back. "You were totally right. We'll stay home."

"And miss Littlejohn's trivia night?" Beale shook his head. "Nah, we'll go, and then we'll come back." He winked. "I think they call that edging."

I think they called this *screwed*.

Beale pulled his Jeep into the gravel parking lot of a little bar on Cooter Key just after sunset. The place was relatively tiny—a single low turquoise building with a slightly pitched roof and wooden shutters, bordered on two sides by an L-shaped patio half again as large as the bar itself—but it was packed to the rafters. Light and laughter spilled out each wide-open window and led us up the conch-lined path from the lot.

The crowd on the patio seemed mostly to be tourists—either that or folks around here really loved wearing I-Heart-Cooter T-shirts—but when we got inside, the vibe was a bit different, and the faces were already familiar just from hanging around town for a few days. A group of bikers sat in the corner and nodded at Beale when we walked in. Bubba Irvine and his wife, Lety, who owned the Concha, called out our names, and a bunch of older men and women playing a board game looked up and waved cheerily. Dale Jennings, Littlejohn's cousin, turned away from the television over the bar and embraced me like a long-lost relative.

"Trey! Dude, you're here! LJ said you were coming, but after the time he got sun poisoning and thought I was Big Bird, I ain't ever sure if he's serious anymore. We're gonna murder these Cooter clowns and mop the floor with their entrails," he said gleefully.

There was a lot to unpack there, and I debated explaining how mopping worked, but before I could open my mouth, Maddie McKetcham threw herself into my arms, blonde curls bouncing dramatically.

"Oh, Trey, thank *goodness*. Juju, Carolyn, Grandma, and Mr. Wynott were discussing your party? And I offered to make homemade decorations, you know? Like maybe a sign with the tiniest bit of glitter and stuff, since signs are kinda my thing? And also maybe streamers? In coordinating colors? But Mr. Wynott said nonsense 'cause that was tacky and they'd want elegant tablescapes." She crossed her arms. "Glitter is *not* tacky."

"Pssht," Dale scoffed. "'Course it's not. Marius don't know nothin. 'Sides, ya can't decide on decorations and tablescapes until ya have a theme. Trey, what's our theme?"

They looked at me expectantly.

I gave Beale a look that said, *Help a fake soul mate out?*

And he gave me a smiling look that said, *You've got this, ringer*, which was not at all helpful.

Truth to tell, the Mason I'd known before would probably want elegant, but the Mason who'd voluntarily committed himself to a blue-collar beau and a full-time life with these folks?

"The theme is... homemade glitter," I said firmly. "So your decorations would be perfectly suitable. And if Mr. Wynott has concerns about that, he may address them with me directly."

Marius Wynott had impressed me the first time I met him because he wore a waistcoat like nobody's business, and I'd give him points for that, but I was deducting points for abysmal people skills.

"Yay! I'll tell them," Maddie said. "Oh, and also? Ms. Charbonnier says nobody added her to the Facebook group for the party, and how's she gonna make sure no one else is bringing ambrosia if she's not in the group?"

I sighed. "Ms. Charbonnier is Bernie, right?"

Maddie nodded.

"Hmmm." I pulled out my brand-new phone and opened my very new "Trey" Facebook profile. The irony of having a profile for my alias when I'd avoided even creating a profile for *myself* all these years was not lost on me, but that wasn't remotely the weirdest part of the situation.

Yesterday at the Bean, Dale had officially made me an administrator of the Whispering Key Happenings Facebook group. This was a trifle concerning since I'd only been here four days—and Jesus Christ, when I stopped to think about that my brain got stuck, 'cause I'd once spent four *weeks* debating which kind of underwear to purchase and what each choice said about me as a person—and I'd told Dale maybe a visitor to the island wasn't the best choice of admin.

Dale had looked all kinds of confused. "But you and Beale are soul mates."

"Erm. Yeeeesss," I'd hedged. "But possibly long-distance soul mates for the foreseeable future?"

Dale had looked back and forth from me to Beale, whose arm happened to be around my shoulders at the time, then tipped his head back and laughed uproariously. "Ah, laws, that was a good one, Trey. You'll be permanent by Christmas. Just make sure new members answer the challenge questions correctly before you let 'em in, m'kay?" He'd thumped Beale on the shoulder appreciatively as he'd walked off.

I hadn't been sure how to take that. To be honest, even a day and a half later, I still wasn't, but that hadn't stopped me from doing the job.

"I've got her join request here," I told Maddie. "She's in."

"Trey! Getcha self over here!" Littlejohn yelled from the back of the bar. "It's almost trivia time!"

Beale nudged me in that direction with a little smile. "Go on, ringer. Wow 'em with your variety of knowledge."

Littlejohn jumped up and wrapped his arms around me as soon as we got within hugging distance, just as Dale had done. I was pretty sure I'd been embraced more in the past week than in the last thirty-five years. It was incredibly off-putting.

Mostly.

But I hugged him back because it would have been churlish not to.

I took a seat between Dale and Lorenna at the Whispering Key table and said my hellos to Lorenna, Marius, and Juju, while Beale shook hands with people at the Cooter Key table I hadn't met yet. I listened with half an ear to Marius chattering excitedly about some historian coming to town in a couple of months to write the history of Whispering Key and "our treasure."

It was funny to me how proprietary the town was about it. Beale's family (and Mason) had found the treasure, they were the ones who'd profited from it, but anytime I'd heard it mentioned, it was with a kind of pride. Like when something good happened to one resident, it happened to all of them.

It was bizarre. Cultlike. *Wrong.*

Buuuut I was starting to understand how Mason had been adopted into this little community so quickly... and why he'd adopted them right back.

I was profoundly grateful when the kid from the bar carried over a tray of pitchers and empty margarita glasses and set them on our table. I needed a drink rather badly.

"You can put those down right here by me, honey," Lorenna McKetcham said with a leer, "'cause if I don't drink my fill before Jonquil Pepper gets here, I won't be getting any a'tall."

The kid and I exchanged an amused look, and I offered a hand to shake. "I'm To—*Trey.*" Fuck, that was becoming annoying.

"Nice to meet you. I'm—"

"Heya, Silvio," Beale said, giving the kid a friendly pat on the shoulder.

Silvio? Holy, bedazzled Britney Spears. This... this... decidedly-not-thirty-five-year-old *child* was Bountiful-Bootied Silvio?

It was a sign of my distractedness that I hadn't even pondered the perky-assed implications of spending the evening at this bar, otherwise I would have dressed much more effectively.

I super casually leaned back in my chair, trying to get a look at the guy's nether regions—solely for research purposes—but he'd already turned toward Beale with a slack-jawed, adoring expression on his tiny, probably underaged face.

"Oh, heya, Beale!" His voice was like the shrill shriek of crows as they circled their prey.

Beale glanced around the table, then shrugged at me. "No free seats. I'll just—"

"You can come sit at the bar with me!" Crow-Baby offered. "I'd be happy to have the compan—"

"Absolutely not." I stood, grabbed Beale's arm, dragged him over to my chair, and shoved him down in it without conscious thought. "Plenty of room right here at the table."

Beale looked up at me, blue eyes dancing in a way that said *I know exactly what you're thinking and I like it,* which was kinda funny 'cause I hadn't fully articulated my motivations to myself yet, and I was trying hard not to.

"But now there's nowhere for you to sit, Trey," Dale said, all concerned.

"Sure there is," I insisted... then I plopped myself down on Beale's lap.

I could feel Beale's laughter against my back, and it was nearly as delightful as Silvio's narrowed eyes.

"And you are?" Child of the Crows demanded.

I smiled a smile that said I would cheerfully mop the floor with his entrails which, okay, credit to Dale, actually maybe worked as a metaphor. "Trey, precious. Remember we were introduced a minute ago?"

"He's Beale's soul mate," Littlejohn supplied.

"They met at a summer camp twelve years ago," Lorenna added. "And fell in love."

"Beale wrote letters to him afterward, every day for a year," Maddie proclaimed, clasping her hands under her chin. "But Trey's heartless mother intercepted them, because Beale is from Florida and Trey's family hates Floridians."

I blinked. This story got better and better with each retelling. Pretty sure this was a rip-off of *The Notebook*, but I was here for it.

"We stayed true to one another in our hearts," I told Silvio solemnly. Then I deliberately misquoted the movie. "If he's a plover, I'm a plover."

Littlejohn frowned. "What's that mean? Ain't plovers endangered?"

"Shush, LJ. Don't you know that shit don't have to mean nothin' if it sounds romantical?" Dale gave me a fond look. "And I think Trey and Beale are a great couple—"

"Oh." I brushed some nonexistent lint off my shirt. "Well, thank you, Da—"

"—even if they *are* kind of a May-December pairing."

"Uh, excuse you?" I scowled. "Jesus Christ, Dale. May-*June*! July at most."

Beale tickled my waist, and I jolted. "Settle down, soul mate."

"Payback will be swift and merciless," I informed him with narrowed eyes.

And just like every time we'd been in public, everyone around us stopped what they were doing to heave a collective sigh at our cuteness or some shit.

Now this *was* actually off-putting. Me claiming Beale by planting myself like a flag on his lap was one thing, but I wasn't sure how I felt about the whole island watching us share fake soul mate moments... moments that felt so real, even I had to remind myself they were fake.

When Silvio offered to pull over another chair beside Beale's so I could concentrate during trivia, I accepted.

About five minutes before the trivia started, Jonquil Pepper rushed in, all apologies, and we had to squeeze in another chair.

"Sorry I'm late, y'all, but look what I've got." She pulled out a stack of bright-pink fliers printed in Comic Sans with a clip-art picture of the Golden Gate Bridge below it.

"Whispering Key Bridge Committee," I read. I looked around the table and found Jonquil already sucking back her first margarita. "What's this? What bridge?"

"The main bridge that connects Whispering Key to the mainland," Marius said, as though this should be self-explanatory.

"See, maybe three years ago now—" Dale began.

"Six," Maddie corrected.

"More like eight, I think." Beale's voice was soft and a little sad.

"Has it been that long?" Dale whistled low, like the passage of time was a new idea for him. "Maybe so."

"Three to eight years ago... what?" I prompted.

"The bridge washed out in a storm," Beale explained. "It's not safe anymore. So now we have to come over here to Cooter Key, and take the Cooter Key Bridge to the mainland, which takes way longer—"

"Hours, sometimes," Jonquil interjected. "If the drawbridge between here and Whispering Key is up."

Beale leaned back in his seat, and his bicep rubbed against mine which was annoyingly thrilling. "It's restricted tourism and made deliveries tricky. Made it real hard for people to live on the island and commute to the mainland for work, too. You probably noticed that when you came in from the airport that it was kinda roundabout."

I shook my head. "It's the first time I've been here, so I never dreamed there'd be a different, faster way. I bet most tourists just figure this is the way it's always been, too. Why hasn't it been fixed? Isn't that up to the state?"

"Should be, but there's so few of us out here, and so many bigger fish to fry, it's been a nightmare getting the government to approve the funding." Dale shook his head. "Big Rafe's tried a billion times, but no dice."

"So now a few of us private citizens are taking the situation in hand. The Bridge Committee meets every second Thursday morning at the Bean to talk fundraising strategy." Jonquil set an enormous coffee can wrapped in construction paper in the center of the table beside the fliers. "No donation too small."

"Wow." Dale nodded, impressed. "Great idea."

I blinked.

"I can give Bubba and Lety a stack of fliers and a can for the Concha, and I bet Scotty will put a can at the Bean," Lorenna said.

"Wait." I frowned, shaking my head. "Wait, sorry, how much is the bridge going to cost?"

"Big Rafe says it'll be about six million, give or take? Plus a couple thousand to get a survey done and whatnot," Jonquil said cheerfully. She refilled her margarita glass from the pitcher. "But he's fronting half a million of his own money from the treasure, and he's paying for an architect to design it all up, so we're halfway there, really."

"Hmm." Math wasn't my strong suit, but I felt like it wasn't Ms. Pepper's either. "I know some people back in the city who might be interested in donating to a good cause." For example, me.

"Really?" Jonquil's face creased with a smile. "Trey, that would be amazing!"

I waved this away. "But I don't see your website on this flier. Or how to donate."

She tapped the can with the bottom of her glass. "This can right here!"

I pursed my lips, trying to figure out how to say this nicely. It was safe to say that "nice" was not my specialty.

"Jonquil, precious, you can't collect 5.5 million dollars a quarter at a time unless you have over twenty million people donating. No one in their right mind will make a big donation to an organization spearheaded by a retired kindergarten teacher with a coffee can. You need an actual board of directors. And you might need to talk to a legal representative about becoming a recognized charity so that donors can get a tax deduction for their trouble. And while you're at it, I think getting an artist's rendering of the actual proposed bridge would add an air of legitimacy *and* generate considerably more interest in... um..."

I looked up to find the entire table staring at me with wide eyes. Possibly I'd underthrown to hit "nice," but Jesus, what did people expect from me?

"Sorry," I began. "I have a habit of giving advice—"

Jonquil interrupted me. "All in favor of having Trey be the head of the Whispering Key Bridge Committee, say aye!"

A chorus of ayes filled the bar, including some from the Cooter Key table which should totes *not* get a vote.

"Oh, but I... um... I'm not a resident here," I reminded them. I looked at Beale a little desperately, hoping for a save. "I'm only here for the week."

"Psssht. You'll be back," Dale said confidently, just as he had when I tried stepping away from the Facebook group, and I felt overwhelmed both by the feeling that I was not remotely the man they thought I was... and also the feeling of really wishing I were.

Needless to say, margaritas were my friends after that—my very, very best, best friends, and I loved them above all things—and the rest of the night passed in a blur.

I got a bunch of trivia questions right. I also got a couple wrong.

I vaguely remembered arguing that no normal human knew what a neap tide was and doubling down when Beale said he did by loudly proclaiming that Beale was a "fucking big-dicked superhero and mortals can't be judged by your standards."

I was also pretty confident that at one point I told Lorenna obnoxiously that we could not be friends if she didn't know the words to at least one song from *Hamilton,* then leaned over and gave her the login information for my music account so she could "educate herself." She'd laughed and called me a good egg.

I knew for sure, though, that with every question I leaned a little further into Beale's side and enjoyed the scent of his cologne a little more. I knew for sure that I was transfixed by the way his thumb rubbed soothing circles on my neck, and the way his breath felt against my ear when he whispered that he couldn't wait to get me in bed. I knew for sure that I hadn't felt this comfortable or safe in approximately *ever*, and that I was going to miss the fuck out of this when it ended.

So, when CelebTV News flashed on the television above the bar during a commercial break, showing the back of my head and that ridiculous tattoo poised above the crotch of "pop-folk star Jayd Rollins," and some helpful patron said, "Holy shit! It's Jayd again! And who the heck is *Tommy*?" I may have panicked just a little at the idea that Beale would see it, not because I was afraid he wouldn't keep my secret, but because I was afraid of… something else entirely.

So I very deliberately moved back to Beale's lap, delighting in his surprised, welcoming smile, wrapped my arms around his neck, and kissed him with every ounce of the foolish yearning I'd accidentally allowed myself to feel. And in that second I truly *hoped* every person in the bar was watching us... because this was the version of Toby Elford I wanted them to see.

10

BEALE

Czarina's StarCharts for Today
Patience, Virgo! The best teachers listen as much as they speak.

"I know what I want to do with you today." I threw a jingling cat toy into the hallway, and the second Marjorie ran after it, I grabbed the swim trunks she'd been "protecting" off the bed and pulled them on.

Toby, who was picking up our assorted clothes from the corner of the guest bedroom, paused to give me a flirtatious grin. "Oh, really? You ready to go again already, Goodman?"

I snorted. God, he made me happy.

"Not that." Although, you know, these days I was *always* down for that. I had zero hesitation when Toby was involved. "I meant an activity where you can work on your tan."

We'd been so busy for the last couple of days, what with trivia, and town meetings, and me taking a couple of shifts running Goodmen Outfitters' tour boat around the island, and Toby being the unofficial social events coordinator for Whispering Key, Toby had joked the night before that he was the only person in the world who'd leave Florida paler than he'd arrived.

Meanwhile, I'd started thinking maybe I didn't want him to leave at all.

He straightened, narrowed his eyes, and set his hands on his hips. "What kind of activity?"

"I..." Somewhere around Monday, he'd developed a line of freckles across his nose that were the cutest, most distracting thing ever. I wanted to boop them with my fingertip. I also knew better than to mention this on pain of death.

"You, what?" he demanded. "Finish the thought, Goodman."

His scowl made me grin. "So suspicious."

Toby went back to gathering up clothes. "Wonder why. Possibly because we've already re-enacted *Titanic*? Or because we were nearly *stranded* on a deserted island? Or because you fed me vegan seitan hotdogs yesterday and *claimed* it was an accident? Or—?"

I laughed out loud. "We absolutely were not stranded, you enjoyed the seitan before you knew what it was, and nothing has tried to murder you in hours and hours. You even have your credit card back now. I'm starting to think you enjoy being almost-murdered, Toby."

"Nonsense. I do not have a murder fetish, thank you very much, and I am the perfect amount of suspicious." He dumped the pile of our clothes on the bed and started sorting them for the wash, doing this little domestic task for the both of us like it was a normal, everyday thing, and I liked that way more than was healthy. "But if I *were* absurd like that, you'd be the deluded fool who *liked* my overly suspicious ass, and that's worse." He looked up like he'd startled himself. "I mean... you like me well enough to sleep with me. That kind of like."

I threw myself chest-down on the bed, stacked my fists under my chin, and watched him steadily. "I do like you, Toby." I liked him very much. Maybe too much. Certainly more than I knew what to do with.

Toby Elford was a snarky little rain cloud of a human, and it shouldn't have been possible for him to light up my days, but he did.

"*Pfft*. Of course you do." He slapped his ass lightly. "Who wouldn't like this? Crazy people, that's who."

I shook my head and watched him swallow while his face turned red and he tried so, so hard to pretend it was all a joke.

"That's not what I mean, and you know it. I like you. As a person. A lot." I liked his humor. I liked the soft heart of him that kept peeking out from his prickly shell.

Toby darted his gaze to mine like he was pretty sure this was the setup to some kind of joke and wasn't sure what to do when he found I was serious. "Ugh, fine! We can do whatever you want. You don't have to butter me up."

I did an ab curl and sat up so I could stroke a thumb over his cheek. Toby was really attractive when he was prickly... and he was almost always prickly. "Keep an open mind. You might actually find this activity kind of fun."

Eventually.

"Oh, no doubt." He waved a hand airily. "Hunting pythons or wrestling baby alligators or whatever's on the agenda will no doubt make me feel *fully alive*. Figures I couldn't have landed myself a fake soul mate who enjoyed mimosas and a high-quality cucumber facial mas—" He shook out a pair of shorts and something clacked against the mattress. "What's this?"

I grabbed for the brightly colored strand eagerly. "No *way*! That's my bracelet! I thought this was gone for good." I clasped my left wrist which had been naked for nearly a week. "It must've fallen into my pocket after all. I can't believe you found it."

Or that the Universe had meant for him to find it.

Toby snorted. "And here I thought you kept rubbing your wrist 'cause I made you nervous."

I ignored this, since it wasn't entirely wrong, and spread the bracelet on my palm to show him.

"Check it out: lapis lazuli for confidence, moonstone for intuition and clairvoyance, sapphire for serenity and peace of mind."

"It's beautiful."

I nodded. "It was a gift from my mom before she died. The last thing she ever gave me."

Toby trailed a finger over the stones, then looked up at me with a half-smile. "Aww. Kind of a lucky charm, then?"

"Kinda. More like... a promise. See, the stones protect me from negative energy, and just feeling the bracelet there reminds me not to give in and take the easy road. My mom believed the Universe had great things in store for me, and settling for anything less would be like letting her down."

"Ah." Toby frowned. "And what does 'great things' entail, precisely?"

"I don't know yet *precisely*. A soul mate. A life path." I grinned. "I guess I'll figure it out when the Universe shows them to me, huh?"

"Ah," Toby said again. He hesitated, then shrugged. "Well, I hope I didn't mess it up when I touched it like I did the big green one the other day."

I held the beads in my palm and worried them lightly with my thumb. "You didn't mess anything up. You couldn't. Even if you had somehow attuned the stones to you, I like your energy. It's soothing. Like sunshine."

Toby's face blanked except for one raised eyebrow. "Soothing."

"Yeah. But that's a good thing," I assured him.

"Is it, Beale? Is it really?" Toby set his hands on his hips. "Is your ultimate goal in life to be *soothed,* precious? Do you live to be told you have the energy of one of your cups of Sleepytime tea? *Soothing.* Fuck that. A clarinet solo is soothing. My energy is *raw,* and it's *carnal,* and... and... and... it's *lustful.* Almost entirely lustful. Understand?"

I pressed my lips together against laughter, but I was pretty sure he could see it spilling from my eyes. "Maybe soothing was the wrong word," I agreed. In reality, being around Toby was more like existing on a continuum between amusement and frustration, arousal and annoyance, but it was really fucking *fun.*

I'd always been a content sort of person by nature, but I wasn't sure I'd ever felt as much as I did with Toby. Want and need and protectiveness and anger and… joy. It threw me off balance, but in a good way. It made me feel awake and aware and really alive.

"Finish up fast, okay?" I rolled to my feet and gave him a quick peck on the cheek before heading for the door. "Then put on your bathing suit and meet me outside."

"I don't know how else to say this but in English, Goodman. No fucking way are you teaching me to swim."

Toby stood on the cement at the edge of the pool, looking sexy as anything and wearing nothing but tiny red swim trunks and a pissed-off expression.

I pushed my wet hair back from my face and tucked my tongue into my cheek. "But you said we could do *anything* I wanted."

Toby shook his head. "Beale. Precious. *Angel.* Sweetness. There was a distinct sexual overtone to my agreement, because I felt there was a sexual overtone to your proposition." He pursed his lips. "Or there fucking *should* have been. I have so much to teach you, my Virgo."

I grinned. Before this week, I'd never really understood how Mason and Fenn's constant teasing seemed to make them both better—stronger—but now I got it. There was no judgment in Toby's teases, and it was hard to be offended when I could sense so much genuine appreciation every time he looked at me.

In fact, Toby was a lot like Marjorie—all hisses and side-eyes, bone-deep loyalty and a need for affection... which was another thing I wasn't gonna tell him on pain of death.

"In retrospect, I don't have time for... water frolicking." Toby stared down at the water balefully. "I have work to do."

"Work, huh? Because you maybe mentioned once or a hundred times that you were going to be in the Maldives this week. On vacation."

He licked his lips. "Yes. Well. I *was*. But since I'm *not*, I should probably use my time wisely and get ahead. Besides, imagine if I were to sink to a watery grave right here in the pool this morning, and all those letters went unanswered?" He shook his head once in the negative. "I couldn't live with that on my conscience."

I rubbed my chin. "Mmhmm. I can see how that would be a real concern."

"Excellent! Then we agree—"

"Except you wouldn't have to live with it on your conscience, 'cause you'd be dead."

"Oh." He frowned. "Then I would be a very malcontented spirit. A poltergeist, I expect. Or—"

"Toby, I'm not going to let anything bad happen to you," I promised. "And you know what's great about the water? You can think about your Hagatha responses while you float. Kill two birds with one stone."

Toby sighed and took a single step down into the water so it lapped at his ankles. "No more metaphors about killing and ghosts when referring to my pool-based endeavors, Goodman." He swallowed. "Fine. I'm in. Now what?"

I bit the inside of my cheek hard, because I was *not* going to laugh about this. Not yet, anyway. "Now you get all the way in. Until your feet touch the bottom."

"I was afraid you were going to say that." He took a step down, and then another, clinging to the railing beside the wide steps. But when he was nearly ass-deep, he hesitated again.

"One more." I held out a hand to help him down. "Come on. It's so refreshing in here."

"Nonsense. It's *wet*." He grabbed my hand. "Off-puttingly wet."

"It is very wet," I agreed solemnly. "That's an unavoidable part of the swimming experience."

Toby took the final step, and when his feet touched bottom, he shivered. Without thinking, I wrapped my arms around him to warm him, though the sun was so hellishly hot, I knew he wasn't really cold.

"You're doing really well," I whispered.

Toby's nostrils flared. "I'm being ridiculous. I'm well aware that I'm being ridiculous. Don't coddle me, Beale."

He tried to push out of my arms, but I held him tighter. "Whoa! You're not being ridiculous. Christ, baby, everyone has things they're scared of. And unlike house pets and rogue microwaves, water is a thing that's actually *good* to have a healthy concern about. Did you ever fall in a pool or something? Maybe as a kid?"

He mumbled something against my chest that sounded like, "My dad pushed me in."

"What?"

Toby shrugged. "That was how he learned to swim, so it was how he taught me and my little brother. It worked for Russ; not so much for me. Probably because Russ could recite the entire Litany of the Saints by age eight and I couldn't. All those sins weigh a person down." He gave a panicked little laugh at his own joke.

To be honest, the "sink or swim" method was how my dad had taught me and my brothers, and I'd never given it much thought, but it seemed totally barbaric while I was holding a shivering Toby in my arms.

"Okay, let's try this. Turn around and lean back against me... yeah, just like that. Now let your feet come up and I'll hold you. We're gonna float, and that'll help you get used to the feeling of the water, and remember you're buoyant, okay?"

"I'm buoyant. *Super*. Buoyant and soothing. It's like you've read the deepest dreams of my heart this morning, Beale. It's like you've instinctively understood my—*aahhh!* Don't drop me!" he yelled as I pulled my feet up. "I'll behave."

"Not gonna drop you," I crooned. "Trust me."

He laughed shakily, his hands grasping the forearm I'd wrapped around his chest. "Oh, trust you. Certainly. Easy peasy. I trust you, Beale, it's the overwhelming quantity of wet shit surrounding us I don't trust. Don't suppose you have an extra lucky charm lying around? Preferably a tiny stone embedded in a pair of those floaty arm things children wear?"

He was joking, but I could feel in every line of his body how stressed he was, so I backed us up against the side of the pool in the shallow end, and without thinking about it too much, I removed my bracelet to clasp it around his wrist.

"Wait, what are you doing? No, that's yours, Beale. I—"

"Shhh. I'm only lending it to you for today." I wrapped my hand around the bracelet, holding it against his skin. "It's for good luck, okay? And whenever you catch sight of it, you'll remember that I'm not gonna let anything happen to you."

For once, I seemed to have shocked Toby silent, because he stared at the bracelet on his wrist and relaxed against me without a word, letting me tow him toward the deep end.

"What's the weirdest Hagatha letter you ever got?" I asked. We'd reached the center of the pool, and I was treading water for both of us, but I didn't want him to think about it too much. I should have known better.

"Don't try to distract me in the murder pool, Goodman."

I laughed and squeezed him closer. God, he was adorable. So adorable I couldn't resist pressing a kiss to the silly tattoo on his shoulder. "I suppose it was only a matter of time, really, until you accused something else of murder, but you're still alive, you know. For now."

One of these days, I was going to ask him about that tattoo —a permanently inked sexy cartoon character was so unlike the man I was coming to know, I felt like there had to be a story involved—but Toby didn't like being questioned about anything, and I'd been really hesitant to push the issue. This was temporary, so it was none of my business. Fascinating as the man was, he was not meant for me.

I tried to picture, for a second, how much more perfect a situation like this would feel when I was actually experiencing it with my soul mate... but I couldn't. I figured it was like looking at a crystal that was flawless to the naked eye, only to be told there was something even better out there. It was hard to imagine.

"Once I got a letter from a guy who wanted me to send him my sock so he could come in it." Toby's words startled me from my thoughts. "Pretty sure that was the weirdest."

"Gross. That must've been upsetting."

"Sure." He sighed sadly. "I'm upset every time I see that single sock in my drawer."

"Toby!" I poked him gently in the side, and he squirmed and flailed dramatically. "Be serious."

"Alright, alright! Jesus. Surely this kind of aggressive questioning is banned by the Geneva convention. Yes, it really happened, but no, *obviously*, I wrote him back and said that wasn't appropriate." He relaxed back against me again. "Because maybe he was a kid or something, you know? Don't want to embarrass someone who might not know better." He thought for a second, then cleared his throat and added, "But mostly because it was a liability issue, of course."

"Of course. Not like you *cared* or anything." I snorted. "Drop the act, because I've figured out your secret, Toby Elford. Beneath that raw, carnal, prickly exterior, you're a giant ball of mush and you *care* about things."

I could *feel* Toby rolling his eyes, though I couldn't see them. "Of course I care about *some* things! I care about Mason. And the fate of the polar ice caps. And having job stability. Making sure that every human has the same basic rights. My cute apartment with its ultra-plush mattress and pretty view. Um... not drowning? That's damn important. So there's, like, twenty-seven things I care about right there."

"You might have forgotten a couple, because your love for your plush mattress doesn't explain why you'd reply to someone whose letter wasn't getting published."

"*Ultra*-plush," he corrected. "And I happen to reply to all the letters, even the ones that don't get published. But don't read into that, Beale," he hurried to add. "I'm no saint. The best part of my job is that I get to be a snarky know-it-all to people for money. 'Oh, you're sad your granddaughter is marrying someone you disapprove of, so you're not paying for the wedding? Let me tell you where you can stick your trust fund, Ebenezer.' Or, 'Oh, you want me to say it's okay not to invite your neighbors to your barbecue because they practice a different religion and you don't wanna take ten seconds to ask their dietary requirements? Ask yourself, Sally, if that's what Jesus would have done.' But I imagine the people who write me want to be seen, you know? Acknowledged. And even the assholes deserve a minute of my time, if only to set them down a peg or two. Doesn't make me a saint, though, darling. On the contrary."

God. The man really had no clue. Toby was the one who didn't see himself clearly. I kinda understood why—his family sounded like assholes, he couldn't tell anyone about the specifics of his job, and he probably felt like he was completely alone—but I wished I could make him see himself the way I saw him.

"Toby, you're really smart and insightful—"

"Oh. Wow. That's nice of you to—"

"—so I totally don't get how you can be so dumb about this. You're not a saint, but you're a really caring person."

Toby sighed. "Precious, if you persist in seeing me through rose-colored glasses, far be it from me to—" Toby's phone, which was sitting on a bench near the pool, chimed with an incoming text, and he sighed again, louder this time. "I'll bet you five American dollars Jonquil Pepper just had a flash of inspiration that we need a tuba soloist for the party and wants my buy-in."

I laughed and rubbed my nose against his neck. "And you're gonna tell her that's an amazing idea, but maybe not for this particular party?"

"Yes, probably," he grumbled. "Because it's more expedient—"

"But it isn't. Not at all. It's because you, Toby Elford, *care*. You actually like the lunatics on this island."

For a long minute, Toby seemed to ponder this, and then he admitted, "I don't dislike Whispering Key. I didn't expect to be able to say that, but there's a certain charm in people embracing you immediately. It's a far cry from New York."

"Yeah? How long does it take to fit in there?"

He chuckled lightly. "I'll let you know when it happens."

I turned us in a wide circle, so Toby's legs fanned out, making ripples in the water. "So why not move? You can do your job anywhere, right? Why not relocate to Whispering Key? I mean," I added quickly, "a place *like* Whispering Key."

"There *isn't* anywhere else like Whispering Key. At least not that I've ever encountered."

"So stay here, then." I tried to sound casual, like my heart wasn't beating out of my chest at the idea of keeping this thing between us going for longer. "I mean, there's no reason you can't stay even after Mason comes back, right?"

"For a little while, I suppose. I might have to, depending on how things work out back in the city."

Have to was not the same as *want* to, and I realized I wanted him to want to be here, even after whatever bullshit with his ex-boyfriend... or ex-boyfriends... or whoever the hell he was running from... was over. I wanted him to choose this place. I knew this thing between us was only temporary, but I wanted him in my life anyway.

"You still haven't told me what's going on in the city," I reminded him, and his body tensed in my arms. "But isn't there something you can do to fix the situation with the two guys? Or will it resolve itself?"

"Eh. Time will tell," he said vaguely.

"You could tell me what's going on. I would help you with anyth—"

He shook his head firmly. "No, Beale, I couldn't. It's a... a relatively minor personal problem that has nothing whatsoever to do with you, okay?"

"Yeah." Logically, I knew he was right, but it felt instinctively wrong, like some ass-backward part of me wanted everything that involved him to involve me, too, just because we were sleeping together. "Okay."

"Besides—" Toby shot me a sly look over his shoulder. "—if we start talking about all the shit I'd rather not talk about, then we'll have to talk about all the stuff *you'd* rather not talk about."

I wondered if he turned the conversation away from himself all the time on purpose or if it was instinctive. Still, I bit.

"What's that supposed to mean?"

That sly look again. "Do you *really* want to know?"

"Why not?" I turned us in a tight circle again. I couldn't think of much I wouldn't want to discuss with Toby. "If I don't like it, I could always drop you," I teased, holding him tighter.

"Well, I was thinking about your career concerns." Toby gripped my arm, like he wasn't quite sure if I was teasing. "You remember when we were plover-spotting the other day, and I said something along the lines of, 'Beale, fake conquistador of my soul, what does a plover look like?' And then you showed me what I should be looking for, including the forehead markings that say they're down to mate?"

"Of course that's the part you remember," I said irritably. Leave it to Toby to actually find maybe the one thing I really *didn't* want to discuss with him. "Yeah, so?"

"So… if you hadn't shown me, how would I have known what I was looking for? I could have been counting bald eagles."

"There are no bald eagles here," I scoffed.

"The Universe doesn't magically give you things," Toby continued, undeterred. "You tell it what you want, right? What you visualize is what you get."

I scowled. What was he getting at? I mean, *obviously* that was the way things worked. I'd visualized myself happy and fulfilled a *lot*. But the Universe took its own sweet time.

"I told you before, everyone has an opinion on what I ought to be doing for a career, but I *like* doing lots of different things. I'm happy doing lots of things. Until I know what the path is—"

"No, no, no. Beale. Precious. That *is* the path. That's my point. You're there. Revel in it. Glory in it. This *is* your grand future. You told the Universe you wanted a bunch of things, and it provided a bunch of things. The future is *here*."

I frowned at the water. "I don't think it's that easy."

"Who decides when you're happy enough, Beale? You do. You decide when you're as happy as you want to be. You don't need to have crazy ambitions if they don't feel authentic. Most people would kill to have plenty of money and spend each day doing things that make them happy. What more could you want?"

You.

I disregarded the thought immediately, but it was so ridiculous, my rhythm was thrown off and we floundered for a second.

"Sweet mother of dragons, I thought you were kidding about the dropping thing!" Toby cried.

"I was. I had a... a cramp. Sort of. Continue what you were saying."

"Hmph. I'm not sure if—"

"Toby."

"Look, there's a part of me that very much wishes I could stay here, Beale, but I can't. For one thing, I've lied about my identity and our relationship to absolutely everyone on the island. It's gonna be bad enough when I inevitably fake-break-up with you," he said mournfully, and my heart skipped a beat. "It'll be even worse when they learn I'm not who I said I was. Plus, I'm meant for city life. Do you know, there's not a Neiman Marcus around here for miles? You, on the other hand... you know where you belong, and it's here."

"It is. The idea of even *visiting* a city like New York gives me hives," I told him honestly. "There's an energy here on the island—an interconnectedness maybe—that feels right to me. Like I'd starve without it."

"So *own* it. The beauty of having lots of money is doing whatever you want, right? When you're rich, you're not weird, you're eccentric. So stick to your guns. Why limit yourself? If I had millions, I'd devote myself to doing nothing but visiting luxury resorts around the world so I could rank them. I'd enjoy every single minute without a care."

Five days ago, I might have believed that.

I stared down at his wet hair, at the smooth length of his torso glowing beneath the water, at the darker line of my tanned forearms wrapped around him as he leaned against me, and at the bracelet of colorful stones wrapped around his wrist. It loosened something in my chest to see it there.

"No, you wouldn't."

Toby opened his mouth, then shut it again. "Alright, no I wouldn't." He sounded surprised and maybe a little reluctant to admit it. "Or not just that. But I'll tell you what I wouldn't do: I wouldn't spend a single second worrying about the opinion of anyone who wanted to make life decisions for me. That way lies madness." He patted my forearm. "And both Hagatha *and* Toby say that, for whatever our opinions are worth."

The vulnerability in his voice made me want to hug the crap out of him, but I could just imagine how he'd react to that—like Marjorie when she was frightened, razor claws and all.

"Toby, Hagatha *is* you. Honestly, anyone who'd spent a couple hours with you would spot the similarities. You have the same voice. You have the same heart. Maybe if you stopped running away from your alter ego, you'd understand what other people like so much about you. Maybe *you* need to own *that*."

He cleared his throat. "In any case, this has been quite passably enjoyable, Goodman, but surely our swimming lesson is over now?"

"Floating's not the same as swimming, Toby," I warned.

"An excellent point, but I'm concerned for the state of my skin." He held up his pruny fingers.

I almost sighed. The time limit on Toby's patience for serious discussion seemed to have expired. But in the end, maybe that was for the best. Maybe there was something to be said for just enjoying something, especially when you knew it wouldn't last long.

We'd drifted back to the shallow end, so Toby put his feet on the bottom and stood. "I feel like it's only fair that I should choose our next activity."

"You already serenaded me with Broadway's greatest hits yesterday, and once a week is probably my limit," I warned, though I was pretty sure I could tolerate it as many times as necessary. He was adorable when he reached for the high notes.

He mock-pouted. "I wasn't going to sing... probably."

"And I told you I'm not helping to make decorations for the party. My hands are too big for paper crafts."

"Yeah, we figured that out pretty fast on Monday." He wrinkled his nose and wrapped his arms around my neck. "Your origami stars were... unique. But there are many, many things your big hands *are* very good at, Beale."

"Is that so?" I lifted one eyebrow. "Anything in particular?"

"Oh, rescuing me from murder cats. Um. Fixing murder boats. Swimming lessons—" He backed me up against the wall.

"In the murder pool?" I guessed. I spread my legs so he could fit against me better.

"Exactly."

"I'm sensing a pattern here, Toby, and it's concerning."

"You're also good at decidedly un-murder-y things. And you might recall providing me with a comprehensive list of sexual fantasies the other day. I believe a blow job was discussed, for starters."

For starters. Yeah, I remembered that list in great detail, specifically the part that had involved me fucking him, which was something we hadn't done yet this week. My dick started to swell despite the cool water.

"You got my attention." I coasted a hand down over the ass of those tiny red shorts and held him in place so I could stroke myself against him. "Tell me more."

He tugged my hair to get better access to the tendon at the side of my neck and bit down gently. "I'm more of a show-er than a tell-er, baby. Come see." He spun away from me and headed for the stairs.

I narrowed my eyes. Up to this point, Toby had mostly directed our sexual encounters, which had been totally fine with me. More than fine. *So* much more than fine. His confidence and take-charge attitude had given *me* confidence. But today, I felt the need to remind him that I had a few tricks up my sleeve, as well, and I always tried to listen to my instincts.

I caught him when he was about to put his foot on the bottom step and lifted him from behind with one arm around his chest.

"Sweet Jesus, Beale! What the hell are you—?"

"It's all coming back to me now." I ran a hand from his chest to his abs, then down over the front of his bathing suit. He sucked in a breath through his teeth and bucked against my hold. "I'm remembering there was a pool-related component to the fantasy list."

"W-we don't have supplies," he said weakly. "We should—"

"Take advantage of the contractors not coming until this afternoon and enjoy some more time in nature? Someone once told me you were Outdoorsy Barbie." I delved my fingers into his bathing suit and stroked his length. "I couldn't agree more."

It only took a couple of strokes before his entire body melted back against me like butter in the hot sun.

"Oh, fuck, Beale. *Fuck*, that's so good."

I nudged him onto his hands and knees on the stairs, with his lower legs still in the water. "Look at you, already half-hard for me. That cannot be comfy in those shorts. Let me help you out."

"Wait, wait, not *here*. Not in the—"

I had his suit pulled down in what I thought was record time considering how fucking tight it was, and since it was right there in front of my face, just begging for attention, I bit his ass cheek lightly.

"—pool," he finished weakly. He gave me a look over his shoulder like he wasn't quite sure who I was anymore, and I grinned because I liked keeping him on his toes. Or his hands and knees, as the case might be.

I grabbed his bountiful, *exceptional* ass with both hands, spreading his cheeks, and then I teased his hot hole with my tongue over and over.

"Oh, holy fuck," he moaned. "Holy fuck. You're... you... How? *Gah.*"

Yeah, I definitely enjoyed this side of Toby.

"You remember we do have the internet here, right, baby?" I laughed lightly, making him moan again. "And that I might be a virgin, but I'm not a *total* virgin."

"Mmmph." Toby shot me a glare over his shoulder. "Less talky-talky, Goodman. If you're gonna do a job, do it—*oh, good God.*"

I laughed again. I'd sort of wondered if this was a thing I'd be any good at, or if I'd even enjoy it, back when it had been a theoretical thing—something that happened to other people on the opposite side of a laptop screen. Hearing Toby's loud groans, watching him pound the side of his fist against the concrete, feeling him push back against my tongue, it felt profoundly *right* to be able to do this for him, to give this tightly controlled man a moment of uninhibited freedom.

I pushed my thumb against his rim as I licked at him and imagined how it would feel when it was my dick pushing inside him instead. The thought was so fucking exciting I felt my cock pulse in my shorts.

"Want to fuck you," I told him. "Shit, Toby. Wanna be inside you so bad."

"Y-yeah. Yes. Yeah. Do it," he ground out, spreading his knees wider. I spit on his hole so I could push two fingers inside him along with my tongue, stretching him further. He'd let me finger him before—in fact, because Toby was Toby, he'd practically drawn me a map to his prostate—but this time when I hit it, he let out a wail so long and keening, it startled the birds from the trees.

"Fuck, yes. More. Come on, Beale. *Please*. Do it." He balanced himself on one hand so he could jerk himself with the other.

But Toby was right—we needed supplies, including vast amounts of lube at the very least, for me to take him, so that was going to have to wait a minute... but Toby couldn't.

I reached around him and knocked his hand out of the way so I could wrap one hand around his length while I worked his ass with the other. He stutter-moaned, and the sound ricocheted through me, setting up an ache in my balls.

He was one hundred percent mine in that moment, and it was a fucking heady feeling. *This* was what had been missing from every sexual encounter in my past. The feeling of being open and vulnerable with someone, the absolute knowledge that they were open and vulnerable to me. This was the feeling I'd never expected to find outside of my soul mate, the thing I'd never been able to articulate because I hadn't experienced it.

And I still wouldn't have, if not for Toby.

I nudged him up so he was kneeling with his back to my chest. I loved this position with him always, whether we were floating in a pool or standing in the kitchen, because it calmed this need I had to protect him—like the prickliest man in Florida needed *my* protection, right?—and also because Toby turned to putty when I put my mouth on the tendon at the join of his shoulder.

Now I liked it for a very different reason. His body weight pushed my fingers more deeply inside of him, deep enough that he gave another one of those wild moans, while my view over his shoulder was of the head of his cock peeking out the top of my closed fist.

Size difference for the win.

"You are the hottest thing I've ever seen. Your skin is like honey, and I want to lick every inch. Your cock in my hand is perfection. You feel that?" I slid my dick against his ass cheek, leaving a thick trail of precum there. "I'm gonna be inside you soon, and this ass feels so perfect I might never leave it.

Toby bit his lip and tipped his head back on my shoulder, working himself against me. He lifted up, thrusting into my fist, then lowered back down to rub my fingers against his prostate, over and over again. It felt strangely like fucking and being fucked at the same time, and I had never been so turned on in my life, even in this whole crazy week.

It felt like I was going to explode if I didn't get a hand, or a mouth, or sweet Jesus, an ass, on my cock immediately, but at the same time I never wanted this feeling to end. Toby used sex as a weapon, as a tool, as a distraction... but ironically, he was never more honest than he was when he was having sex... at least, when he was having it with me. It was really tempting to believe that I was the difference, that this was as special to him as it was for me.

"Come for me, baby," I whispered in his ear. "I wanna see it. I wanna feel it." Then I bit down on the side of his neck.

His hole clenched around me like a vise, his dick went off like a rocket, he screamed my name into the hot sunshine, and deep inside me, some lock that had been shut tight for a really long time finally opened.

Toby collapsed down onto his hands again. "I do believe... I've been convinced... of my buoyancy...'cause I feel like I'm floating." He sounded drunk. "And my chakras... are as open... as any man's have ever been. Really, ten out of ten for swimming pools. I've seen the light."

And though my dick was hard enough to hammer nails, I couldn't help but laugh.

11

TOBY

Help Me Hagatha
(*Unsent*)

Dear Aunt Hagatha:

Help! I'm pretty sure I've gone and fallen for a guy who's way too good for me. What do I do?

"That Guy" in Whispering Key

Dear Guy,

You hope like hell he doesn't figure it out, you poor sad sack.

Do better,
Haggie

"You wait right there, precious, and do... whatever thoughts of me inspire you to do. I've got everything we need in my toiletry bag." I tossed the stunning man on the bed my most seductive smile—the best I could muster, anyway, when I smelled like coconut and chlorine, and my hair was doing plovers-alone-knew-what—and scurried out of the bedroom.

I examined myself in the mirror. I looked well fucked in every way that a man could be. Eyes overbright? Check. Hair artfully arranged in a wood chipper chic style? Super check. Goofy smile stuck to my lips like I'd just won the biggest prize at a fair I hadn't known I'd be attending? Enormous, outrageous, sanity-threatening check.

I blew out a shaking breath and grabbed my toiletry case, only knocking *half* my Sunday Riley skincare regimen in the sink in the process. Deep down at the bottom of the bag were several strings of condoms I'd packed on top of the case last week in a variety of sizes, knowing I'd find someone fuckably cute and totally forgettable to pass time with in the Maldives. Instead, I was here in Whispering Key, Florida, ready to be fucked by a virgin, and my goddamn hands were shaking.

I remembered Beale calling my energy soothing, and I wished I could summon just a tiny fucking shred of "soothing," because I was a nervous wreck and it was all his fault.

How dare he attempt to take me seriously as a person?

How dare he hold me like he was afraid I might fly away?

How dare he be all hearts and flowers perfect, when everything about our fake relationship was so very clearly impossible, including the fact that when I'd had the opportunity to tell the truth, I'd purposely *lied* and told him the situation in New York was "a relatively minor personal problem" that had nothing to do with him?

I had no clue how to handle this because it was totally outside my frame of reference. I didn't have *real* relationships, let alone fake relationships. Jesus Christ in a blanket, I didn't even do friends other than Mason. I didn't do... trust, and I wasn't sure how to start.

Beale was the one person in the world who knew me as Toby *and* as Hagatha, and he not only liked both parts, he saw them as two halves of a whole. Even *I* didn't do that. It was weird enough to have someone like me; it was next to impossible to believe that someone liked *all* of me. It was an equation that would not equate.

"And it's not gonna equate, even if you stand here pondering it for a hundred years," I told my reflection. "So focus on Beale and make this perfect, asshole."

I huffed. If Beale could hear me, he'd probably say this was more evidence that I was a nice person. Good people like Beale always thought other people were good too.

My motivations, though, were entirely selfish. I wanted it to be perfect because I wanted him to remember it that way. You always remembered your first, right? Well, I wanted no one who came along after me—no gorgeous hunk of big-dicked, soul-matey enchantment—to ever compare. It was only fair, since that orgasm out by the pool had been one of the most gratifying sexual encounters of my entire life, and there was no way I was going to forget that, even long after I was back in the city, carrying a giant, unrequited crush as a souvenir.

"Toby?"

I whirled to find Beale leaning against the bathroom door frame, gloriously naked, fully aroused, and watching me make sad faces at myself in the damn mirror. By the hair of Justin Bieber circa 2012, was I to be allowed to maintain no vestige of my dignity this week?

"You okay?"

"Yes! Yes, fine. Obviously. Just getting the supplies, and… things." I clutched the extra-large condoms in my hand. "Um. Where did we leave the lube earlier?"

Beale looked down at the counter, approximately two inches from my right hand. "There?"

"Oh." A burst of desperate laughter bubbled up from my chest and got caught in my throat. "Ha. Silly me."

"Toby," Beale repeated. He took a step toward me, so I looked up and our gazes locked. Those kind, patient blue eyes seemed to see all my silly, selfish, chaotic thoughts, and I realized I was willing to give up all my dignity this week. Every last shred. And it would be worth it, just for this chance to be with someone who made me feel cherished and safe and seen and wanted. So very wanted.

"I'm nervous," I blurted. "I don't know why! I'm the furthest thing from a virgin you could find."

"Well, I'm not nervous." He closed the distance between us so he could chafe my chilly arms with his big hands. His cock poked my belly, but he ignored it. "You know why?"

I shook my head.

"Because it's you, Toby."

I blinked. "If this is about my soothing energy..."

Beale shook his head and lifted both hands to cradle my jaw as if I was something infinitely precious. Then he leaned down and kissed me—hot and hungry and *real*.

I'd been kissed a thousand times. Maybe ten thousand. Hell, even a hundred times by Beale this week alone. Still, this one felt different. Like Beale was trying to tell me something. Like I was trying to tell him something back.

The next thing I knew, I was ass-down in the center of the bed and Beale had covered me with his body. He pressed hot openmouthed kisses to every part of me he could reach —my nipple, my bicep, the sharp jut of my hip, the thick cord of my neck that he'd figured out slayed me. He whispered sweet, silly things against my skin—how beautiful I was, how lucky he was, how special I was, how badly he wanted me—like he hoped the words would sink inside me, and I'd have sworn a couple of them did. I felt marked by him every place the words touched, as surely as if they'd been written in indelible ink.

By the time he made his way down my body to my cock, I was fully hard again and moving restlessly against the sheets. Then he opened his mouth over my cock, and I swear to fuck, I saw stars. I didn't realize I'd been trying to move away from the gorgeous torture of it until I felt his hand splayed against my belly, holding me down and making me take it.

"Holy shit, Beale." My voice was slurred, wrecked. "Please." I wasn't sure what I was asking for—for him to fuck me, for him to bring his cock to my lips so I could taste him, for him to end this quickly because it had all become way too real when we were nothing but a lie on top of a lie. "Let me touch you. Let me make you feel good."

Beale lifted his head, and his hair fell across his forehead. He grinned rakishly with spit-slick lips and reached for the lube so he could coat his fingers. "I'm onto you, you know," he said casually.

My eyes widened. I had no idea what he meant. Was he talking about the thing with Jayd? Or the fucking feelsy-crush-thing I was pretty sure was giving me bulging heart-eyes every time I looked at him? Or...

"You don't like anyone to pay too much attention to you, do you?"

I swallowed. What the fuck was that? Who made startling, heart-squeezing pronouncements of things a casual hookup would *never* notice about one, accompanied by a devastating smile, in the middle of particularly good sex? It was rude. Unforgivable. Not fucking *done*.

"You said I was a drama queen," I reminded him in a lusty frog croak that was approximately as sexy as you'd think it was.

"'Cause you are." He stopped to run his teeth over my nipple, and I shuddered. "But that's just another way of distracting me from what you're really feeling, isn't it? The same way you turn the tables on me every time we're talking about you." He sucked hard at my other nipple. "The same way you're more comfortable when you're the one giving pleasure than when you're receiving."

Dear sweet baby Jesus, if I suddenly became *that guy* who cried during sex, I was gonna... fuck. I didn't even know.

Find a sword and fall on it? Swear off sex forever? Something powerful and atrocious and...

"But that's not happening today, Tobias Elford. Because you are the absolute center of my attention. And I like everything I see."

I made a noise that was halfway between a moan and a sob—okay, more of a sob trying valiantly to be a moan—that turned into a full-on epic porn-star squeal the minute his fingers breached my hole. He'd done such a spectacular job of loosening me up earlier that it barely burned, and the pressure of his big fingers inside me was ten out of ten epic stars.

"Fuck me," I begged. "Please, Beale. Please, baby."

He ripped open a condom and took a second to figure out which way it rolled on, which was literally the most painfully beautiful moment I'd ever experienced because it reminded me that this was *Beale*, who'd never be able to say he'd never done this before to anyone ever again.

I held my leg to my chest as he lined up against me, and watched him swallow hard. I thought he might ask if I was sure I wanted this, or if I was really ready, but whatever he saw on my face—those damn heart-eyes, I swear—clearly removed any reluctance, and he slowly, slowly pushed inside me, filling me up.

"Ohhhhh, Toby." His eyes nearly rolled back into his head, and he said the words like a magical spell. Weirdly enough, they felt that way, too. "This feels... fucking incredible."

"I know. *Shit*. And it's gonna feel even better when you move, baby." I wrapped my legs around his waist, braced my arms on his biceps, and set my heels on his ass like I could spur him to fuck me. "Trust me."

His eyes blinked open and settled on mine, and all I could think was that no one had ever seen that beauty quite that way before. And then he pulled back and rocked into me, and I couldn't think of a single fucking thing.

Beale Goodman was loud, and God, I loved it. I loved him shouting my name so hard the cat was probably having a conniption somewhere. I loved him staring down at me like I was a gift. I loved the feeling of his muscles bunching beneath my fingers as he drilled into me with a skill that no newbie should have had.

"I can't... help it..." he gritted out. "I'm gonna come, Toby. You've gotta come first."

He reached a hand between us and wrapped it around my dick to jerk me off. It was sloppy and totally uncoordinated and so magnificent that when I came, and he came half a minute later, I had to turn my face toward the pillow for a second. You couldn't be *that guy* if no one saw the tears, right?

12

BEALE

"Afternoon, Beale!" Scotty gave me a cheerful smile as I strolled up to the counter at the Bean. He looked behind me expectantly, and his smile fell just a little. "Trey not with you today?"

I smiled. Whispering Key was not a place where things usually changed very fast, if ever. The cell signal was spotty, ten-year-old cars were considered new, folks still thought of Rafe as being married and treated Gage like he was twelve. But somehow Toby—*Trey*—had become a fixture in less than a week.

I couldn't say I was unhappy about it; he'd kinda become kind of a fixture in my life, too. It was thrilling...

The same way a roller coaster was thrilling when you were heading for the drop.

"Not today. The guys and I just got back from running a tour." I nodded at my brothers, who'd grabbed their favorite table in the back. "Last I saw him, Trey was at Mason and Fenn's place with the party committee. The contractors finished work inside the main house just in time for Mason and Fenn to come home tonight, and Trey and the committee are hanging fairy lights and decorations around the yard."

Scotty turned to make our coffees without needing to ask our orders but gave a dubious glance at the sky outside. "He'd best be careful with that. Gonna rain soon."

"Oh, Trey knows," I assured him. "He's got the whole thing down to a science. 'Paper products must stay in the house until the *final moments*, Beale. Like crafting a *soufflé*, Beale.'" I grinned. "Needless to say, I was told my help was not necessary." And I hadn't felt sad about that in the slightest.

Scotty laughed and put our drinks on a tray. "Well, when you get home, tell him I got the ingredients to make that coffee he wanted the other day. I googled it, and it turns out the thing only sounded fancy. It was actually simple as anything."

That was pretty on-brand for Toby.

"I'll let him know, Scotty. See you tonight?"

"Wouldn't miss it."

When I got to the four-seat table, Rafe had arranged himself with his eyes closed, his head tipped back to the wall, and his feet stretched over a second chair, so I grabbed the seat next to Gage, who was busily scrolling something on his phone and set the drinks in the middle of the table.

"You gonna make it to the party tonight, Rafael?" I kicked lightly at the chair with his feet on it. "Think you might need a nap?"

Rafe cracked open one brown eye. "Listen to you. One week ago—a mere seven days—you were all 'Parties are bad. I hate parties.'"

"I do." I twisted the cups to find the one with my name on it. "They are."

"Uh-huh. And yet, you're not having a panic attack or making plans to flee the island." Rafe dropped his feet and leaned toward me. "Hmm. Let's think about what's changed."

"Let's not."

"Oh, no, I'm with Rafe on this one." Gage shut off his phone and set it facedown. "Let's talk about the color-coordinated, designer-shoe-wearing, party-planning elephant in the room."

I sipped my tea and stared at the bright July day outside the window.

"Things seem to have gotten serious between you remarkably fast, even for two people who knew each other years ago." Rafe picked three packets of sugar out of the container by his elbow and added them to his iced coffee. He tasted it, then reached for three more. "Even for soul mates."

"So, are you happy?" Gage asked.

Was I?

That morning, I'd woken up with Toby wrapped around me, which had become our norm. The sky outside had been rose-tinged with sunrise, and I'd known I'd curse myself for putting off my run until the day got hotter, but it had been really hard to force myself away from the man in my arms. I'd stared down at Toby's face, which I'd already mapped a dozen times over the past week in moments like that, and remembered Mason was coming home tonight. Tonight, Toby would tell *Mason* about the problem he was facing in New York—the one he wouldn't explain to me. Tonight, Toby and Mason would figure out a solution—one that might involve Toby leaving for good. All the frustration that had built up over the past week at feeling myself grow closer to Toby—but also *not,* thanks to these giant, gaping holes— ate at me. It gave me a tight feeling in my chest that felt like a portent. Like something bad was coming.

And then, Toby's dark eyes had fluttered open, and the instant he saw me, he'd smiled like the thing he'd been dreaming of had come to life. Just like every other day this week, I'd told myself that maybe I didn't need to know *all* the details of his life or his problems. He'd trusted me with his identity as Hagatha. He'd told me about his family. We'd had in-depth conversations on all kinds of topics, and he'd even sung me silly show tunes. Maybe what I knew was the *real* Toby, one those idiots in New York hadn't gotten to know, and maybe that was enough.

"Yeah," I said quietly. "I'm happy."

Rafe and Gage exchanged a smiling look, and I rolled my eyes.

"I thought you were against the whole soul mate thing, Rafael. Make up your mind."

"See, ironically enough, that's exactly what I had against the soul mate thing. I wanted you to stop waiting around and make up your mind, and now you have. I don't care if he's your soul mate or your Grindr hookup, as long as you're happy. Because drifting isn't the same as happy, Beale."

I thought of Toby, floating in the pool yesterday, and how floating and swimming weren't the same thing. I nodded once.

"Well, I'm fucking jealous," Gage said, sipping at his own coffee. "Not only did you get yourself a hot soul mate, you found one who's heading up the fundraising committee for the bridge *and* coordinating your party. I'm pissed Grandma never sent me to Adventure Camp."

"You went to Nerdy Nerd Camp that one time." Rafe waved a hand. "Not Grandma's fault you never hooked a dude like Trey."

"It was called the Center for Advanced Technologically Talented Youth," Gage corrected, throwing a straw wrapper at him.

"Ah, yes. How could I forget your 'CATTY Camp' shirt?"

Gage held up a hand. "I'm not talking to you about this. Back to *Trey*, who is about to become my favorite brother."

"Uh. Brother might be pushing it." I hunched forward spinning my coffee cup on the table. "Let's wait and see if he decides to stay, okay?"

Rafe snorted. "Beale. He's singlehandedly spearheading your party—"

"Not singlehandedly," I protested. "He's got an army of volunteers."

"I was *born* on this island, Beale, and nothing could make me attempt to coordinate a volunteer army of Whispering Keysters." Rafe shuddered. "That's love."

I swallowed hard. It wasn't love. Of course not. But how foolish did it make me that I almost wished it was? Toby wasn't my soul mate, and I knew that, but...

"Remember, not all of us volunteered. Trey had no problem conscripting the two of us to go pick up Fenn and Mason at the airport at seven." He motioned between himself and Rafe. "Then we have to text him when we're twenty minutes out so he can get everyone ready to yell surprise."

"Would be nice if Fenn acknowledged my fucking text and confirmed the time," Rafe said sourly.

"Sure, but why would he when *not* answering pisses you off so nicely?" Gage gave him a sweet smile.

"Anyway, tell Trey to let us know if he needs anything before then," Rafe said. "Everyone I invited is showing up around eight."

"I'll let him know, but I'd be shocked if he hasn't thought of everything. He's really good at taking care of people." I found myself smiling again. He pretended Hagatha's caring and deep emotions weren't him, but they so were. No one who got all emotional when he orgasmed could be heartless. I refused to believe it. And if that was the case... maybe he cared for me a little.

Or more than a little.

"You know," Rafe said, staring at my face thoughtfully, probably because I was grinning like a sap, "the whole time Aimee lived here, at least while we were married... she never tried to fit in the way Trey has. She had an idea of what this town was based on those summers when we were kids, but she didn't like the reality. Trey does. I'm glad for you, man. Really."

I swallowed.

"So, does this mean you forgive her for leaving?" Gage blinked innocently and sipped his coffee.

"Fuck no. It means I'm giving Trey my blessing. Things with Aimee were different. She should have talked to me. The running away is the part I can't forgive."

"Maybe she had her reasons, Rafe." I shrugged. "You don't know what was going on in her head. She took it hard when mom died, and you were angry a lot. Maybe she wasn't strong enough to talk to you about what was going on. Maybe she felt guilty for feeling the way she did. Who knows?"

Rafe's nostrils flared and his jaw worked, but finally he nodded. "You have a point."

"And frankly, it's the same with Jayd," I pointed out, since I was on a roll. "If the situations were reversed, either of us would have kept a secret about where you'd gone."

"Please. You're shit at secret keeping, Beale, everyone knows this." Rafe waved a hand dismissively. He sipped his coffee, wrinkled his nose, and reached for more sugar. "And Jayd's not so great at keeping certain secrets anymore either."

I took a deep breath and remembered Toby the other day on the boat, reminding me that I was *smart*, and that no one should make me feel less than. "Actually, I'm really not. I did shitty in school, and I have different beliefs about the Universe than you do, but I'm not an idiot. It's annoying when people make ignorant comments like that. They're not fair, and they're not true."

Gage and Rafe both blinked at me like I'd sprouted a third head, but after a minute, Rafe's mouth curled up at one corner. "Well, damn. Alright, then. How long have you been holding on to that?"

Probably longer than I cared to admit.

I cleared my throat, uncomfortable. "Never mind. What were you saying before? Something about Jayd not keeping a secret?" If Jayd had changed his mind and told Rafe where Aimee was, I was pretty sure I'd have known about it.

Gage made a disapproving noise, and Rafe grinned.

"I meant the tabloid story," he said. "About him being gay."

"Wait." I blinked and looked to Gage for more information. "The what?"

Gage sighed and opened his mouth to explain, but Rafe cut in. "How the hell can you not know this? It was in the local paper, and I even caught it on that CelebTV News thing a couple times. It's all anyone on the island is talking about. It's all anyone in the *world* is talking about. Do you know what year it is, Beale? How many fingers am I holding up?"

"Ohhh." Come to think of it, I vaguely remembered something about Jayd being on the television at Blue Smoke a week ago. I also remembered Rafe flatly denying it then and *again* when Dale showed him the newspaper right here at the Bean the next day. "Yeah, no, I heard he was in the news. I missed the details." I'd been kinda busy.

"He's been *busy*, Rafael," Gage said slyly, like he could read my mind.

Rafe laughed, but there was no bitterness in it, so I laughed along.

True story, I hadn't thought of much this week that wasn't Toby. Even now, my first thought hearing this was to wonder what Toby would think when he heard about Jayd.

"If *you* were getting action a little more regularly, Rafe, you'd have more important things to think about than Jay's—" Gage broke off when his phone chimed, and he glanced down at it guiltily. "—sex life."

"Uh-huh." Rafe snorted. "Go on and check it. That's the chime that means Jay's done some shit somewhere in the world, isn't it?"

Gage flushed. "What? Why would you—?"

"Because I'm not the only one who's been obsessed with Jay's sex life." Rafe's smile was cutting.

"Hey! I'm only concerned because of the Extravaganza coming. Dad put you and me in charge of the concert, and—"

"Yes, yes, because he's a sadist. Spare me the reminder." Rafe waved a hand and reached for more sugar packets. "Well, go on. You know you wanna look."

Gage didn't need to be told twice—he picked up his phone eagerly. Meanwhile, I debated pulling out my own phone to see if Toby wanted me to bring him home anything, like a coffee or maybe a late lunch. I wondered if he'd appreciate it. I wondered if we had time for him to show me his appreciation appropriately before people started showing up for the party.

It was a whole new way of thinking about life, having someone by my side and... fuck it, I really wanted to keep that, keep *him*. Maybe I hadn't made it clear enough to Toby that I wanted him to stay here permanently, even after his mess in New York was cleaned up. Maybe I could be more convincing.

I could find him high-speed internet, if working with the hot spot was too much of a drag. Hell, I could buy a house and outfit it with the *highest*-speed internet—a field of satellite dishes in the backyard, if necessary.

"You're grinning again," Rafe pointed out unhelpfully, stirring his coffee with his straw.

I shot him a look. "If you put any more sugar in there, that coffee is going to stand up on its own and walk out."

Rafe scowled. "It's not crunchy enough yet."

"Yuck. I don't even drink coffee and I shudder on behalf of all people who do," I informed him.

Gage gasped. "Jayd's publicity company is canceling his remaining tour dates, and he's gone into hiding." He looked up at Rafe. "We need to contact him to make sure he's still coming for the Extravaganza."

Rafe snorted. "No, we don't. Let him cancel. Too bad, so sad. Answer to a prayer, if you ask me."

"I *didn't* ask you. We've already sold tickets to the concert, Rafael. Jesus. Dad's gonna explode. And besides all of that, Jay's in hiding someplace in Colorado, which sounds like the opposite of healthy behavior. Don't you care about him at *all*?"

Rafe swallowed hard and looked away. "He's a shithead, Gage. Whether he's a straight shithead, a gay shithead, or any other color of the shithead rainbow doesn't matter to me in the slightest."

"That's just lovely. Your support is noted." Gage shook his head and put his phone to his ear. "I'm calling Dad. No one should have to hide out in the middle of nowhere because a photographer caught him messing around with a guy at a gay club in New York."

The New York thing caught my attention, even when I'd been trying to tune out Gage and Rafe's squabbling. I wondered how many clubs like that Toby had been to and whether he missed them.

"Jayd is hardly innocent here, Gagie-poo. Remember, he was the one who got a blow job in a public place." Rafe finally achieved the proper level of sugar sludge and sipped his drink happily.

A blow job. In a club? I tried to picture that—Toby on his knees for me where anyone could see—and just the thought made heat climb up my chest. God, an intimate act like that, with an audience? A primal part of me thought I might enjoy claiming Toby like that, but the rest of me—

"You're blushing."

I blinked out of my daydream and scowled at Rafe.

"Hey, what's with the play-by-play?" I demanded. "Don't you have anything better to do? Other unfortunate former friends to cackle over? Other brothers to micromanage?"

"Nope." Rafe popped the *p* obnoxiously. "Gage is immune to my micromanagement, and I only have one former friend stupid enough to hook up with a guy who'd get an X-rated Where's Waldo tattoo on his shoulder." Rafe snorted, inviting me in on the joke.

I smiled back instinctively in the second it took my brain to process what he'd said. Then I blinked. And blinked some more.

"P-pardon?" I finally managed to say, pushing out the words with lungs that no longer remembered how to work right. "Say again?"

"Oh, shit, that's right! You haven't seen it." Rafe shook his head, still chuckling to himself. He called something up on his phone and spun it on the sticky Formica table to face me. "Take a gander."

I didn't want to look, I really didn't. I somehow instinctively knew what I would see, and my mind resisted. But gravity dragged my gaze down to the tabletop, to the grainy picture on Rafe's phone screen.

It was unmistakably Toby.

His head was turned almost fully away from the camera, but I'd kissed the hinge of that jaw, I'd traced the shell of that ear with my tongue, I'd bitten that shoulder tendon with its one-two-three freckles in a line, like Orion's Belt pointing down to that one-of-a-kind tattoo.

Still, I couldn't totally believe it.

I picked up the phone and tried to enlarge the image with fingers that were suddenly weirdly numb and cold. My stomach roiled and burned as I took in the look on Jayd's face, noted how his eyes were squeezed shut but his mouth open like he was feeling incredible pain... or pleasure.

My blow jobs change lives.

Blood pulsed in my ears like the roar of the ocean.

It wasn't like Toby had ever hidden the fact that he'd had sex with everything that moved, but knowing it and seeing it were vastly different. And maybe that made me a jealous asshole—okay, no, *definitely* that made me a jealous asshole—but it was still true.

And seeing him like this with someone else when I'd just two minutes before been thinking of it with him and *me*? It took me out at the knees.

I'm meant for city life...

My throat went thick as I realized just how deluded I'd been. Just how foolish.

Scene after scene crashed through my mind. Toby in the sunlight, Toby laughing, Toby clinging to me.

Circumstances involving a man and... another man... The details are unimportant here.

It's a... a relatively minor personal problem that has nothing whatsoever to do with you, okay?

I trust you, Beale.

I trust you, Beale.

I trust you, Beale.

Except he didn't. He hadn't.

Not with this.

And what's more, he'd lied.

He knew—*knew*—that Jayd had been part of my family. He knew Jayd was someone I cared about, and he'd kept the whole thing from me.

He'd let me fall for him... and he'd played me.

You're smart, Beale. No one has the right to make you feel less than.

The irony was bitter. No offhanded comment from anyone in this town had ever made me

feel as foolish as Toby had.

"Beale?" Gage frowned up at me, phone still pressed to his ear, which was when I noticed that I'd stood up. "You okay?"

"Yeah, good. Never better. I'm gonna let you two deal with this. I need to go—"

I nodded toward the door, and then I headed in that direction without waiting for a reply.

"Wait." Rafe hurried after me and caught my wrist. "You look like you've seen a ghost, and you're not leaving until you talk to me. If you're pissed at Jayd, nobody gets that better than I do, okay? Tell me—"

"No!" I yelled way louder than I'd intended to, shaking off Rafe's restraining hand. "Just let me go, okay?"

All eyes in the place turned toward me, and I knew what they were thinking. Beale Goodman didn't lose his temper.

Beale Goodman never physically intimidated anyone. Beale Goodman was careful to use his words.

But Beale Goodman had never felt the way I currently felt either. Like I'd been fooled and betrayed. Like anger and helplessness were bubbling inside me, and I was coming out of my skin—

"I'll see you guys later." I turned and slammed my way out the door.

—like all the words in the Universe wouldn't be enough to explain things, let alone fix them.

13

TOBY

Help Me Hagatha
(Unsent)

Dear Aunt Hagatha:

I lied to my boyfriend and I feel like shit. Do I come clean, or—?

Still Me in Whispering Key

Dear Me,

You don't actually *have* a boyfriend, Toby. Probably because you lie to people. This is why we can't have nice things.

Consider a new career, maybe, and stock up on ice cream,
Other-Toby

"Trey, I laid out all the chafing dishes under the tent and labeled them, just like you suggested." Maddie McKetcham, who'd declared herself my party-planning protégé, bounced on the balls of her feet and made her ponytail sway.

"Excellent." I jotted this down on my clipboard. "Who's hanging the bunting?"

"Me," Juju Irvine yelled from a ladder. "I threaded it with the twinkle lights, just like you said."

"Perfect." I checked off a box. "Alright, coolers—"

"Got 'em, boss," Littlejohn said, coming out of the guest-house with two giant bags of ice. "Cleaned and filled."

"Wow. You guys are doing gr—"

My phone rang, and I winced when I saw Jeanette's name on the display.

Some idiot had possibly—misguidedly—called in to work this morning after Beale left, hoping for a casual chat with my editor so I could see whether HiWire had gotten any closer to connecting Tattooed Tommy from the tabloids to real-life me, and had possibly—also misguidedly—left my new phone number on her voicemail. She'd called back almost immediately, but in the intervening period I'd had a quick panic attack and realized I didn't really want to know what anyone knew, so I'd declined the call.

It was too much to hope that she'd give up easily, though.

"Hey, Trey," Littlejohn said, jogging over. "I don't want to freak you out, but I think we have a problem."

"Okay?"

"We've got the food tables."

"Yes."

"And the gift table."

"Under the tent in case of rain. Right."

"And we have a table for the drinks."

"Yep. With you so far. What's the problem?"

"Two words, man." He looked at me expectantly.

"Am I supposed to guess them? Is this… charades?"

"Trey, man." He motioned with his two hands like he was showing me the future. "*Body. Shots.*"

I blinked, tilted my head, then blinked some more. "No, sorry. Still not getting it."

"You know, where people lie down, and…"

"I'm familiar with the concept, LJ." From college bars, mostly.

"Well, where are we setting them up? Or is this like… a body shot free-for-all?" He snorted like he couldn't imagine such a thing.

Before I could answer, Jeanette called again, and my heart rate spiked as I declined the call. Two calls in two minutes? Not good.

"I… really don't know what the body shot protocol here is, LJ, but in general, I think housewarmings are a non-body-shot occasion in most parts of the world, but—*shit*," I muttered as Jeanette called a third time.

"Everything cool, Trey?" LJ frowned.

I silenced my phone and gave Littlejohn a smile. "Yeah, totally. Just my boss." I rolled my eyes. "You know how it goes."

"Mmmm, nope. Put all my money in bitcoin back in '09 and cashed out in '17. Ain't worked a day since." He winked, and I stared at him. "But just remember, you need anything—money, fresh passport, SpaghettiOs—I'm your guy. M'kay?"

I blinked and shook my head, amused and weirdly moved. I'd never had anyone offer me a fake passport before. "Yeah, Littlejohn. Okay. Thank you."

He clapped me on the shoulder just as Jeanette called again, and I motioned at the patio by Mason's house. "I'd better get this."

I walked a few feet away before engaging the call. "Jeanette! Oh my God, honey, how have you been this week? Are you *languishing* for want of me?"

"Tobias—"

I could tell from that one word that she was none too pleased, so I hurried on. "Sorry about the confusion earlier. I called you, then I was suddenly busy *all* morning. And, um, afternoon. And honestly, I'm *still* busy, but I didn't want you to think I was ignoring you when—"

"Tobias, stop. Patricia in HR got a call this morning asking about you by name: Tobias Elford. Someone wanted to confirm your employment."

Ah, motherfucker.

"*Did* they? Ha. Well. Good gracious. I'm... I'm... I'm *stunned*, that's what I am. The lawlessness. The fraudulence! I—"

"Tobias, need I remind you that you are under contract with HiWire for five more years? It's a contract that cannot be broken unless you are convicted of murder, and even then, I'd find you."

"Well, yes, darling, I'm aware." I frowned, genuinely bewildered as to where she was going with this.

"We traced the phone number back to BlazeNewz, so either you're planning to jump ship and take the column to Blaze, which would imply you'd broken your nondisclosure agreement, or else you somehow managed to leak that you're Hagatha, and would also imply you'd broken the NDA. Which is it?"

"Orrrrr, door number three, someone's checking my identity for a totally separate purpose. HiWire *is* my legal employer of record on my credit report, you know."

"Hmm. Well, Patricia refused to confirm your employment, in any case. So, while I'm giving you reminders that you might find pertinent to your life, let me remind you that we are *all* sunk if your identity gets out. Ratings would plummet. No one wants advice from a middle-aged man with no partner, no children... not even a pet."

Middle-aged? That was low.

"Ah, Jeanette. You are a ray of sunshine lighting the cold and empty darkness of my existence. What would I do without your constant encouragement? And for your information, I have recently acquired a pet." Temporarily. "She's a cat. Her name is Marjorie. She's *feral*."

"Hmm," she said dubiously. "You have so much in common. Anyway, just remember what I said, alright? You *need* HiWire."

I clenched the phone in my hand. I remembered what Beale had said about embracing Hagatha. About owning it. "And HiWire needs *me*." I swallowed hard. "And while I would never willingly break the NDA, if someone has somehow found out, we'll simply have to deal with it. Your threats only go so far."

Jeanette made a frustrated noise. "What the hell happened to you in the past week? Is there something noxious in the air in the Maldives?"

"I'm not in the Maldives," I informed her. "I decided to visit a friend out of town, instead."

"*A* friend." She snorted. "You mean your *one* friend who lives Upstate somewhere?"

Except he didn't, because Mason had moved down here. "No, actually. I haven't seen Mase in months. A different friend."

"Hmm," she said once more, like she couldn't believe more than one person put up with me.

Honestly, I couldn't believe it either, but evidence suggested it was, indeed, possible. I had Littlejohn now. Maddie. Mason...

Beale.

"Fine," Jeanette sighed. "Keep your secrets. But I expect you back next week or so, and no more calls from our rivals."

After she disconnected, I grabbed a hank of my own hair and tugged roughly.

Next week was the new timeline, and I sure as hell hoped Mason had a good idea of how to get this resolved by then, because from what I'd read online earlier, it didn't seem like Jayd would be coming forward anytime soon.

Keep your secrets, she'd said. But the trouble was, I didn't *want* to keep my secrets anymore. I had to tell Beale what was going on. We'd passed a point, sometime in the middle of sex last night, or maybe long before that and I'd pretended not to notice, where keeping secrets started to feel a lot like betrayal. I had to tell him and Mason the whole sordid story when Mase got home tonight. I'd let the chips fall where they might.

Beale picked that exact moment to walk into the backyard, and my heart gave a crazy stutter before it settled into a feeling of rightness.

He looked good, yes, and it was impossible not to notice it, but it wasn't just that. As insanely sappy as it sounded—and yes, I was not unaware of how very, *very* sappy it sounded—life just seemed more possible when Beale was around.

And Jesus, wasn't that a scary thought for a man who'd avoided relationships for his entire life? Still, the way I'd felt this morning waking up in Beale's arms—safe, warm, happy—was probably worth the constant terror. Right now, after the conversation with Jeanette, I craved his arms around me.

Beale caught sight of me, and I smiled. I expected him to smile back and head my way, but he stopped to talk to Levi somebody and then with sweet, blind-as-a-bat Barbara Patenaude.

I bit my lip. That wasn't weird. He was being polite. Besides, my legs worked, too, right? I could go to him.

So I did.

Except when he saw me coming, he excused himself from Barbara and went to hold Juju's stepladder.

Okay, no, that was definitely weird. I wondered if something had gone wrong on his tour or with his brothers. I wondered if he was upset and didn't want to show it.

"Heya," I said, sliding into the typical Whispering Key greeting, even though I was pretty sure I'd never greeted anyone that way in my life before. I wrapped an arm around his waist in a supportive way.

Beale's body stiffened, and that... okay, that was 100 percent weird.

"Hi," Beale said. "Um. Kinda busy holding a ladder here."

Ooookay. In the hierarchy of brushoffs, that one was... transparently transparent. Even Juju looked down from where she was hanging bunting to blink at him. "It's a four-foot ladder, honey. I told you, it's fine."

"You can't be too careful," Beale said, resolutely holding the ladder with both hands. He wouldn't meet my gaze.

He didn't seem angry. He didn't seem upset. He seemed... disconnected. And that was when the penny dropped, and I took a step back.

Oh, Lord. It had been a week tomorrow since we started this, hadn't it? So short, and yet... maybe too long for Beale? Had he remembered that I wasn't his soul mate? Better question: how the heck had I forgotten, even for a minute, that he was holding out for someone way better than the likes of me?

I looked down at the bracelet on my arm, the bracelet Beale had lent me just yesterday and that I'd conveniently forgotten to give back because I liked seeing it on my wrist so much, and felt ridiculous, reactionary tears prick behind my eyes.

Well, fuck.

Was this how Cinderella felt after the ball?

And, in the end, I hadn't even had to share with him the full extent of the poor choices that had brought me here, which was kind of a relief. I wouldn't have to tell Beale about Jayd Rollins, 'cause Beale had remembered I was a bad bet all on his own.

"Hey, Trey! Silvio's here and he's brought some vodka. Also, Jon Davis has a tray of brownies," Barbara called, like she'd set herself up as the royal announcer for the party.

I summoned a smile. "Acceptable offerings. Let them pass."

I'd swear I heard Beale make an amused sound, but when I looked back at him, his face was blank and his eyes—those expressive eyes that could tell me entire paragraphs with just one glance—were empty, which was so unlike the Beale I thought I knew that I felt a deep ache in my solar plexus.

I wondered idly what kind of yoga move could fix that, but it didn't matter. I'd probably kill myself if I tried it.

Whatever. This was okay. This was good. This was *fine*. This I could handle. And better sooner than later.

It was not my first rejection rodeo—fuck, not even my twenty-first—and I needed to cowboy up, in a sexy, refined, Timothy Olyphant cowboy sort of way, obviously, and handle this with dignity. If there was one thing I was good at —one skill I could add to my unofficial resume thanks to catty friends in high school, losers I dated in college, and my family back in Ohio—it was this. I knew how to smile vaguely, nod along with whatever they said, and give the overall impression that parting ways had been my idea in the first place.

Step one: stop looking like a needy asshole.

So, I made myself busy, throwing myself into the last of the preparations in the way that only a person who really didn't want to think about his own life could. I didn't glance in Beale's direction. I smiled hard and laughed harder. I directed my volunteer decorators with aplomb. Several people made the effort to tell me how great the decorations were and how yummy the food was, and I made a mental note to send out a thank-you message to my Facebook group.

And through it all, even though Beale was less than a hundred feet away, I ached for him like he was on the damn moon.

This rodeo was gonna suck.

The downside of having half the town on the party committee was that there really wasn't a point where I could slip away to get changed. But when a few early birds showed up and someone switched the sound system on, and then Lorenna and Jeremy-Someone started dancing, I realized that unless I wanted to experience this party in a manky tank top and casual shorts, I needed to grab a shower while I could.

I passed Littlejohn my clipboard and asked him to hold down the fort and keep everyone out of the guesthouse so I could change quickly... and then I nearly bumped into the guy I'd been avoiding, who was heading into the guesthouse at the same time.

"Oh. Uh. After you," Beale said, and though I would not admit it aloud even under the rudest torture, those few, rough, fumbling syllables felt like raindrops on parched skin.

"Oh, no, you go." I smiled tightly. "I can wait. If you're gonna shower, I mean. I'll... wait here."

"I should, probably. Yeah. Good call." He rubbed the back of his neck. "I'll just... do that?"

"Sure."

God, this awkwardness was terrible.

I'd slept in this man's arms last night. I'd kissed him goodbye this morning with a smile and a "call me if you need anything," and I'd let myself start to think thoughts about how I could maybe... have this. Have *him*. For my own.

Stupid, stupid. I was nobody's endgame. Nobody's motherfucking soul mate.

I was desperate to know what had changed, but I was fucking terrified to know what had changed.

I wanted him to keep talking and also to just go away before he shredded my self-control.

But apparently I enjoyed the pain more than my sanity, because I found myself saying, "But what do you think of the decorations, though? Be honest."

"'Be honest,' huh?" Beale's jaw worked like I'd asked him a totally different question. "That's... wow." He blew out a breath. "*Honestly,* I think the decorations are great, *Trey.* I think Mason will love them. I think no one could have pulled this off like you did. But then, I've thought you were pretty extraordinary from the first moment we met."

I stared at him in surprise. He'd spoken those pretty words like a challenge. Like the opening salvo in some war. Like he was pissed that I was extraordinary, and more pissed that he had to acknowledge it. I had no idea how to respond to that. It was one thing for him to be "it's been fun but it's over" distant, but another thing entirely for him to be angry.

What the hell was that about?

"Well. How kind of you to say," I managed to reply. "I—"

"It's really not. I—*ah, fuck it.*" Beale grabbed my face in his two big paws, speared his fingers in my hair, and kissed me until my ears rang. He tasted like green tea and bright anger, and as he kissed me, that anger leached into me, too.

How dare he be mad at me! How dare he kiss me like this when *he* was the one pulling away?

I wrapped my arms around his neck and pulled myself up so I could put my legs around his waist. Beale caught me with both hands under my ass in the way I guess I'd instinctively known he would—even if he was mad at me, even if he was acting distant—and I groaned, reveling in the feeling.

Someone nearby whooped and someone else laughed, and I barely heard it because Beale was kissing me with passion and a kind of aggression I'd never experienced with him before.

He carried me into the guesthouse, where the air-conditioning was cool on my overheated skin, and broke apart just long enough to say, "Keep everyone out, LJ," and for Littlejohn to say, "Already told Trey I would."

Then Beale slammed the door behind us... and we were alone.

14

BEALE

Czarina's StarCharts for Today
Virgo, your greatest gifts are your listening ear and your loyal heart. But are you listening to the truth or to your own fears?

What the fuck was I doing?

I'd driven here, absolutely ready to confront Toby and demand answers, forgetting that the place would be littered with volunteers. So I'd tried avoiding him, except that hadn't worked either, so now all of a sudden I was kissing him like he was oxygen and I was a fire.

His weight in my arms and the smooth, solid heat of him against my chest felt so right it was hard to stop, but I had to. I was angry, when I hardly ever got angry. I couldn't imagine having sex with someone in this state. It probably wasn't healthy... right?

I pulled him off my body, which was a little like pulling a remora off a shark, and set him on the tiled floor in the living room, where the two of us stared at each other, panting.

One time, maybe a year ago, at the same flea market where I bought my variscite, I walked by a woman doing Tarot readings, and she'd offered me a single-card draw for free. I'd learned as a kid that some "fortune tellers" would tell you whatever junk you wanted to hear just to get you to spend more for a full reading, but this lady had a vibe about her, a kind of clarity to her aura, so I'd gamely drawn a card.

"Ace of wands." The woman had frowned, and her earrings had tinkled as she tilted her head like she was trying to see inside mine. "I see new beginnings for you. Passion beyond passion. But remember that when hot passion collides with a cool and patient spirit..." She'd brought her hands together in a loud clap, like booming thunder, and grinned. "Remember that destruction leads to new beginnings, too."

I'd politely excused myself after that because the woman clearly didn't know what she was talking about. Passion? Destructive? *Me*? Never.

Until now.

Toby's big brown eyes were fever-shiny, his cheeks were flushed pink, his hair was a violent mess, and his lips were bright red. He wore that wary, vulnerable look that had slayed me the first night we met and—shocker—slayed me even now when I felt like he'd played me for a fool.

Fuck, I wanted him so much. I shouldn't, but I did. And it might destroy me, but I was going to see it through.

Forgetting all about what might be right or healthy, I was on him again in a second, pushing him against the wall across from the little sofa, kneading his ass with both hands, and moaning when he rubbed his half-hard dick against my thigh. I wanted to get closer to him, to feel that completeness one more time before... before whatever happened next.

"Come on," I muttered, pulling him toward the bathroom. Just that morning, we'd been careful to hide the lube and condoms in Toby's toiletry case under the sink for the duration of the party, giggling like a pair of kids who didn't care very much if they got caught. Now, I grabbed the case and practically threw it on the vanity, rifling through it thoughtlessly.

"Hey," Toby croaked. "Hey, chill. Beale!" He grabbed the case from my hand and frowned at me severely as he removed the things I wanted. "Look, the stuff's right here, but before we do this, we need to talk. We need to—"

I kissed him again, hard, pouring all my hurt and anger and fear into the kiss, and Toby clutched at my shoulders for a beautiful half second before pushing me away once more.

"Wait," he panted. "Wait. Look, angry sex is probably enjoyable, and I'm not opposed to giving it a whirl, but I think it would be advisable for me to know why you're mad at me beforehand."

I rubbed both hands over my face and forced out a frustrated growl between clenched teeth. Then I turned on my heel and stalked back to the kitchen where I slammed open the refrigerator door and took out a bottle of water.

"Seriously, Goodman, what the actual fuck?" Toby demanded, tossing the lube and condoms on the counter so he could set his hands on his hips.

I downed half the bottle in one go, then slapped the bottle down on the counter so hard water sprayed out the top.

Shit. I was not a slammy person. I was for sure not a growly person. I didn't like or want to be either of those things. A person my size couldn't *afford* to be either of those things.

I needed to calm down, but I didn't know how. My insides were throbbing with hurt, and it felt like everything I wanted was slipping away somehow. I wanted to yell at Toby, but I didn't. I wanted to push him away, but I couldn't bring myself to.

"For God's sake, why did you come here, Toby?" The words came out like a whisper even though I wanted to yell.

Toby swallowed. "Well." He licked his kiss-swollen lips carefully and watched me warily, like I'd asked a trick question. "I recall us discussing this already several times, precious. I came here because of a... a difficult situation."

I nodded once and told myself this answer was no different than what I'd expected. "With two guys."

He started to nod but stopped himself. "Actually, three, not including myself. It's all... complicated." Then he actually waved a hand, like the whole thing was so much water under the bridge, when he fucking knew it wasn't.

"Then *simplify* it!" I demanded.

"What for?" Toby's eyes blazed with sudden anger. "I understand you're new to this, but if you're done with me, Beale darling, you just say you're done. That's the polite thing to do. We don't rehash every step of the past week just so you can feel better about choosing to end it, especially when we never made any promises to begin with. We're both big boys who knew this wasn't going to last very long. You've got a *real* soul mate headed your way, and I… well, I'll find some other way to keep myself occupied, don't you worry."

He gave me a teasing smirk, and it was only much, much later that I'd ask myself if that expression ever reached his eyes. In the moment, I was so fucking *infuriated* he could say things like that when I could have sworn he cared about me, damn it—and yes, also because I was so *jealous* of every lucky man who'd take my place and bask in all those teasing smiles that should've been mine—that I, Beale glass-half-full Goodman, who prided himself on the way every negative emotion rolled right off my back, lost my ever-loving mind.

"You felt pretty fucking real to me," I said, in a voice gone all gruff and scratchy, and then I kissed him again, deep and hungry, like this was the last time, because maybe it was.

Shockingly, Toby's resistance melted away after the first second, and he threw his arms around me with a groan that sounded like a sob.

I stripped his shirt off in a rush and was only dimly aware when mine came off, too, because Toby raked his nails down my back. It was brutal and perfect. I bit down on the side of his neck, and his knees quaked, so of course I lifted him up, held him against me, and did it again.

I laid him out on the countertop like my own personal feast. I held his wrists to the smooth surface and sucked on his nipples, relishing every harsh inhalation and shuddering moan of my name. The skin over his abs was golden and gorgeous as it rippled beneath my lips.

I grabbed the waistband of his shorts with two hands, and without a word, Toby braced a foot on the counter so I could peel them down. They hit the floor with a loud *thunk* that said he might need another new cell phone. *Oops.*

He shivered when the bare skin of his ass hit the cold counter, and I murmured sympathy against the join of his thigh. Then I pushed his legs apart and pulled him toward me.

"Tell me you want this," I murmured. My hands held his hips, and my thumbs traced circles mere inches from the root of his straining cock, but I wouldn't go further unless he said for sure that he—

"Of *course* I do. Fuck, Beale. I always—*oh, Jesus*," he sobbed, clunking his head back against the counter and grabbing my head in his hands as I sucked him into my mouth. I felt ultrapowerful and helpless at the same time because he was so goddamn beautiful and I wanted him endlessly.

The bitter salt tang of his precum was like a fucking aphrodisiac, and I went at him with shit tons of enthusiasm and zero finesse, but he didn't seem to mind, if the restless motion of his legs and the bucking of his hips was anything to go by. He wanted to be in control, but he needed to realize he couldn't be in charge of every-damn-thing.

I rolled his balls in my hand as I worked, and he slapped one hand to the countertop like he was counting down to a drum solo while he pulled my hair with the other. It was almost funny, but I didn't feel like laughing. Instead, I popped off his dick and started jacking him with my hand. "I want inside you."

Toby tried to focus his gaze on my face, but no matter how much he blinked, he couldn't seem to get there. "Yeah," he breathed. "Yeah."

I uncapped the lube and pushed his legs back so I could see his hole. I worked his dick with one hand while I fingered him with the other, and every time I tagged his prostate, I watched in awe as wave after wave of bliss rolled across his beautiful face.

"Please, Beale," Toby begged, and fuck, I just wished he could be half as honest in everything else as he was in this. I had deep feelings for this man—for some version of this man—and I didn't know whether I was falling for the real one or my fantasy.

He wriggled off the counter and dropped to his knees, pulling my shorts down to my ankles. I couldn't spread my legs far enough to account for our height difference, so I hunched over, grabbing the counter behind his head, and let him suck me fully hard... which took a ridiculously short amount of time. Then Toby grabbed the condom off the counter and rolled it on me.

I kissed him again briefly, then turned him around and pushed his chest to the counter where his back had been. I drizzled more lube over his hole, stretching his rim even further with my thumbs just because I enjoyed the sight so damn much. Toby pushed his ass back against my fingers and made greedy little "*hunh hunh*" whimpers that went straight to my cock, so I pulled his cheeks apart with two hands and slid my dick along his crease, giving myself the friction I needed.

"C'mon," Toby said a few seconds later. "Come on, baby, please."

"Baby" in that pleading voice sent a shiver through my whole body, and I couldn't wait any longer. I lined myself up with his hole and slowly, slowly pushed inside.

"Yes. *Yes*. You. This. So good, Beale," he moaned, spreading his hands out on the counter. He was warm and snug, and my entire body flushed hot as I entered him because I knew exactly what he meant. *This*—this feeling with this man and no other—was exactly what I wanted. Forever.

"Ah, Toby. Fuck, baby." I stretched my arms out, too, so my palm fit over the back of his hands. When I threaded our fingers together, Toby curled his hands into fists, locking us tight, and I felt the anger and confusion leach out of me. At least for the moment, we were the only two people on the entire planet who mattered.

I fucked him hard, pistoning my hips, reveling in the earthy slap of flesh on flesh. Every drag of my cock against his prostate made Toby whine, and the knowledge that I was doing that to him, making him lose control, made me feel twelve feet tall. I reached around him and grabbed his poor, neglected dick, jerking him in time to my thrusts.

"Say my name," I instructed. "Say it."

"Beale."

"Again."

"*Beale*."

"Yes, *me*. Yes, Toby. Fuck. You just don't know..." I swallowed hard, biting back all the things I couldn't say, like "please stay with me" and "please make this work" and "I love you."

"I know," he groaned, "I fucking know."

And when he came all over my hand, I thought maybe, possibly, he did, so I followed him over the edge half a minute later, with a shout that rang through the little house.

I pulled out of him gently and dealt with the condom, but Toby hadn't moved from where he rested cheek-down on the counter. I pulled up my shorts and moved back to drape myself over him again.

"Ah, Toby," I murmured against that goofy tattoo on his shoulder.

"Oh, Beale," he sigh-panted, and it sounded sleepy, almost amused.

He pressed a single, lingering kiss to my forearm where it rested on the counter next to his, and I smiled.

Then the door to the fucking house opened and Barbara Patenaude yelled, "Hey, Trey! Mason, Fenn, Rafe, and Gage are here!" two fucking seconds before all four of them walked in.

Mother. Fucker.

I lifted my head, and Rafe's eyes widened before he clapped his hands over them. "Gage? Gage! Tell me they're doing yoga again!"

"Oooh, sorry, bro. This time it's, ah... not yoga." Gage's voice threaded with laughter. "Wow."

"Step outside," I yelled. "And where the hell is Littlejohn? I thought he was guarding the door."

"I'm right here!" Littlejohn said, stepping inside the room, too, because what we needed was *more* of an audience. "But Mason and Fenn own the house, so, ya know... I was a li'l bit unclear as to whether I had the right to bar the door." He paused. "Y'okay there, Trey?"

"Delightful," Toby said from beneath me, still hiding his face. "Never better."

"Beale, what the hell is going on here?" Mason demanded.

"Baby, if you don't know..." Fenn scratched his eyebrow with his index finger.

Mason elbowed him lightly. "I meant, what's going on *here*. At our *home*. Where we *live*. And where all of Whispering Key, and part of Cooter Key, too, are right now congregating around our pool, discussing whether it's too early to do body shots and where Bobo and the Stallions should put the keg!"

"Oh for fuck's sake! I told them exactly where to put the—" Toby pushed up off the counter, and Mason's eyes widened. "—um... keg? Heya, Mason."

Shit. Shit shit shit.

"Toby?" Mason said, frozen in disbelief.

"Could everyone get out of here right now?" I demanded. "The man's naked. Jesus Christ, you can have this conversation in a minute."

"Who's Toby?" Rafe demanded. "That's Trey. Beale's soul mate."

Oh, delightful.

"Trey?" Mason shook his head. "No. That's my friend Toby from college."

"Oh my God, Doc's college friend is Beale's soul mate? What a small world this is! Wait'll I tell the girls!" Barbara scurried out to share this news, and I smacked my forehead.

"Toby," Mason said. "What the fuck—?"

"Can you get me my shorts, please?" Toby whispered over his shoulder, and I swept them up off the floor along with his shirt and handed them to him.

"Hey, hey." Littlejohn rocked back on his heels. "Don't go talkin' that way to my friend Trey, Doc. You can use a civil tone."

Mason scowled. "When I find my best friend—"

"You sure he's *your* best friend?" Littlejohn asked. "'Cause I was the one who fed him Pizza Bites in his time of need."

Toby buttoned his shorts and scrubbed a hand through his hair. "There's enough of me to go around, guys."

Mason shot him a glare. "Well, *that's* patently obvious to anyone who's seen the news recently."

"Hey!" Littlejohn, Toby, and I said at the same time. I was pretty sure Littlejohn had no idea what Mason was talking about, he was just being loyal to Toby.

But who was Toby loyal to?

"Mason," Toby continued calmly. "I can explain everything, okay? Just... give me a minute to change."

Fenn wrapped an arm around Mason's shoulders and whispered something that made Mason take a deep breath and let it out again slowly. "Fine. You have ten minutes. And then I want an explanation."

Didn't we all?

15

TOBY

Help Me Hagatha
(Unsent)

Dear Aunt Hagatha:

**So, about that lie thing. Let's say I didn't come clean when
I could have...**

Hopeless Case in Whispering Key

Dear Hopeless,

I'm guessing the guy you want deserves better than that.
Maybe he should get it.

Take your own advice for once,
Auntie H.

Common wisdom says that when you find yourself in a hole, it's important that you stop digging. Since we've already established that I am neither common nor wise, you can imagine that I did neither.

"So, um." I trailed Beale to the bathroom. "About that me-being-on-the-news thing Mason mentioned a minute ago? It's kind of a funny story—"

Beale turned the shower on and dropped his shorts on the floor. "A story about how you were giving Jayd Rollins head at a bar in New York and got caught by the paparazzi, right before you came to Whispering Key, and then lied to me about it?" He tilted his head thoughtfully. "Would we call that funny?"

My stomach lifted up to my throat and then plummeted to somewhere around my knees. "You knew all along?"

"Me? Nah. I'm not that smart. I only found out about two hours ago, give or take a counter fuck." Beale's deep voice thrummed with hurt. "Humor was not my first reaction. Or my second."

He yanked the curtain aside and stepped under the water, so I shucked my clothes, too, and stepped in after him, but he was already rinsing the soap off his body. "It wasn't funny-funny, obviously, Beale. More like horrifying-funny."

"I can imagine. Now take that and multiply it by being the guy you treated like an idiot for the past week. A *minor personal issue*?" He scrubbed at his hair ruthlessly, and shampoo suds flew everywhere.

"Yes, kind of." I pressed my lips together. "I hoped it would be."

"That had nothing whatsoever to do with me?" He stuck his head under the spray.

"It didn't!" I insisted, soaping myself quickly. "Honestly, Beale, it had nothing to do with this. With *us*. I know you're angry, and I don't blame you—"

"Oh, *thank you*, Toby. Thank you for not *blaming* me—" He stepped out and slung a towel around his waist. "—for being upset that my—fuck, what even *are* you, *Trey*? My fake soul mate? The guy I've been messing around with?—doesn't trust me at all."

"Not true!" I shook my head vehemently and tried to grab his arm, but he shook me off and stalked out of the room. I rinsed off quickly, grabbed a towel, and followed him to the bedroom.

"Please listen, Beale, *please*. That's not what happened. It was a setup. I wasn't at that club to hang with Jayd—I've spoken maybe five words to the guy in my entire life, and I didn't have any kind of sexual *anything* with him. In fact, I went to that club with the guy sitting next to Jayd in the picture, and he yanked me into Jayd's lap so that the paparazzo could take the shot. Jayd was fully clothed."

"You were half-naked," he said roughly.

"Yes, because I was dancing at a club," I repeated, trying to keep my patience. "A gay club called Dive, specifically, where the clientele are not always dressed in suits and ties and sweaters, because *they are dancing at a club*." I swallowed hard. "And the fact that it was—is—a gay club is exactly why I wasn't going to tell you the story. By confirming that Jayd was there—"

"I don't want to hear this right now, Toby. I'm angry. And I thought I got over being angry, back when we were—" He waved a hand at the kitchen.

"Fucking like bunnies?" I supplied.

He yanked a T-shirt out of the closet, not caring that three others fell to the floor. "Yeah. But it turns out I'm not over it at all. I'm... hurt. I opened up to you. I cared about you. And..." He licked his lips. "Look, I know this was never a long-term thing in your mind, like you said earlier—"

My mouth opened, but I couldn't force a single syllable out.

"—but I really thought you cared about me and that we had *something*. Friendship, or respect, or like... damn, I don't know." He wrinkled his nose like he was horrified he'd admitted that. "I feel like a fool."

The past tense of "I cared about you" was not lost on me... but it was the last word that squeezed my chest so hard I couldn't draw a deep breath. "You are not a fool," I whispered. "Fuck, Beale."

He grabbed a pair of worn-in cargo shorts from the closet, too, and as he yanked them on, I felt that kind of melancholy feeling you get when you wonder if you've appreciated a thing enough while you had it.

Jesus. Pining for raggedy cargo shorts would be a new lifetime low for me.

"How long did you honestly think you could keep this a secret?" Beale asked softly. "Or maybe it didn't matter to you, as long as you were back in New York before I caught on, leaving *me* to explain to everyone around here who you really are?"

"It wasn't like that, either! God, please understand. I didn't want to have to tell you, Beale. I was... I was embarrassed, okay? I got duped by this guy, and I panicked and... it wasn't my proudest moment. But I also didn't want to share about Jayd until *he* was ready to make a statement. I didn't want to out him—"

"Well, it's good to know you were thinking of *someone*." He sounded bitter, and my Beale—*fuck*. He was not my Beale and never would be—was not a bitter person.

"Hey!" I scowled. "You *said* motive matters, Beale! The other day on the boat, you *said* there were no villains. How can that be true for the bad guy in every movie ever, but not for *me*?"

He shook his head sadly. "Because this was real life, Toby. And this was important. At least for me it was."

I blinked back the tears that threatened to fall. I wanted to say that it was important to me too, but I didn't know how to say it convincingly. I made a living using words and telling other people what to do, but when it came to myself? To being honest with a man who deserved the best of everything? All my words dried up.

If Aunt Hagatha were here, she'd have said...

Oh, who fucking knew? She was *me*, and we were both idiots.

Just a few minutes ago, I'd felt closer to Beale than I'd ever been to another person. Now there was a giant chasm opening between us, thanks to me, and I was clinging to one side with my hands and the other side with my feet, and I was not strong enough to keep things together. There was a reason I didn't do relationships, after all. A reason why Mason was the only person in existence who'd ever put up with me for very long.

So, I fell back on what came naturally: I nodded stoically and forced my voice to be light... though I wasn't sure I quite got there. "Well. Comfort yourself with the knowledge that there is a man out there somewhere who would've handled this better. Your *real* soul mate wouldn't have fucked this up, right? He would have known exactly what to say and what to do that would be fair to everyone." I shrugged one shoulder. "This is merely further proof that I'm not him."

Beale stared at me for a second, then whispered, "Yeah, I guess." He nodded and cleared his throat. "Anyway. I'm done talking about this right now. I'm gonna go help... someone. With something."

"Good. Yes." I nodded also. We were a great nodding duo. A pair of life-sized bobbleheads. "You should. I'm gonna go pay the piper." I leaned toward him and stage-whispered, "Mason is the piper."

"I figured. I guess I'll see you around."

Ugh. That hurt. A sharp, metallic tang filled my nose, and I was pretty sure tears would come soonishly. In my entire life, I'd never wanted anything as much as I wanted him to smile at me and wrap those big arms around me and be my safe place again. What a fucking sap Whispering Key had made me. The sooner I left, the better.

"Sure. I'm hard to miss, darling. Enjoy the party."

Beale looked me up and down, from my bare, damp chest,

to the towel around my waist, to the tips of my toes. Then he nodded once and walked out.

I shut the bedroom door softly behind him and locked it tight, then sat on the bed and stared at my hands for a long moment, waiting for tears to come. I was pretty sure I loved Beale Goodman, and I knew that because him walking out felt a lot like when my family had asked me to leave.

Apparently some of us were destined to only see love in the negative, in the void left by its absence.

What a cheerful thought.

The bed jostled as Marjorie jumped up from wherever she'd been hiding and butted her head against my chest looking for pets.

"You come to comfort me? You're a good girl," I told her, scratching her soft head until she closed her eyes in ecstasy. "Don't listen to anyone who says otherwise, okay? And promise you won't like anyone better than me, no matter how soul-matey they are, m'kay?"

Marjorie gave a chainsaw cough that indicated agreement and commiseration.

"Toby!" Mason shouted from the living room, and I sighed.

Marjorie hissed, which was thoughtful of her.

"Coming," I yelled. I pulled on my Alexander McQueen jeans with the gray stripe, a deconstructed floral shirt, and pair of leather slip-on Louboutins, because I had a fairly good idea how this conversation would go, and I required tactical armor.

And then, because I also had a fairly good idea how this conversation would *end,* I opened my suitcase on the bed and chucked the rest of my clothes in haphazardly. All I needed was my toiletry case to make a clean getaway.

I opened the door just as Mason was about to knock. His usually tidy hair was a mess, like he'd been running his hands through it, and his polo shirt was wrinkled from travel, but he looked... good. Happy. Not in the moment, obviously, since his expression suggested he was ready to commit all kinds of violence, but deep-down happy and lit-up from the inside, probably thanks to Fenn.

I caught a glimpse of myself in the mirror, all red-rimmed eyes and zero hair product. Further proof that relationships were like wide-legged pants or anything mustard yellow: fine for some, but a positively hideous look on me. I should have known better.

I did know better.

Yet here I was.

"Hey." I gave him a little smile as I stood back from the door. "How was O'Leary?"

"Oh. It was nice, actually. Seeing Fenn hold the baby was..." He scowled. "Stop. Don't distract me right now, Toby. What the heck is going on? Imagine me seeing my best friend's tattoo on the news three days ago and then calling and texting him a billion times, but he never replied. I was nearly ready to detour to the fucking city before we came home, asshole."

I winced. I'd been thinking that I didn't want my sudden appearance in Florida to ruin Mason's time Upstate. I hadn't really considered that Mason would find out anyway and be worried. I guessed I'd been looking at a lot of things wrong.

"I'm sorry. My phone died. Was murdered, really." Just saying that made me think of Beale's teasing, and I nearly cried again as I sank down on the bed.

I took a deep breath and explained the whole story about Dive, and Jayd, and the paparazzi. I explained how I'd come here to ask Mason's help, and how Littlejohn had helped me get into the guesthouse. All the important facts except the giant, Hagatha-shaped one.

"The guesthouse," Mason said, breaking his silence. "Where Beale was staying." He stood against the wall by the closet, arms folded over his chest.

"Yeah." I found myself strangely reluctant to provide details. Beale could if he wanted to, but as far as I was concerned, what had happened between us was ours and no one else's. "Beale took mercy on me and agreed to let me stay. He, um, knows that I'm your friend Toby. I didn't tell him why I came here, though. Once I realized the Goodmans knew Jayd, I decided I *couldn't...*" I trailed off and took a deep breath. "Anyway. His brothers randomly decided I must be his first love from summer camp years ago, so we went with that because I didn't want anyone else to know I was Toby. I figured if they knew, they'd call you to come home and that would ruin your fun." Marjorie curled up beside me, and I stroked her fur absently.

Mason's eyes narrowed to slits. "Ruin *my* fun, Toby? Or *yours*?"

"Huh?"

"Were you or were you not fucking Beale Goodman in the kitchen twenty minutes ago?"

"I..." I opened my mouth and shut it again. "I mean, in the interest of accuracy, I wasn't doing the fucking."

"Tobias!"

"Yes, yes, fine. Obviously I was, but that's neither here nor there." I'd decided not to ruin Mason's trip before Beale and I had ever done... anything.

"Neither here nor there? Do you know what you've done? Do you know what kind of person Beale is?"

"Yes, of course I know. I told you, I've spent the whole week with him. He's—" Amazing. Brilliant. Talented. Mischievous. Gorgeous. Compassionate.

"Thoughtful and kind, Toby. Sweet and good and, like... *wholesome*." Mason's voice had this reverent tone, like he was discussing some kind of religious vision instead of an actual human.

I wrinkled my nose. Nothing he said was wrong per se, but if he thought that was *all* Beale was, he was blind.

"You make him sound like a chocolate chip cookie, Mason. God. He's also really, really smart and capable." And then because I refused to get all schmoopy over a guy who'd basically dumped me—I mean, not without cause, but still—I examined my nails closely as I added, "And he's not as innocent as you might think. Just sayin'."

"Ugh," Mason groaned. "I do *not* wanna know that. Tobias, I understand that you change sex partners as often as most people change underwear, but you need to understand that for most of us, it means something. For *Beale* it means *everything*. He's not one of your conquests back in the city, and it was pure selfishness for you to take advant—"

"Mase, stop. Beale and I... it wasn't whatever you're thinking. I told you, he knows who I am. He knows... me." Honestly, better than Mason did in a way, since despite our years of friendship and how much I trusted Mason with other things, I'd only ever told him I was a writer, not what I wrote. Mason could be a wee bit judgmental over anything that didn't fit in a loafer-sized box in his mind. "I really don't need a lecture right now. I need your help."

"*My* help? What do you want *me* to do?"

"I don't know, man! If I knew, I'd have done it. You're the one with a cool head in a crisis, right? You're the one, of the two of us, who always knows the empirically *right* thing to do. You're the yin to my yang. The Squidward to my SpongeBob. The Mary Kate to my Ashley. The Aziraphale to my Crowley." I dragged the toe of my shoe along the floor. "I need you to tell me how to fix things back in New York so the paparazzi will leave me alone and I can go back to my life, but without outing someone who didn't do anything wrong."

"Toby, I wish I knew." Mason blew out a breath. "That's way out of my realm of expertise. And I'm honestly still a little bit overwhelmed at coming back from a trip to find the entire town out on my back lawn—" He pressed his fingertips to his eye sockets. "—and, not to keep harping on this, *my best friend fucking Fenn's best friend.*"

"Once again, I wasn't actually—"

"Oh, for heaven's sake! I can't help you sort your shit this time, okay? It's beyond me. But you can't keep hiding here. You *do* need to go back and deal with it, 'cause it doesn't seem to be going away on its own. Maybe ask Aunt Hagatha."

Oh, the irony.

I made myself nod calmly, like my heart wasn't aching. "Yeah, okay." I forced a smile. "See? I knew you'd know what I should do, precious." Turned out the incident at Dive had been the least of my fuckups this week. The veritable tip of the fuckup iceberg. I'd fucked things up with Beale, and now it seemed I'd fucked up my one and only friendship, too.

"Look, Mase." I stood up and laid a hand on Mason's bicep. His face was so familiar to me, even after not seeing him in months, and his picture would always be found in my personal dictionary beside the word *friend*, so I didn't want to say goodbye with him still angry at me or, worse, at Beale or Rafe or any of the party planners. "A whole lot of people came together and worked really hard to make this housewarming party happen for you and Fenn because they love you guys. I understand that it's overwhelming, and that the timing is absolutely deplorable. I also understand you're frustrated because you think I've seduced Beale for sport or something, but I'll repeat for the record: it wasn't that." Not at all. "Though, for what it's worth, I *do* know that he deserves way better than the likes of me, and Beale knows it, too."

"Wait, that's not..." Mason frowned. "I didn't say—"

"I heard everything you didn't say," I assured him. "My point is that Lety from the Concha has been slaving away over some soup thing she swears is your favorite, and Jonquil hasn't slept in days because in between coming up with random ideas to save the bridge, she keeps dreaming the balloons will catch fire, and the Stallions MC missed out on a run in Miami this weekend because they wanted to be here to thank you for patching up Bobo's leg. And I don't tell you that to make you feel guilty at all, just to say, try to look past the crazy and see the love, okay?"

In them *and* in me.

"Toby," Mason began. "If I made you feel like—"

"Hey, Mase? Baby?" Fenn appeared in the doorway. "Oh, hey, Toby. Nice to meet you officially. Not sure I said that earlier, what with you being, ah... busy."

"Yep." I smiled sadly. "Same here."

He shifted his attention back to Mason, and his eyes—blue, like Beale's, though not nearly as pretty—softened. He took one of Mason's hands in his and stroked his other hand over Mason's cheekbone. What would it be like to have someone look at you like that? I was pretty sure I wouldn't get to know.

"I know you're tired, love, but everyone got us house-warming gifts—like, a hundred of them—and Dale wants us to open his." He shrugged, all helpless amusement.

"Okay, but I was in the middle of—" Mason looked uncertainly from me to Fenn.

"*Pfft.* Go on!" I made a shooing motion with my hands.

"Open those gifts. I've seen what Dale got you, and you're gonna love it." He totally would *not* love it.

"You sure?" Mason lifted an eyebrow. "We'll finish this later?"

"You know where to find me." Back in the city, where I belonged.

Still, he hesitated. "I'm sorry if it seemed like—"

"Like you were being protective of Beale?" I smiled. "Don't be silly. I'm really glad he has people looking out for him. He deserves that."

"Yeah. Okay." Mason slid his hand into Fenn's. "Thanks, Toby."

"Always, darling."

As soon as he left, I zipped up my suitcase and made a phone call.

"Nope, I still don't get it," Littlejohn said. "Why're you leaving?"

I sighed.

The windshield wipers on the freaking Mercedes SUV LJ had been hiding in his detached garage swiped side to side, and I fervently hoped this storm was somehow passing around Whispering Key. I'd seen Beale laughing with Fenn as I snuck away from the party, and I wanted to remember him that way—happy and carefree. I didn't want the party ruined for him, either by my drama or the pesky raindrops.

"I just told you why. I'm not who I've been pretending to be. I'm Mason's friend Toby, not Beale's soul mate, and I have a whole shitstorm with Jayd to deal with back in New York."

"That's nonsense. Ya might not be Trey, but that's just a nickname—I knew it wasn't your real name from the first minute, but I figured I'm a man whose mama named him Littlejohn, so I ain't about to judge someone who chooses something better for himself."

I huffed out a short laugh.

"You showed us who you were every day you were here, Toby," he insisted stubbornly. "An' you might not have started out as Beale's soul mate, but you ended up that way."

"No. That's not..."

"And who cares if you got your picture taken with Jayd? Who cares if you screwed your way through every woodwind in the orchestra? We're real free love on Whispering Key." He gave me a solemn look. "Just ask Lorenna McKetcham."

I blinked. "I'd... truly rather not."

"Alls I'm sayin' is, the guy I got to know was as real as they come. So maybe Trey *is* who you really are, and Toby is the lie."

I snorted. "I almost wish my mother and I still spoke, just so I could explain to her that I'm really Trey and not Tobias." Then I sighed. "I wish it worked that way, Littlejohn, I really do. I, uh..." Oh, what was the harm in admitting it at this point? "I really liked it here. You've been a good friend to me. From the very first Pizza Bite."

"Well, back atcha, Toby. An' I'm gonna think of you..." He sniffled. "Every time I make SpaghettiO Surprise."

It was probably a sign of fatigue and emotional overwhelm that I was weirdly moved by this.

"Well, you have my number," I reminded him. "If you need someone to watch game shows with, you can call me anytime."

"Oh, I will," he said, not in the way that people in the city said it, like you knew they didn't mean it because they figured you didn't mean it either, but serious as a heart attack. "I'll call you all the time. We're friends no matter what name you go by. And I expect a call tonight when you get home safe."

I swallowed hard and my eyes filled up. Damn it all, this had been the weirdest day.

Relationships of all kinds were the official bane of my existence.

Littlejohn reached over and grabbed me by the back of the neck, probably recognizing the shiny stuff spilling from my eyes before I did, and tugged my head against his shoulder. He ruffled my hair with more honest affection than my own dad had ever shown me... and that was when I lost control of myself completely.

LJ didn't say a single word. He just pulled the car to the side of the road and patted my shoulder while I cried.

16

BEALE

I woke up Saturday with a raging headache and a face full of Marjorie's tail.

The party the night before had gone on roughly forever. Even though thunder had rumbled nearby early on, the rain had never materialized, so everyone had stayed and drank, and then stayed and drank some more. I'd stuck around to keep an eye on things, even after Gage, Rafe, and Dad left, and Fenn and Mason went in the house to sleep. Eventually, only the Mahjong Crew and the Stallions MC had been left, whooping and hollering and shooting Jack Daniels as they jigged to "*Devil Went Down to Georgia.*" Finally, in the early morning hours, the calmer and wiser group retired, too, and only Lorenna McKetcham's girls remained.

"I'm going to sleep," I'd told them when Jonquil Pepper had said something about skinny-dipping, because seeing my former kindergarten teacher naked by the light of the full moon was maybe the only thing that would make the evening worse. My face felt sore from forcing a smile so long, and my heart ached.

I had no idea how to feel about Toby, and that was the truth. I'd asked him for honesty, and he'd lied. I'd thought we were getting close, and it turned out he wasn't the person I'd thought I knew at all. I'd given him my heart, even if he didn't know it, and he'd drop-kicked it off a cliff.

So, I'd gone to bed last night full of righteous anger—alone, since Toby had moved all his shit into the main house—but I hadn't been able to sleep. Instead, I'd replayed that incredible, confusing round of kitchen sex over and over in my mind, along with the conversation before and after it. I'd pounded my pillow and debated hauling Toby out of the main house and back to the guest-house to sleep next to me and Marjorie, where he belonged, but I hadn't.

When I finally fell asleep, I dreamed of Toby drowning in the shallow end of the pool, and the look on his face was the same one he'd worn last night when he'd reminded me I had a soul mate waiting for me.

That got my heart racing, and blinking my eyes open to the sight of Marjorie's butt instead of Toby's sly smile only made my snarly mood worse. And that was even before Mason came knocking on the door carrying a tray full of pancakes and syrup, with a sleepy Fenn trailing behind him.

"Where's Toby?" he demanded, looking around like I might

be hiding the man under a piece of furniture. "I made him pancakes to apologize for being cranky last night."

"He's with you." I filled the kettle, turned on the burner, and nodded toward the main house.

"Mmm, that'd be a no," Fenn said with a yawn. "The only bed in the place so far is the one in our room, and I was happily sprawled in it until Mase shouted at me three minutes ago." When Mason shot him a look, he grinned and corrected, "I mean, until my beloved's dulcet tones awakened me like the most beautiful birdsong. And Toby wasn't sleeping on the living room couch, right? My eyes weren't fully open when I shuffled past."

Mason shook his head, brow furrowed, and set the tray of pancakes down on the counter.

Yes, *that* counter. I avoided looking at it.

"But he took his suitcase," I said dumbly. "He has no way off the island. He's gotta be in your house."

"You sure about that?" Fenn scratched his head. "Everyone on the Key seemed to know and like him. Pretty sure he could've gotten anyone to take him to the airport? Or maybe asked to crash on their couch."

"Besides, Toby has plenty of money." Mason rubbed a palm over his forehead tiredly. "He does some kind of writing for a living, and he's got a rainy-day fund that's like the GDP of a small country. If he wanted to leave, he'd find a way. Shit." He slumped onto one of the stools dejectedly. "I should have known he'd leave. That's what he does. When things in his relationships get tough, he backs off. Hell, even when you and I got together, he stopped returning my calls for a little while," he told Fenn, who'd placed a comforting hand on his shoulder. "Toby hates leaving himself open to being hurt."

I got out my phone and texted Littlejohn:

Hey, is Trey with you?

"This doesn't make sense. Toby wanted to talk to you, Mase. He wanted your advice about his problem in New York." My head pounded and I winced. "That's why he came to the Key. He wouldn't have left without talking to you."

"Yeah, well." Mason winced. "He may have tried to ask last night, and I may have been a teensy bit harsh with him."

Fenn snorted. "You think?"

Mase shot him a look, but Fenn didn't back down, and Mason sighed.

"Harsh how?" I asked.

"You don't date people casually, Beale," Mason hedged.

"Right."

"And I care about you very much, which makes me feel a little... protective. Toby's not the kind of person I'd have picked for you, and I maybe snapped at him for taking advantage of you."

"Taking advantage of me? Toby?" He'd lied, sure, and I was angry, but that wasn't the same thing as taking advantage. I'd known who he was and what he wanted from me since the first night we met.

"You've gotta understand, it's not that Toby's a bad person," Mason hurried to say. "He's not! I've known him since college, and beneath that super-snarky, abrasive exterior, he's got a kind and generous side he doesn't show often."

"I know."

"He got his heart broken so often freshman year, I swear he got a permanent callus, which is why... Wait, you know?" He frowned like this sentence didn't compute.

"I know he's a kind, generous person," I clarified. "I didn't know about the heartbreak. Keep going." It tightened my chest to hear it.

"Uh. Well." Mason didn't seem any less confused after my explanation. "I was going to say, he came back to school sophomore year, and it was like a switch had flipped. He didn't let anyone in anymore. He was all about having a good time and being self-reliant after that. And it wasn't a phase. He's been that way for... oh, fifteen years or so? Something like that."

Oh, Toby. Angry as I was, I couldn't hear that without my gut churning.

"Was that after his parents kicked him out?"

"He told you about that?" Mason's eyes went wide. "He didn't tell *me* until years after the fact! I just figured he stayed at school for breaks since he liked it better." He looked affronted.

I shrugged. "He didn't give me details, Mase, he just told me that it happened." And I'd been afraid to push too hard to learn more. "Could you fast-forward to the part where he somehow took advantage of me?"

Mason blew out a breath. "I already told you. Toby's casual about sex, and you're not. I told him he was wrong to mess around with you just because you're hot when he had to know—"

"You think Beale's hot?" Fenn demanded. "Since when?"

"I have eyes, don't I?" Mason arched an eyebrow. "I mean, he's not as hot as *Watt Bartlett*, obviously…"

Fenn's eyes rolled toward the ceiling. "This again?"

"This *forever*," Mason said haughtily. "You don't get to make eyes at my brother's friend and expect me to ignore it."

"I have never 'made eyes' at anyone in my life, except possibly you." Fenn crowded Mason, standing between his legs, and tried to kiss him.

Mason turned his head. "Oh, really? Even though, as you have reminded me no less than four times this week, Watt has an iconic 1966 Chevy Corvette in his barn that he wants you to see next time we visit?"

"But I'd bet he hasn't got a pair of loafers to his name," Fenn said solemnly. "And I find I have very specific tastes these days."

Mason snorted, but his mouth turned up at one corner. He slid a hand up Fenn's chest. "That's true love right there."

"It really is."

Blurgh. "Focus, people," I demanded. "And not on Fenn's shoe fetish. Mason, finish. You told off your best friend because he and I chose to have sex?"

Fenn shifted to one side, and Mason tilted his head against Fenn's chest. He looked at me and sighed guiltily.

"I jumped to conclusions. I told Toby you were sweet and good..." He wrinkled his nose. "Toby said I described you like a cookie, and he was right. I should have listened better when he said you were capable."

Toby saw you, a voice in the back of my head said. *He did care about you. And can you blame him for not trusting you when you pushed him away like every other person in his entire life has, from his family to his exes, the second he didn't meet some crazy standard of perfection?* The voice, which sounded suspiciously like Toby's, reminded me, *"You said motive matters, Beale!"*

"Toby was right," I said softly. "Mase, I love you, but I'm an adult human being capable of making decisions, and I don't need protecting. I knew who Toby was before anything happened between us. He didn't lie about that. The only thing he lied about was Jayd."

"And from what Mason said, that situation wasn't really his fault either," Fenn said, stroking a comforting hand down Mason's back. "For better or worse, he had reasons for not telling you. He was trying to protect Jayd from being outed. And if he knew about the bullshit between Young Rafe and Jayd..."

My stomach sank. "He did. I told him."

Fenn grimaced. "Then Toby was doing you a favor by not asking you to keep a secret he thought might test your loyalty."

I tried hard to hold on to my anger, since the alternative was feeling guilty and sad. "He still should have told me. If he'd told me, I'd have..." I broke off and shook my head.

God, I wasn't sure. And if I wasn't sure, how the heck should Toby have been?

My anger evaporated entirely.

"I was wrong," Mason admitted softly.

"Yeah," I agreed. That seemed to be going around.

"I need to go find him." Mason nodded resolutely and headed for the door. "Or at least call him. Apologize profusely."

"Right behind you, Loafers," Fenn said, grabbing a pancake off the tray and stuffing it in his mouth.

In the bathroom, I found Toby's toiletry bag right where we'd left it the night before. I lifted the bag to my nose so I could take a breath of his sexy cologne—the happiest breath I'd taken all morning—and I got a crazy surge of hope because he wouldn't just have left this stuff behind. That meant he was coming back, right?

But when I brought the bag into the bedroom, my heart dropped again because my bracelet sat on the dresser, coiled atop a note that said simply, *Beale: Your soul mate is one lucky guy. Thank you for everything, and I'm truly sorry. —Toby*

I stared at the stones for a long moment before I picked the bracelet up and held it tightly in my hand. It seemed crazy that just a few days ago, I'd felt such an intense connection to these stones when now they felt empty.

I felt empty.

My phone buzzed with a notification.

LITTLEJOHN

Not with me. Dropped him at the airport last night and he's back in NYC. You done fucked it up, Goodman.

I clutched the phone in my fist and threw my head back to the ceiling.

I remembered Toby on the boat the other day, talking about his family. Saying he'd left town after they'd hurt him and he'd never gone back.

LITTLEJOHN

He was in tears, in case that matters.

I shut my eyes tight and sucked in a breath. It mattered. Fuck, just thinking about Toby crying made me want to cry, too, and in that minute, when it was way too late, the truth hit me: I'd fallen in love with Toby Elford.

He was *not* the soul mate I'd intended to manifest for myself. He was snarky and cutting, self-absorbed and high-strung. He didn't trust me. He might never love me back.

But none of that seemed to matter to my heart.

Toby had told me that I was enough, even when everyone else seemed to be saying something different. He'd helped me clear the stumbling blocks in my mind so I could choose what *I* wanted for my life, even if what I wanted was what I already had. He'd believed in me and made *me* believe in me.

The man deserved more than an apology... he deserved to have someone clear a path for him.

It was time for me to stop waiting for the Universe to hand me good things; it was time for me to start making them happen.

17

TOBY

Help Me Hagatha (Issue #2444)

Dear Aunt Hagatha:

I'm having trouble with my cat. Every time my boyfriend stays over, she pees on his belongings, and it's really starting to cause a strain in our relationship. He's tried to be patient, and I understand why he's upset, but I love my pet and I hate to think of surrendering her. There doesn't appear to be a simple solution here. What should I do?

Pitiful in Platte

Dear Pitiful,

Simple and easy are two different things, but if you truly love your cat, you'll fight for her. When you love hard, you'll fight harder, even when it seems hopeless. I suggest talking to your vet. Also, check out the articles linked below. I'll be thinking of you. Check back soon.

Love,
Hagatha

"Tobias, are you even listening?" Jeanette's disembodied voice came through the phone as I sprawled on my sofa, staring out my ginormous curved window at the city skyline.

That view over Chelsea, which was worth at least a couple million dollars of the apartment's 3.5-million price tag, looked wrong.

The sky wasn't blue enough.

Big, blocky buildings littered the horizon where palm trees should have swayed.

Nothing in my cramped apartment smelled like coconut sunscreen or fresh air.

Even the roar of engines and honking cars muted by the thick glass windows jarred me, when a few weeks ago, they'd been my usual evening lullaby.

I'd been back in New York for five days. Not a single appliance, dubiously domesticated cat, or rogue watercraft in the city had tried to murder me in all that time, which was probably for the best since there were no shining-armored knights around to save me, but somehow the lack of death-defying experiences made my days feel flat...

Or, fine, maybe it was the lack of knights.

Either way, nothing about my life worked right anymore. My ultra-plush mattress was hard as a rock when Beale wasn't holding me, I couldn't watch movies without wanting to redeem the villains, for all the good that would do, and it was hard to fall asleep and even harder still to wake up. I was getting grocery deliveries of Peanut Butter Party ice cream with such regularity that I'd told Franz the doorman to just give the delivery guys my key when they came through, and I swore I could feel the cholesterol hardening my arteries in real time.

In short, I was unhappy to report that breakups—even fake breakups of impossible relationships—were no more fun at thirty-five than at nineteen, and in fact, they seemed to get worse as you aged.

Like chicken pox, or whichever pox it was.

At least when I was a teenager, the most reactionary thing I'd done to get over a breakup was to find a rebound hookup. Now I was contemplating far more drastic action, like quitting my job and moving to Malé for real.

Someone needed to call Aunt Hagatha to stage an intervention.

Oh, wait.

"Tobias!"

I sighed and turned toward the ceiling. "Jeanette, precious, my eardrums are perfectly functional," I informed her. "I gather that you're displeased with the content of my column today." I studied my nails in the late-afternoon sunlight. "I'm not sure why. It was thoughtful, responsible advice, and I linked to subject matter experts. My commenters seem to relate to it."

"Your twenty commenters."

"Mmhmm."

"When you usually have hundreds, Tobias. Sometimes over a thousand."

"What can I tell you?" I sighed again. Sighing was a super-underutilized way of coping with stress. Much like Peanut Butter Party. "Quality's more important than quantity, darling."

Jeanette made a noise halfway between a growl and the whistle of a teakettle. "Not. To. Our. Advertisers," she bit out. "But alright, fine, let's talk quality. This response is perfectly unoffensive, but it's trite. '*When you love hard, you'll fight harder*'? Seriously? I'm almost positive I read that inside a chocolate wrapper. People expect more of Hagatha."

This was extremely annoying because "*When you love hard, you'll fight harder, even when it seems hopeless*" was something Littlejohn had said a few days back on one of our nightly *Jeopardy!* calls, and I'd actually found it kind of chest-squeezingly profound in the moment... though, come to think of it, he *had* been gobbling chocolate while we'd chatted, goddamn it.

Next thing you knew, I'd be getting teary-eyed over Hallmark cards. Where would this emotional bullshittery end?

"Been thinkin' Veronica Hampton might just be the lady for me, Trey," Littlejohn had said. "She rollerblades like a dream, she's fair at trivia, and she agreed to be the sexy Scully to my badass Mulder come Halloween. I'm a simple man. I don't need much more."

"That's enough for anyone," I'd agreed. "Have you made her SpaghettiO Surprise?"

"Mmm... not'chet," he'd hedged around a mouthful of candy. "I was savin' that for something special."

"Nah. If you think she's the one, you can't hedge your bets, trust me." I'd brandished my ice cream spoon and spoken with way too much confidence for a man who'd sunk his own relationship like an inflatable dinghy. "If she likes it, you'll know the tea. Our fears make us our own worst enemies."

"True enough, and when you love hard, you'll fight harder, even when it seems hopeless. Which makes a body wonder... why the heck ain't you back on the Key yet?"

I hadn't had an answer.

Littlejohn had assured me multiple times over the past few days that no one hated me—that, in fact, no one on Whispering Key outside LJ, Mason, Fenn, and the three Goodman brothers even knew I'd been involved in the Jayd scandal, and Maddie McKetcham thought it was *absofreaking adorbs* that I was somehow, impossibly, both Mason's college roommate Toby *and* Beale's summer camp lover Trey. LJ had even explained my abrupt departure, saying I'd had an emergency back in the city.

But how in the world was I meant to go back and "fight harder" when I wasn't sure there was anything to fight for anymore?

Mason had called a bunch and texted several times, telling me he loved me and apologizing again for being harsh. I'd texted him back to say I got it, because I did, and that I wasn't upset, because I wasn't. Not at him. Not at Beale. Not at anyone except myself.

Even if no one else on the island hated me, Beale had to hate me, right? I'd made him feel foolish when I *knew* that was the thing he hated most in the world. I'd held on to my secrets when I knew how much he valued trust.

I would hate me. Hell, I *did* hate me.

I'd had something really good at the edge of my fingertips, something that was maybe almost—oh, who was I kidding? Something that was *totally*—love, and I hadn't been careful with it. Beale deserved so much better.

And as if that weren't enough to keep me from ever dragging my dumpster fire of drama back to the Key, there was still the issue of the paparazzi. I'd sort of expected them to be camped out on my doorstep when I got back to the city, but they hadn't caught up to me yet. There'd been a moment earlier in the week when I'd thought maybe the world had moved on, but then Jayd had been caught with some other guy—in freakin' Colorado, of all random places—and suddenly my ridiculous tattoo was all over the news again. Where's Waldo? Right freakin' here.

I was going to get the damn thing covered—which was what I should have done in the first place, if I hadn't panicked. Maybe I could find a tattoo artist who'd turn Waldo and his hat into a mountain. Or a replica of the Washington Monument. Or an enormous, erect phallus. Something meaningful like that.

Anyway, I'd tried contacting Jayd's management team to get in touch with him, but they had no idea where he was either, and apparently I wasn't the only one he was avoiding. In short, it was becoming pretty clear that Jayd didn't have a plan for coming out; he simply didn't plan to come out at all... which meant my life wasn't going to be any less dicey anytime soon.

"Tobias, I know you're still there." Jeanette's voice was an uninvited guest crashing my truly epic pity party. "I can hear you breathing. So listen up. I don't know what happened down in Florida, but it seems like you packed Aunt Hagatha in your checked luggage and the airline lost her. I need you to find her again. The column is not called Toby's Mediocre Musings."

I clenched my free hand into a fist and sat up straight, letting anger burn off some of my self-pity. It was funny how everyone in the world wanted something from me—a laugh, a fuck, a shoulder to cry on—but no one wanted all the shitty parts that came along with cute, fun Toby.

Except Beale. And look what I'd done with that.

"And if your plan," Jeanette continued mercilessly, "is to tank the column so I'll let you out of your contract, think again. I'm willing to give you lots of latitude, Tobias, and I'm even willing to renegotiate certain terms, including your salary, but I'm not letting you run away. To put it in chocolate wrapper language, I love the Hagatha column hard, and I'll fight harder." She snort-laughed at her own joke. "So pull your head out of your ass, understand?"

I opened my mouth to tell her where she could shove her understanding when my phone beeped. I'd like to say my heart didn't give a crazy leap when I saw it was a Florida number, but that would be an utter lie.

"Jeanette, I'll call you back," I said, not giving her time to respond before I hit End and Accept. "Hello?"

"Heya, Trey! It's Jonquil. Jonquil Pepper. Littlejohn gave me your number."

"Oh. Hey…a." I tried not to let my disappointment show and braced myself, expecting… I wasn't sure what. A reprimand? A string of curse words?

"Honey, it's so good to hear you! We miss you."

Okay, definitely not that. "You… do?"

"'Course! Listen, I'm calling about the flyers for the bridge fundraiser. We got the rendering back from the architect Big Rafe hired, but I'm not sure where I'm meant to send it? I'm thinking we need to get this started this week, what with everything happening, but you're in charge, so I guess maybe I'll just send it to you and let you forward it on?" she asked hopefully.

"Oh. Sure." I swallowed. "I… I missed you, too," I rushed out belatedly, then rolled my eyes at myself.

Jeanette might not have been entirely wrong about me losing my sass since I left the Key. I was positively soggy.

"Aww, honey." Jonquil's voice was warm as sunshine. "I'm so sorry, I didn't even think that you must still be busy with your emergency. Is it a family issue? Or work? Are you sick? I would have asked about it first thing, but I didn't want to be nosy. I mean, I *did* want to be nosy, but I held back," she said solemnly. "Until now. And don't you fret about this flyer thing. I'm sure it can wait a day or two if you don't have a chance to handle it right yet."

"No, it's not that. It's just…" I bit my lip. "I figured you'd want someone from the Key to handle this, that's all."

Jonquil sounded bewildered. "But... you *are* from the Key, honey. Or close enough. It's like you're commuting for work, or off at college, or something! This might not be where you get your mail delivered just now, but it will be, once you and Beale get married."

Shit. Littlejohn's explanation of a family emergency hadn't covered the whole Beale-and-I-aren't-together thing, had it?

"Jonquil," I began. "You see..."

"Or not married, per se," she hurried on, like she was worried she'd offended me. "I just meant, until you can be together more permanently, that's all. I hope it's soon. Poor Beale hasn't smiled in days and days, and that's not like him." She sighed sadly. "All the crystals in the Universe can't guard a body from missing the one he cares about, huh?"

My heart twisted, and I let out a little puff of breath like I'd been punched in the stomach.

I'd very specifically *not* asked Littlejohn about Beale, and if I were being honest, the reason I hadn't called Mase to clear the air was because I was afraid he'd volunteer information I didn't want to hear.

Like that Beale was making voodoo dolls in my image using all the toiletries I'd left behind in the pool house bathroom.

Or that he'd finally spoken his soul mate into existence, and they were off on some plover-counting honeymoon, chuckling about that moment of temporary insanity when Beale had screwed around with me.

I hadn't known until Jonquil spoke that thinking of Beale being that unhappy nearly a week later was worse than either of those outcomes.

"Still," Jonquil continued, "when I told him I was gonna call you today, he said that sounded like a great idea, and you always had the best advice even when you didn't think you did, which I thought was real sweet."

Oh, damn. Another gut punch. "He... he said that?" I whispered.

"Sure. He loves you an awful lot. Even Barbara Patenaude could see that, and that woman is a *slave* to her cataracts. You know, I've always said she should've..."

I stared out the window at the beautiful, not-quite-right skyline, and right there, while Jonquil Pepper chattered on about eye surgery or some shit, I had what my mother used to call a come-to-Jesus moment.

I missed Beale. *God*, I missed him.

I wasn't just sad that I'd been dumped by a guy, or feeling salty and unwanted. It wasn't that my pride was injured, or my confidence was bruised. I genuinely missed *him*. Specifically Beale Goodman.

I missed him in a way that I doubted all the Blue Bunny Peanut Butter Party ice cream in the tristate area could soothe.

I missed his smile and his warm embrace.

I missed the way he made me feel safe.

I missed the way everything seemed *possible* with him.

And it didn't matter that I'd been back in New York longer than I'd been in Florida. It didn't matter that we were polar opposites. It didn't matter that I knew better, or that our relationship had been a lie.

This part—the missing-him part—was very real.

A little over two weeks ago, I'd found myself on Whispering Key with none of the things I valued in the world—no money, no contacts, no best friend, no privacy—and instead I'd gotten Beale...

And if I had the chance, I'd trade it all again and consider it a fucking bargain.

But I didn't know how to make Beale give me that chance.

"So anyway, about the bridge," Jonquil finally said. "Guess you've heard there might not be a concert at the Extravaganza after all."

I blinked out of my thoughts halfway to the kitchen area. "Oh?" It was hard to care about the concert, honestly. I needed more ice cream, stat.

"Poor Jayd. I do feel for him."

"Uh-huh." I stood in front of the freezer and shoveled ice cream in my mouth with a giant spoon.

"He went off grid, and now everyone's saying he's in rehab when the boy's never done hard drugs." She paused. "Or not very hard drugs." She paused again. "At least, not back when I knew him."

I shook my head, pretty sure Jayd hadn't been a regular on the Key for fifteen years or something. "Uh-huh."

"And he *says* he doesn't care, but of course he does. I honestly think he's as homesick for the Key as you, sweetie, though he'd never admit it."

"Uh h— *Wait*." I plunked my ice cream carton on the counter and licked some off my finger. "Did you say Jayd *says* he doesn't care?" Unless something had changed in the last hour, Jayd hadn't spoken to the media, so this was news to me. Pretty sure it would be news to his management team, too.

"That's what I said," Jonquil agreed. "But of course he actually *does* care, he just doesn't want us to worry about him. Still, I think it was wise that Big Rafe is sending Gage to fetch him back here, whether he performs or not. He needs to be surrounded by people who care about him."

My heart pounded double-time. "Back up, back up. Big Rafe has talked to Jayd Rollins? Gage is *with* Jayd Rollins?"

"They're family friends, Trey. You know that." She hesitated. "Don't you?"

"No, yes, I knew they were friends. I knew about Rafe and Aimee."

"Right," Jonquil said, sounding relieved.

"But I didn't know they knew where Jayd was *now*." I licked my lips, and the taste of peanut butter was kinda sickening. I wanted to ask where the hell Jayd was and if maybe Jonquil had a phone number so I could call him, but instead what popped out of my mouth was, "God, how does Young Rafe feel about him coming back to the Key? It must be hard."

Because apparently I was a person who thought of others first now? Bizarre.

"Maybe so, but Young Rafe was the one who suggested that Gage should go and fetch him... after Beale gave him a stiff talking-to, of course, as you know."

A giant ball of something like pride filled the empty spots in my chest. I *hadn't* known that, but fuck I wished I had. I wished I'd been there when Beale gave Rafe a talking-to.

"...but I'm not sure anyone can convince Jayd to do the concert, which is why we need the flyers sooner than later."

I frowned and tried to focus. "You're still going to do the fundraiser, then, for sure?"

"Heck, yes. We still need a bridge! And if you care about something, you don't give up, you fight harder. Isn't that what you and Beale did all these years?"

I opened my mouth and shut it again. Once again, the answer was no. Once again, I wished it wasn't.

"That's... a great way to put it," I said, feeling absurdly choky about the whole thing. Apparently Jonquil read chocolate wrappers, too.

"Oh, I can't take credit. It was something I read in Aunt Hagatha this morning. 'Course, she was talking about cats, but that's the thing with Hagatha, I find. You gotta know how to interpret her. Not so different from Beale with his horoscopes, in a way. All depends on how you think the Universe is tryna talk to you, and what you're finally ready to hear, don't you think?" Jonquil chuckled lightly. "Some of us need to hear things a dozen times before it penetrates. So, we'll fight hard, even though it seems hopeless."

I blinked, my mouth hanging open.

"Anywho, about this flyer..."

"Email me the rendering," I said quickly. "In fact, email me everything you have. I'm going to send it to a graphic designer I know, and then I'll talk to a lawyer, just like I promised. But right now... I have something I have to do." Immediately. Before I overthought it and stopped myself.

"Oh! Alright, then, honey. But first, send me your address. I've got a care package for you. Just a few baked goods from Lety and a little something the Mahjong folks painted for you. Don't worry—nothing too risqué. We held Lorenna back."

I gave her my address—hell, I'd have given her anything she wanted—then I booted up my laptop.

I couldn't do anything about the Jayd situation or the paparazzi right then, but maybe... maybe that didn't matter. Maybe I could figure that out in time, and maybe it was just an excuse I was giving myself about why I couldn't take a stand for Beale—for *us*—and apologize, and fight to fix things.

Even though they seemed hopeless.

Maybe nothing I could do would change things between us, and maybe it would, but maybe the outcome didn't matter either. Maybe Beale just needed to know that he was worth fighting for. Maybe I just needed to know that I could stop running and fight.

And sweet Tom Daley in a teeny-tiny Speedo, maybe it was time to take my own advice, because it was a sad day when the Universe had to parrot chocolate-wrapper truisms to you a billion times before you could hear the actual truth of them.

Hagatha was me—not a persona, not someone I pretended to be—and it had taken Beale to show me that, but that didn't mean I had all the answers. Far from it. Sometimes I was sad and lost. Sometimes it was okay for me to ask for help and to admit I'd fucked up. To take things in a whole new direction.

Dear, Jeannie—

I wanna make a change to Thursday's column. I think you'll find the new one is neither boring nor flat, even if it's a tiny bit off-brand. Remember you said you'd work with me?

—T.

18

BEALE

Czarina's StarCharts for Today
*Today's your lucky day, Virgo! The darkest hour is just before
dawn.*

"*Hola*, Beale." Lety greeted me with a bright smile and a menu as I slid onto a stool at the Concha one morning exactly six days after I found out Toby left town. "*Jugo y tostadas?*"

I set my elbows on the counter and nodded. "Yes, please."

I'd been having juice and black bean tostadas at the counter every morning for the past week or so, and while the Concha wasn't my favorite breakfast spot—even Lety got her breakfast at the Bean—it had precisely one thing going for it: I was pretty sure Toby had never darkened the door of this place, whereas being at the Bean made me think of him constantly and miss him more.

Of course, *not* being at the Bean made me remember why I wasn't there, which in turn made me miss Toby more, too.

And, in reality, there wasn't anything that ever made me miss him *less*. Already, my cat, my plovers, and the bed I slept in made me think of him. I'd actually sprayed his pillow with his abandoned cologne the other day, thinking that might help me sleep better, and it had kinda worked... until I'd woken up with his scent in my nose and his side of the bed empty, which had been worse than not sleeping at all.

So I was pretty much doomed to this state until I could fix shit and get him back.

Until I could *earn* him back.

The bell over the door jangled and the few breakfast patrons called out greetings as my brother slid onto the stool beside me.

"Morning, Beale. Coffee, please, Lety?" Rafe asked, summoning a dimpled smile.

Lety winked, and Rafe hunched over the countertop in front of him before turning to look at me.

"How's it going?"

I grunted and shrugged. "You know. Fine."

Rafe nodded. "One more time, and this time make it convincing."

"I'm fine. Really. Why wouldn't I be?"

"Because your soul mate Trey left tow—"

"His name is *Toby*," I interrupted in a low voice. "And he was always going to go back to the city. The soul mate thing was... you know."

Something I'd thought I'd understood, but I hadn't until I'd tried to walk around and live my life with no sunlight in it.

Rafe made a noncommittal noise. "And have you spoken to him?"

"Not yet."

I was waiting until I had something important to tell him. Like, for example, that I'd convinced Jayd Rollins—in a loving, supportive, nonthreatening way—to make some kind of statement about what had happened at the club so Toby could be free from the media scrutiny and choose to be with me—or not—without any of those clouds hanging over his head.

It was supposed to take a day or two.

It hadn't.

"I don't want to discuss it," I insisted. "Move on."

"Okay, then. I heard from Gage earlier. He and Jayd are in Wyoming. They're *hiking*."

I pondered geography for half a second and frowned. "Wait, Wyoming? When they started in Colorado? Pretty sure that's not between here and there."

"Yeah, well. Jayd has his own agenda. What a shock." Rafe's voice was dry as dust.

Lety set down my juice and a mug of coffee for Rafe, and Rafe winked his thanks.

"I thought you were ready to move on from this. You were the one who told Gage you were fine with him going to fetch Jayd."

He lifted an eyebrow. "Revisionist history. You talked to Dad, who talked to Gage..."

"Who still wasn't going to do it because he felt like you'd be angry."

"So then you sat *me* down for a lecture." Rafe sipped his coffee and winced. "Remind me, why are we here and not at the Bean?" he whispered.

I snorted. "I have no idea why *you're* here. And I didn't lecture you. I reminded you why you should give Gage your blessing to go pick Jayd up. He's your oldest friend. He's someone you care about, deep down—"

"Way deep down," he muttered. "Like, six feet under."

"And it seems like maybe he's questioning things, just like you and Gage and I did once, and it'd be good for him to have some support while he does that. Maybe it'll help him feel more comfortable about coming out."

"Or maybe he never will, Beale." Rafe rolled his eyes. "He's famous now. You and me, even Gage, we were scared, but we didn't have nearly as much to lose as Jayd does."

"Yep," I agreed, less than enthusiastically. "Guess that's a possibility, too."

"So why do you care so much about making Jayd comfortable? And do *not*," he added, "give me some shit about helping him out because he's an old friend who deserves support. You're hoping this'll make Toby come back some-how, aren't you?"

"Yeah, maybe," I admitted defiantly. "Maybe I'm hoping when he feels like he's free to choose... he'll choose to come back. Maybe once the way is clear for him, I can tell him that I... I have feelings for him. I know it's a long shot. I know he's got a life of his own in the city, and I don't know if I could be happy there, but... I want to tell him. I want to try."

Rafe nodded slowly and sipped his coffee again. "I hope you're right."

I rolled my eyes. "Come on, don't hold back. This is the part where you tell me I'm ridiculous. This is the part where you tell me that I need to stop believing in fairy tales, and I should stop waiting for the Universe to act. This is the part where you tell me I was foolish to fall for a guy like Toby in the first place, let alone for thinking it would ever work out permanently—"

Rafe shook his head. "Not gonna do that," he said softly. "I want you to be happy, Beale. I wanted you to not be afraid to want something and go for it. That's all. That's... that's it. You know, when Aimee left..." He blew out a breath. "The God's honest truth is, I was almost relieved. And I felt so, so guilty about that. Felt guilty about *everything*. Our relationship hadn't been good for a while, but I'd figured it was circum-stances, you know? Money was tight, we were all struggling. I figured things would sort themselves out." He grimaced down at his coffee. "And they did, but not in a way I ever expected, and I had a lot of regrets. Did I not tell her I loved her enough? Did I just not love her enough, period? Part of the reason I blame Jayd is because I mostly blame myself."

He looked up at me. "But only part of the reason," he said severely.

"Of course," I agreed.

"Anyway, the worst part of Aimee leaving was wondering if there was something I could have done to make her stay, Beale. So if you care about him…"

I gave Rafe a long, measured look, and he grinned.

"Oh ho! So it's like *that,* is it? Fine, if you *loooove* him—" He shoved my shoulder good-naturedly. "—then you need to keep trying. But I don't get why you're waiting on Jayd. Shit, go find Tr—Toby," he corrected. "Do it today."

I shook my head stubbornly. "I need to do this for him first. I need to clear this obstacle. He can't make a real choice if he's concerned the media will find him and…" I bit my tongue before revealing Toby's identity as Hagatha. "I want to make the situation safe first."

"Pretty sure telling him he's not alone would go a long way toward making him feel safe. That's what Aunt Hagatha would tell you, righ— Oh. Hang on, Dad's calling."

While Rafe stood up to take the call, I bit my lip and spun my juice glass, thinking about what he'd said. I'd sort of imagined Toby was back in New York, mostly caught up in the whirl of his life again. I remembered our conversation in the pool—how he'd said he couldn't stand to live too far from a big department store—and figured he wasn't missing the Key too much. But was it too much to hope he missed *me*?

Without conscious thought, I found myself with the phone

in my hand, and for the first time in two weeks, I let myself type in the HiWire website.

I'd been a little worried that if I read Hagatha's column knowing it was Toby behind the words, I'd miss him so badly I wouldn't let myself stick to the plan and do things in the right order, make things good for him the way he deserved. But just then, every instinct screamed at me to do it, and I couldn't resist.

"Holy shit," I muttered, as soon as the page loaded and I read the first couple of lines. I read it through… then read it again a second time. My heart beat like crazy, and I jumped to my feet. "Rafe? Come on! We need to get to Littlejohn's."

19

TOBY

Help Me Hagatha (Issue #2450)

Dear Readers,

For the past ten years, I've published five columns a week,
forty-nine weeks a year. That makes two-thousand-four-
hundred times I've told someone what to do, so you might
well believe that Auntie has her own life sorted out, and
that I am always kind, and brave, and practice what I
preach.

Not so much.

Recently, I told a lie to a man I care about. It was a tiny lie.
A lie of omission. To protect someone. And the truth was
nobody else's business. I had a billion reasons, a billion
excuses. But in the end, when the lie came to light (and
readers, they *always* come to light), I hurt this man I care
about.

But that wasn't the worst part.

When I should have owned up and apologized for my error, when I should have dropped to my knees and begged for forgiveness, when I should have barred the door (in a law-abiding, consensual sort of way) and insisted we not leave until we'd hashed out the truth, instead I let the lie stand and ran away to protect my heart... only to find I'd left the foolish thing behind in his keeping.

So, to that good man I hurt: I'm sorry I let you down. We are real. We are important. I thought you deserved someone more perfect than me, but it occurred to me that what you deserve is someone who really, really loves you... and there is no one who'll do that better than I will. If you let me, I'll prove it to you.

Readers, thanks for sticking with me, even when I mess up... because we all mess up.

Love always,
Hagatha

Look, it wasn't like I'd been expecting Beale to storm the HiWire offices with a half-dozen buff, lightly oiled, and scantily dressed friends, each carrying a bouquet of red roses, to perform a highly choreographed flash-mob dance routine...

Or not exactly that, anyway.

For one thing, I was pretty sure he didn't know where the office was, and for another, he knew my identity was a secret, for a third, I didn't think he knew any Bruno Mars lyrics, which was kind of a requirement. And if that weren't enough, there was the small matter of him never venturing farther north of Whispering Key than the Florida state line.

But I'd kind of expected a phone call.

Or a text.

Or a message delivered via trained plover.

Something.

I'd definitely expected something.

I'd woken up thrilled to greet the sun for the first time in weeks, so secure in the knowledge that I had fixed things that I literally sang in the shower. No, I will not tell you what song. No, we shall never discuss it again.

Fine, it was Taylor Swift's "Shake It Off," if you must know, and I danced so aggressively that I bumped my elbow on the tile quite, quite hard, so that pain still radiated through my forearm even half a day later.

I'd skipped my way to the office—no, not literally—even stopping for coffee at Dot, my favorite local shop. Although there'd been a distinct lack of kitschy decor and overly friendly patrons, I'd managed to enjoy it, mostly because I told myself that soon enough the Bean would be my local shop.

When I'd reached the HiWire offices, Jeanette had actually come to the lobby to greet me. I'd had a momentary flash of panic, because her face had been contorted into a grimace unlike any I'd seen before, but I realized that was because she was over-Botoxed and *smiling* in a way she hadn't since the day I'd signed my contract.

It turned out, readers were flooding my latest post with (mostly) supportive comments and sharing the link on social media. Jeanette's assistant heard some radio hosts chatting about how "Hagatha got personal" during her morning commute, and Buzzfeed had even done a little blurb under the heading "Agony Aunt in Agony," which I believed was stretching the issue.

Pfft. By a lot.

But after my meeting with Jeanette, in which we'd come to an amicable conclusion about my future with HiWire, I'd walked home and looked at the clock—10:30 a.m. And... nothing had happened.

I'd strolled on the building's roof deck. I changed my already clean sheets. I alphabetized the groceries in my nearly empty pantry and took a whole four minutes to decide whether water crackers should be shelved under *W* or *C*.

By then it was eleven o'clock.

I called Mason, just to see if Beale had made any exciting discoveries that morning, but Taffy, Mason's assistant, said Doc Mason was with a patient.

I called Littlejohn, but he didn't answer, and I remembered he'd mentioned an Extravaganza meeting last time we spoke.

In desperation, I called Jonquil, grateful when she chatted to me for thirty minutes about the mockups the graphic designer had sent her and unreasonably disappointed when she had to hang up so she could have tea—"and by tea I mean tequila, honey! Wish you were here!"—with the Mahjong folks.

I tossed my phone on the couch with a sigh and decided to water my houseplants but found I had none.

Who the fuck didn't have a single living organism besides himself in his home? Never had such a busy life seemed so damn empty.

By the time Mason called back around four, I was coming out of my skin.

"Mason, precious! Hello! I just called to catch up. By any chance—" *Have you seen Beale?*

"Hey!" Mason said at the same time, his voice muffled like his mouth was full. "Been a super-busy day here. I'm eating a late lunch while we chat."

"Delightful. I live for the sound of you masticating in my ear. Why so hectic?"

"Mmm." Mason slurped his drink. "One of the Stallions, this guy named Bobo—"

"I know Bobo," I said impatiently, tapping my fingers on the arm of the sofa.

"Oh, that's right! Convenient. Well, he and a couple friends bought a bar."

"What? This week?" Already things were changing without me?

"Yeah. He bought an abandoned property on the Gulfside in the middle of the Key, kind of across from the Gas n' Sundry. Deal went through Monday. Fenn said it's gonna be cute." Mason stopped to swallow. "Anyway, Bobo had a huge barbecue thing last night, and half the town went, and Gloria brought a potato salad, and it sat out a little too long, and… well. As I said, busy day."

I frowned. "Was Beale at the party? Is he okay?"

"Mmm." Mason shoveled more food in his mouth. "Dunno. Pretty sure. Haven't talked to him."

"You don't know if he's okay?" I demanded, jumping to my feet. "How's that possible, Mason? He lives in your backyard. Aren't there *oaths* about this sort of thing?"

Mase sounded amused. "I haven't been in my backyard, Toby. And the licensing board doesn't require me to accost people to find out their potato salad status."

I huffed.

"Besides, Beale's been busy helping Young Rafe plan the Extravaganza since Gage is out of town, and I've hardly seen him in weeks. For what it's worth, Beale and Littlejohn took off in Littlejohn's car this morning toward Cooter Key like the world's oddest *Thelma and Louise* reenactment, and Beale waved happily. Does that satisfy you?"

Beale and Littlejohn, riding off happily. Lovely.

I sat back down hard. "Pfft. *Satisfy*. I don't require satisfaction, Mason. I was… I was… I was merely inquiring after the health of a mutual friend. That's hardly… whatever you think this is." I cleared my throat. "It's called basic human kindness, okay?"

"Ah. It's just that I've so rarely heard you express this 'human kindness' before," he teased.

"Excuse you?"

Mason laughed. "I love you, Toby. I really do. And I think you should call Beale," he said gently. "Just to get closure."

Ah. So closure was the most likely outcome, then? I swallowed against the lump in my throat. "I don't suppose Beale has, um, mentioned me, or...?"

"Not since the day after the party," he said sadly. "But I told you, I haven't seen him. And he did seem really shaken that Saturday morning. And regretf—"

"No, no. No need to elaborate. At all. Something Littlejohn said seemed to indicate that Beale might still be harboring some unresolved concerns, and I was concerned. About those concerns. But all evidence suggests that he's fine, so that's... good. Great. *Perfect.*"

My stomach churned, and the air in my apartment felt stale.

"Toby," Mason sighed. "As your oldest friend, I'm telling you to call Beale—"

"And I will! Goodness, Mason, I certainly will." I waved a hand, though Mase couldn't see me. "His birthday is coming up next month, and I will.... I will call him. I may even sing."

"Today."

"Ha. What? No. Absolutely not." Any confidence I might have had this morning was gone entirely now. In fact, I couldn't believe I'd ever considered that Beale would see my column, let alone that he would be... what? Moved by it? Nonsense. "I can't, Mason, as a matter of fact, because I'm going out to... um..." I hesitated, then decided on the spot. "A club. I haven't been in *weeks*. Men are probably wondering where I am." I was confident that was not the case.

"Toby," Mason said wearily. "Maybe instead..."

"Remember me fondly to everyone down there!" I interrupted cheerily. "Make sure to let anyone who asks know that I am doing well and having just a really, really remarkably wonderful time. I'll speak to you soon, darling. Kisses to Fenn, and tell him he's my favorite."

"Speaking of which, remind me to tell you about Fenn's competition with my new brother-in-law."

I was nearly swayed—*nearly*—but I shook my head. "Next time! Really must dash if I'm going to be beautified by this evening."

Especially since I could sense I'd need a good cry first.

At nine, after a hydrating mask and a bubble bath, I got dressed in my tightest jeans—the ones that showed my bulge to perfection—and my black Berluti Scrittos. I took twenty minutes to fix my hair. And I was stepping out of the Lyft in front of Dive before I realized I was being an idiot.

I didn't want to go to a club. I didn't want a hookup with someone like freakin' Aron, who had started my life down this ridiculous path in the first place. The gorgeous men who thronged the late-summer streets left me cold.

I wanted *Beale*.

And yet the second my feelings touched the edge of potential hurt, I flinched and ran like an animal bumping up against an invisible fence, because I was nothing if not consistent.

My family disowned me? I ran from expectations and hid behind Hagatha.

My heart got broken? I ran from relationships.

Paparazzi came out of the woodwork after the Jayd debacle, and I got scared? I ran away from home to bury my head in the sand.

I fucked things up with Beale? I ran back to the city.

My one attempt to repair things didn't hit right? I was going to chuck everything away again.

Except I wasn't. Not this time.

It wasn't enough to simply fight hard when things seemed hopeless. I was pretty sure you had to keep fighting over and over, which sounded exhausting until I remembered that *Beale* was the prize, and that was worth anything.

So what if he hadn't read my article? So what if my grand gesture had, in the end, fizzled? This wasn't the final nail in the coffin. It was not the end of the line if I didn't allow it to be. I would go back to Whispering Key and sort this.

First thing in the morning.

I pulled out my phone and ordered myself another Peanut Butter Party delivery, stat, vowing it would be my *last*, no matter what happened. Then I got a chicken phall roll from my favorite Indian place on Macdougal and ate it as I walked home, pausing to watch the kittens in the window of the pet store just a block from my building. None of the felines were as antisocial and weirdly adorable as Marjorie, but one was a pretty ginger who sort of reminded me of her, and...

Okay, *fine*. I was a mere mortal, and no more could I take. I couldn't wait for the next day. I couldn't wait another minute. I got out my phone—which was Beale's phone—and dialed his number with a mouth gone dry. I would tell him how I felt. I would apologize. I would ask how *he* felt. I would...

Voicemail.

Fuck.

"Um. Heya, Beale. So, it's me... Toby Elford."

Jesus Christ, how had I ever graduated kindergarten?

"I was just calling to say hi. And Mason said a plague of food poisoning hit the island, so I wondered how you were. And I think I owe you money. And also an apology."

I ran out of breath and choked on my own saliva as I gasped air into my lungs, since my family line had clearly not evolved to the point where we could speak and breathe at the same time.

"So maybe." *Cough.* "You could call me back? My number is..." I coughed some more. "Um. Actually. I guess it's probably already on your phone, since that's how phones work. Ha! Well. Alrighty, then. Hope you're well. Um. Bye."

I closed my eyes and smacked the phone against my forehead repeatedly. Had I actually just left a voice message in which I overtly referenced gastrointestinal illness *and* aspirated my own spit simultaneously?

"Why must you always be such an overachiever, Tobias?" I moaned.

Thank God my readers couldn't see me.

But the good news was that when you hit bottom, there was nowhere to go but up, right?

"Tommy? Tommy! Damn, baby, what're the chances? Been callin' you for weeks!"

The bad news was that so often when you thought you'd hit bottom, you hadn't quite gotten there yet.

I opened my eyes to find Aron standing in front of me on the sidewalk, flanked by a couple other muscleheads. They were all dressed to the nines, like they were out on the prowl, and the look on Aron's face as he stared at me suggested I was a Christmas miracle that had appeared a few months early.

One of the friends jabbed the other in the bicep, and they rolled their eyes behind Aron's back in a knowing way, like they thought their friend was about to score before they even made it to the club.

The very idea made me wanna vomit.

"*Mi angel*, can we talk for a second?" Aron reached out a hand for me, and when I sidestepped, he darted a glance at the others, like he didn't want me to get away but also didn't want to explain my presence to his friends.

I inhaled sharply. Once again, my instincts were screaming at me to walk away, run away, deflect, and retreat, but I made myself stand firm. I wasn't going to do that anymore. Leaving Whispering Key was the last time I would run away.

From now on, I was running *toward* something. Toward Beale.

So instead, I pretended that Beale was standing behind me, his broad chest against my back.

"I told you not to *mi angel* me," I said, folding my arms. "It was bad enough hearing it the night you staged that picture."

"What? Tommy, come on." Aron smiled for his friends' benefit and reached for me again. "Two minutes—"

"Zero minutes, and do not place your hand on me unless you'd like me to explain to your friends *exactly* how a photographer from BlazeNewz helped you pay for that Tom Ford." I gave his suit a critical eye. "Under these streetlights, you look positively jaundiced. Silver is *so* not your color."

He forced a laugh. "Don't be ridiculous, Tommy. I didn't *stage*—"

"Of course, I'm sure your friends will find out all the details when I testify on behalf of Jayd Rollins. I've already given an affidavit that the picture was staged," I lied, not bothering to lower my voice. "I named you and BlazeNewz specifically, and explained all about the deal I was offered to out Jayd for money—"

"Aron, what's he talking about?" One of Aron's friends elbowed him in the side.

Aron seemed too busy staring at me to notice.

"I'm not certain whether his team are planning to go forward with things from a legal standpoint first," I continued blithely, "or just get HiWire News to write up a huge exposé of the situation. First they need to contact your gym to see how they feel about one of their trainers being involved in something like this. And they'll contact that body competition thingy, too—"

"Muscle Men of Manhattan?" Aron's eyes were round. "No."

"Yep." I inspected my nails. "But it won't be so bad. Your bosses might not be happy, and I'm not sure if the Muscle Men will want someone of your moral standing to compete, but at least you have your blood money, right? Better than the choice you gave Jayd."

"Jayd?" Aron's other friend said. "Like, Rollins? Wait, what?"

Aron swallowed and whispered hotly, "But I'm not *out* in the bodybuilding world. They can't run a story with my name that ties me to Muscle Men! That wouldn't be..."

I gave him a look that said he was a hypocrite *and* an asshole.

"...cool," he finished weakly. He ran a hand through his hair, which was a poor choice considering how much product was in it. "Shit. Tommy, *mi*... uh." He cleared his throat and held out his hands in a placating way. "There's no need for any of that. I'm sure we can figure something out."

I tilted my head to one side. "Not my call, Aron, but I don't know why they'd have any interest in helping you out unless you managed to get BlazeNewz to stop showing that picture, and I'm pretty sure *that* could only happen if you admitted you staged it—"

"Y-yeah," he said quickly. "Okay. I'll say I photoshopped it."

"Really?" I slathered my voice with a thick layer of disbelief. "Even if BlazeNewz makes you give their money back?"

"Ah, damn." Aron shut his eyes. "Yeah."

I tried not to show that I was doing an internal victory dance. "Well, I'm not sure if anyone will listen to me, since I'm just the eyewitness to the crime you perpetrated, but I'll mention your intention to the, um... crack legal team." I shrugged. "We'll see what they say." I smiled at his friends. "You all have a lovely night."

"Aron? Dude! The fuck did you do?" I heard the guys mutter as I walked around them and continued down the street.

Halfway down the block, my hands started to shake. I needed Beale so, so, so much. I wanted to tell him the whole story. I could almost picture his smile.

Franz stood outside my building and opened the door when I got close. "Your ice cream order arrived, sir."

"Oh." I gave him a wobbly smile. "Great. Thank you." I was pretty sure I'd die if I tried to eat it now. I was at the stage of emotionality where even ice cream couldn't help me, and I was pretty sure I'd never been here before.

I let myself into my quiet apartment, locked the door behind me, and leaned back against it. The lights of the city outside my window sparkled through my dark apartment, promising all sorts of excitement and adventure. But the adventure I'd committed myself to was way scarier, and I was so excited, I wasn't sure I'd be able to sleep.

I shucked my beautiful shoes and shirt and skintight jeans, set my phone to charge in the living room, and despite the early hour, I lay down in bed, because tomorrow would be a long—

The weight hit my chest, knocking the breath from my body, and then a noise halfway between a chainsaw purr and a smoker's cough filled the apartment.

"No," I said clearly. "No, I am hallucinating. I have consumed too much Peanut Butter Party in a short amount of time. And the cholesterol has caused me to have a lucid dream. Or an un-lucid dream. Holy Kacey Musgraves, I have invented un-lucid dreaming."

"For a man so obsessed with potential murder," came the world's warmest, best, most comforting voice from mere inches away on the other side of my bed, "it was *extremely* easy to stroll into your apartment with a rolling suitcase and a cat carrier. I met the ice cream delivery guy in the lobby, and he let me in."

"Please be real," I whispered, and Marjorie dug her claws into my flesh in a really kind and comforting way, to let me know she was really, actually there, before hopping off the bed and gallomphing across the hardwood floors.

I snickered.

Beale rolled against me a second later, a gorgeous shape in the darkness, and braced his hand in the bed on my opposite side, holding himself over me. He bent his head to my neck and... sniffed? Then his whole upper body sagged against me wearily.

"I didn't actually mean to be asleep when you came in," he told my collarbone. "But I didn't know how late you might be, and I heard your mattress was ultra-plush—"

I snorted.

"And it's just been a really long day." He sighed, his warm breath brushing my skin. "It's been a really long *week*, actually. The longest of my life, and it's all my fault. I came to tell you that. And apologize."

I twined my arms around his neck and let my fingers sift through his long, shaggy hair. Beale inhaled sharply, then moaned quietly like he'd missed being touched as much as I missed touching him. I pulled his head up, found his lips in the darkness, and kissed him. He tasted sleepy-sweet and smelled like home, and something inside me settled into place.

It was scary as fuck to be this happy, but that exquisite fear was all part of the joy.

I pulled back a little and cleared my throat. "That's funny, because I was coming to Florida tomorrow to tell you the exact same thing."

Beale's head came up, though it was probably too dark for him to see me, unless green tea gave him superpowers. "You were?"

I nodded. "I wrote you a column today. You probably didn't—"

"I saw it, baby. That's what convinced me I needed to come right now. See, I was trying to get ahold of Jay, like maybe if I could get him to make a statement and clear up all this stuff, maybe that would be a good way to apologize, but Gage stopped taking my calls, and their drive here from Colorado has turned into an epic road trip. But when I read your words, I thought maybe I didn't need to wait. That maybe you just wanted me."

"I always just want you," I whispered. "And I maybe helped with the Jayd thing." I sketched out what had happened with Aron earlier. "I'm not sure if that will fix things for Jayd or not, but I don't want to wait, Beale."

"Me neither. That's why I... hang on." He levered off me to stand and turned on my bedside lamp. "I wrote a letter for you, too."

He sat on the bed by my waist and riffled through a back-pack there before holding up...

"Excuse you." I snatched it out of his hand. "Is this a vomit bag from the plane?"

"Maybe?" He snatched it back. "My phone died, and I forgot the charger, but I wanted to... I wanted to convince you to give me a second chance, and I figured maybe if I wrote it down, I could make it clearer, so I used what I had. The bag part's not important."

I begged to differ. It was fucking adorable. I wasn't sure if anyone had ever had an airline vomit bag covered in crossed-out scribbles professionally framed before or if I'd be the first. I was very okay with that.

I sat up further and bent over so my chin was on his shoulder and my hands were on his warm skin. "Well, it's important to note that I don't require convincing. But also, please convince me."

Beale shot me a look, his blue eyes hot in the golden light from the lamp. "Promise you won't laugh."

"I solemnly assure you, laughter is the furthest thing from my mind."

"Okay, so... Ahem. Dear Aunt Hagatha—"

I laughed. I couldn't help it.

"Toby!" Beale looked at me severely, though it was clear he was close to laughing, too.

"You didn't tell me it was a Hagatha letter! Sorry! Sorry, sorry." I pressed apologetic kisses to his shoulder and neck, everywhere I could reach. "Go on. No more laughing," I vowed, though laughter and shock and relief still bubbled in my chest.

Then he started reading, and suddenly I was closer to tears than laughter.

"My whole life, I've been waiting to find my soul mate. My other half. I imagined he'd like a lot of the things I liked, and believe mostly what I believed, and that he'd be my refuge from a world that constantly asked me to explain and justify myself. I was sure that once I met him, I'd never feel like I wasn't good enough again, because he'd love me despite all my imperfections. He'd make me feel valued and safe and loved."

I pressed my forehead to Beale's shoulder. I wasn't his soul mate, then. But...

"Instead," he went on, "I met a man who challenged me from the first minute we met. He annoys me. He exasperates me. He makes me nervous. He lights me up. And he's not perfect, just like I'm not perfect, but that just means we fit perfectly. We make each other better."

"Stronger," I whispered against his skin, thinking of fucking Aron, and how good it had felt to stick up for myself.

"Happier," Beale whispered back. "Not just content, but really, honestly happy, Toby, for the first time I can remember. I've stopped waiting for good things to come to me, and I've realized I have the power to make them happen."

"Yeah?" I sniffled in a way that would have been horrifically embarrassing with anyone but Beale. "Well, I've stopped waiting for bad things to come to me, because I realized I have the power to *not* let them happen. And I know I'm not your soul mate, Beale, but—"

"But you *are*." Beale turned toward me. "That's exactly what I was trying to say, and maybe it didn't come out right, but you *are*. You're the only one I want because—"

"I love you," we both said together.

Beale's slow smile was like sunrise in the middle of the night, and I was pretty sure I was smiling just as brightly.

I was such a sap.

But so was Beale, so I was okay with that.

I sniffled again, because that was a thing I did now. "I was going to come to Florida and tell you that I was keeping you, whether you liked it or not, and your soul mate could fight me for you whenever he came along. I decided you needed someone who loved you epically, and I am a very epic sort of person—"

"You are, baby," he agreed solemnly.

"And that you deserved someone who'd fight for you. And I haven't been that person, but I want to be. For you. *With* you."

"Ah, shit." Beale's hand at my neck pulled me forward so he could kiss me, hot and openmouthed. "I love you, Toby," he whispered against my lips. Then he tipped me back against the pillows to straddle me.

"I love you, too." I tilted my head to give him better access as he sucked and nibbled at the skin of my neck. My restless legs rubbed against his, and my hips rolled against him, trying to get friction on my hardening cock. "God. It's absurd. It's... it's... it's—*fuck, yeah, right there*—preposterous, really. It's too fast, and we don't have enough in common, and I don't care."

Beale paused with his nose nuzzled into my armpit, then lifted his face to smile at me. "That was the end of my letter."

"Huh?" I blinked at him. "The what?"

"That was the end of my Dear Hagatha letter." He patted around the mattress and found the world's most precious— and now most wrinkled—vomit bag. "It's too fast, and we don't have enough in common, and I don't care. How can I convince him to take a chance on me? Signed, Not-So-Virgo-Somewhere-Over-West-Virginia-I-Think." Beale threw the bag aside and shrugged. "I kinda lost my creativity at the end there."

He stared down at me expectantly, and my brain was so thoroughly fogged by love and lust and *relief* that it took me a whole second to realize he was waiting for an answer.

For Hagatha's answer.

"Beale, precious? I already told you I don't require convincing, right?"

"Well, yeah…"

"Because I love you and want to be with you?"

"Yeah," he said softly, wonderingly.

"And you love me and want to be with me?"

"Fuck, yes. So much." But he still watched me steadily.

"Right." I cleared my throat and rolled my eyes just a little.

Good Lord, the things I did to hook up with a hot guy.

With one particular hot guy.

With *this* particular hot guy, who'd be the one and only guy in my life from here on out, if I had anything to say about it.

"Dear Not So Virgo, I know what will make the man you love agree to pretty much anything, especially when it's something he's already agreed to and wants as much as you do."

Beale quirked an eyebrow at me, and I reached up to push his hair off his face.

God, he really was beautiful. God, I really was lucky.

"Blow jobs," I whispered encouragingly. "They change lives."

EPILOGUE

Help Me Hagatha
(Hagatha's private files)

Dear Aunt Hagatha:

Is it possible to be happier than we are right now?

Beale in Bed
(As in, *our* ultra-plush bed.)
(All alone.)

Dear Beale,

Your methods of reminding me when it's time to stop working grow more devious. I approve. I'll be there in thirty seconds. Don't start without me... or actually, *do*.

I love you,
Toby

"Four point eight million!" Jonquil exclaimed, her eyes as round and wide as the martini glass in front of her as she took in the latest fundraising tallies. "Four point eight *million*?"

Marius Wynott and Dale Jennings exchanged an approving smile. My brother Rafe grinned and said, "Hells, yes." Shannon Tate, who was back on the Key for the summer to reopen her art gallery, shook her head in amazement. My dad's eyes got so shiny, he had to mop them with a cocktail napkin and nearly turned over a pitcher of beer in the process. Mason, who Toby had drafted to be part of the committee using what he called Best Friend's Privilege, saved the beer and only looked a little startled when my dad yelled, "I love this bar!" and turned to cry into his shoulder instead.

The Whispering Key Bridge Fundraising Committee now met biweekly at Fisher's Wreck, Bobo Fisher's new beachfront bar. Shocking literally everyone, Bobo mixed a mean martini, and since Bobo was dating Jonquil's niece, Corey, that meant the committee got their first two rounds of drinks comped.

Since I was living with the head of the committee, this also extended to me, though I happily drank water and passed my drinks on to Toby. A tipsy Toby was a playful Toby, and a playful Toby tended to do wonderful, horrible things like smudge dirt on his forehead to simulate breeding plumage, jump into bed on top of me, throw my book on the floor, and tell me he'd been a naughty plover.

Suffice it to say, I was really glad the actual snowy plovers wouldn't be breeding again for a solid six months, because I wasn't sure I could even see one without hearing Toby whisper, "Breed me, plover hunter," in my ear and having exactly the response you'd expect.

Toby leaned against my side in the red pleather booth and sipped his dirty martini happily. My bracelet of protective stones was back on his wrist where it belonged, and he insisted he'd never take it off. "No offense to Scotty at the Bean, who supplies me with my daily coffee and is therefore the most important man in my life aside from *you*, but this was a definite upgrade in meeting locations."

I wrapped an arm around his shoulders to pull him more firmly against me. The Bean didn't have booths like this. "Agreed."

"Trey." Jonquil clasped Toby's iPad to her chest like a beloved child. "Is this... *Can* this be right?"

He nodded. "The fine accountants at Trout, Comstock, and Purchess don't lie, sweetness. I'm fairly certain they don't even know how to joke."

She squeezed her eyes shut and inhaled slowly, hugging the iPad. "Toby-Trey Elford, you are a true hero, setting all this up."

I bit my lip. Toby had acquired himself a nickname, and I thought it was adorable. I wasn't quite sure how Toby-Trey felt about it.

Toby shook his head and set his drink down. "Oh, I can't take any credit for that. The letter was all Beale's idea, and Aunt Hagatha's followers were beyond generous."

"I just can't believe she published it!" Littlejohn's girlfriend, Veronica, managed to sound really glad and really horrified at the same time. "I think hitting up her readers for donations like that is kinda tacky. But I mean, I'm glad for y'all and for John. Obviously." She touched her ample cleavage and smiled up at Littlejohn prettily, and you could practically see the cartoon swirls in her eyes, he was so hypnotized.

Meanwhile, Toby's smile hardened to the point where I had to poke him in the ribs.

He glanced over his shoulder and gave me a look that said, *What?*

I narrowed my eyes a little. *I thought we were giving her the benefit of the doubt for LJ's sake. I thought we were reserving judgment.*

Toby inhaled and set his head in a way that screamed, *Benefit revoked because his name is* Littlejohn, *not John.*

Which, honestly, was a really good point.

"Oh, I don't know, *Ronnie*," Toby said. "I think Hagatha encouraging readers to write in about their favorite little-known charities is an amazing idea."

"Veronica," she corrected. "Not Ronnie."

"Oh, silly me! I thought we were playing some kind of name-shortening game! My bad. I'm new to small-town life." Toby's smile was the kind of slow poison that wouldn't catch her until she got home. "But as for why Hagatha chose Beale's letter..." He gave me a mischievous look. "I find Beale a *very* persuasive letter writer."

I shook my head slowly. The man I loved was pure trouble and drama and every other thing I'd thought I never wanted, and in a few minutes, I'd get to take him home to our new home—a gorgeous, single-story, huge-windowed place we'd rented from Littlejohn that Toby had promptly dubbed the Terracotta Palace, and where a professionally framed vomit bag now hung in our bedroom alongside a printout of Hagatha's letter to me.

I couldn't have been happier.

The '80s rock ballad playing over the speakers cut out, and there was the sudden whine of feedback as someone—oh, good Lord, my dad—unearthed a microphone.

"I now declare this meeting of the Whispering Key Bridge Fundraising Committee *closed*! And I'd hereby like to open the Whispering Key Welcome Party in honor of Toby-Trey Elford!"

The entire bar erupted in a chorus of "Surprise!"

My cousin, Fenn, appeared from somewhere, along with Lety, Bubba, Scotty, Jeremy, Barbara, Carolyn, Taffy, and Orry—more Whispering Keysters than I could even count —and all of them came over to tell Toby how glad they were that he'd picked up stakes in New York and moved down here.

Honestly, it had been a near-run thing as far as I was concerned. When I'd packed Marjorie up and brought her to New York, I'd had the idea in mind that if I somehow got Toby to take a chance on me, I'd happily stay, even if I had no idea what that would look like.

But when I'd told Toby so, he'd looked at me like I was several sandwiches shy of a picnic. "Permanently? Under no circumstances, Beale Goodman. Jonquil would fly up and smack us. Since you're here, it'd be great to show you around this weekend, but I talked to my boss today and told her if all went well, I'd be moving to Florida. We can sublet the apartment and maybe sell it eventually."

And all of that had sounded really, really good, but the best part had been the *we*.

Maddie McKetcham ran up to our table carrying an enormous banner that read TEALE 4EVA! in bright purple glitter.

Toby reached for my hand and gave me a look that said, *What the fuck is going on?*

I gave him a return look that said, *Around here, baby? Who the hell knows?*

"Madeline," Toby said, staring at the sign. "What a truly... triumphant work of art. Thank you."

Maddie beamed. "I *knew* you'd like Teale better than Boby for y'all's ship name."

"Our ship name." Toby closed his eyes and nodded. "That's... yes. Remarkable."

"Littlejohn had us vote."

Littlejohn nodded. "Ronnie here thought 'Boby,' but I wasn't so sure."

"Veronica," his girlfriend, who was probably not going to be his girlfriend for very long, reminded him.

"That's right, honeybunch. But you've gotta admit Ronnie's catchy."

Veronica looked like she didn't "gotta" do anything of the sort.

"We have *presents for you*," my dad shouted into the microphone, loud enough to startle any dolphins in the vicinity. "But Doc Mason said you wouldn't be ready to entertain at your place yet, so we decided to surprise you here!"

Toby mouthed the words "Thank you" to Mase across the table, and Mason winked.

Dale Jennings placed a hand on Veronica's and Littlejohn's chairs and leaned in. "Betcha can't guess what I got you," he said with an eyebrow wiggle.

Toby blinked. "Is it a seashell-covered toilet seat?"

Dale grinned and nodded slowly. "Aw yeah. You know it. And? Don't tell Doc Mason, but I got both you boys a year's supply of *ferrymones*, for to help your prowesses." He paused, and when Toby and I stared at him, he elaborated, "Your *sexual* prowesses."

"Gotcha. Yeah. That's... I can't even..." I shook my head. "Wow."

"Well said, soul mate," Toby said, shooting me another one of his speaking glances. "Wow, indeed."

"I'm literally sitting right here, Dale," Mason said. He shook his head.

"And my cousin Marian knitted you a bed for your little one!" Dale continued, pretending he couldn't hear Mase.

I wrapped my arms around Toby, buried my head in his neck, and pretended I couldn't hear *Dale*.

At some point Bobo came over and asked Young Rafe about Gage's road trip. He mentioned his nephew was coming to town and asked about our plans for the tour business, but I didn't pay much attention. The man in my arms was so intoxicating, it wasn't hard to tune everything else out...

Except my dad with his microphone.

"Okay, everyone, we're gonna start the dancing soon—"

That got me to lift my head because dancing with a guy I loved was something I'd never done before, and suddenly I really wanted to.

"—but first, the Bridge Fundraising Committee has just taken a very quick secret vote—"

Toby looked at me, I looked at him, and we both looked at Mason, who grinned and shrugged.

"—and we've decided to name the new bridge after our Toby! It will be called the Toby-Trey Elford Memorial Bridge!"

Toby gave me a wide-eyed look that said, *Memorial?* at the same time Gloria leaned over to whisper something to my dad.

"Er. I mean. It'll be named whatever Toby would like to name it," he corrected.

All eyes turned to Toby, who floundered for half a second. He looked at me and then fingered the bracelet on his wrist. Then he looked up at my dad and smiled. "I think it should be called the Goodman Bridge, sir."

"The... Why, thank you, Tobias. That's... that's... beautiful." My dad broke off, too overcome to continue. His already leaky eyes leaked a little more, and I knew Toby had just earned himself a permanent spot at the top of the Favorite Goodman Son list. "Cue the music!" he choked out.

Littlejohn leaned across the table. "Awful nice'a you to name it after Big Rafe. He's been a good mayor." He nodded once, then clapped his hands and stood up. "Time for dancing!"

Veronica stood up quickly also. "Alright!"

"Oh." Littlejohn seemed startled, like he'd forgotten she was there. "Okay, then."

"Trouble in paradise already with those two." Marius Wynott pursed his lips and shook his head as LJ and Veronica headed for the makeshift dance floor at the back of the bar. He leaned across me to tell Toby, "I know you're too polite to tell everyone you named the bridge for Resolute Goodman, the founder of Whispering Key, so it'll stay our little secret." He tapped the side of his nose. "But your nod to history does you credit." He slid out his side of the booth.

Toby pressed his lips together. "The island was founded by Resolute Goodman?"

"And Jacob Godfrey," Mason agreed. "They're the ones who buried the treasure we found."

"Pfft. I knew that."

"Of course you did, baby." I ruffled his hair. "That's why your nod to history does you credit."

Fenn came over to wrap his arms around Mason from

behind and drop a kiss on his head. "Heya, Loafers." A rain of glitter fell off his hair and landed in Mason's lap.

"Ack." Mason brushed the glitter away. "Fenn Reardon, have you been having Zoom unicorn parties with my niece again?"

Fenn rolled his lips together and blinked guiltily. "Possibly?"

Mason shook his head. "Was it magical?"

"Obviously." Fenn grinned. "I'm getting a drink. You want your usual?"

Mason nodded, and Fenn kissed him again before heading to the bar. Mason turned to watch him go, and an unmistakable smile played around his mouth.

When he turned back, he gave Toby a knowing smile. "You're naming the bridge after Beale, aren't you? No, no!" He held up a hand. "Neither confirm nor deny. I'm your best friend, and I know the truth. You're in love, so it just makes sense. You know, at first I didn't see you two together, and that was my fault. Sometimes the weirdest pairings just... work." He looked over his shoulder at his glittery boyfriend. "I'm so glad you're here, Toby."

"Me, too," Toby said softly.

"Welcome to Whispering Key."

When Fenn came back, Toby and I excused ourselves to go try out the dance floor, and holding him in my arms as we spun to the music was every bit as amazing as I'd hoped it would be. Thanks to the martinis, Toby couldn't stop himself from grinning goofily up at me, and if he hadn't been wearing a blue jumpsuit that cost nearly as much as a mortgage payment, I would have said the man in my arms bore hardly any resemblance to the guy who first washed up on Whispering Key.

He crooked a finger up at me, and I leaned down so he could whisper in my ear.

"I have a secret to tell you."

"Oh, yeah?" I held him tighter and breathed him in. Coconut lime Toby. Delicious.

"The night of Mason's party, when Mase and I were talking, Fenn walked in and he gave Mason this *look*."

"A look."

"You know, a *look*-look. Like Mason was the most important person on the planet. That kind of look. And I wished someone would look at me that way."

I pulled back just far enough to see his face. "You mean the way I look at you? Like I know you better than anyone and love every single thing I know?"

Toby's mouth opened and shut wordlessly for half a minute before he managed, "You think you know me that well?"

"I know I do. You might be the king of trivia, but I am the king of *Toby* trivia."

"*Pffft. No. Pffft.* That's not even. *Pfft.*"

I laughed. "For example? I know that a minute ago when Dale said he was giving us supplements to improve our prowesses, you were thinking that if our prowesses were any more prowessful, we'd die."

Toby coughed weakly. "That... was a lucky guess."

"Uh-huh. And I know that when you said you wanted to name that bridge Goodman Bridge, you weren't thinking of naming it after my dad, even though you care about him, or about Resolute Goodman, even though you're real devoted to the history of the island."

"Oh, yeah? You think Mason was right, then?" He gave me an arch look. "You think I wanna name it after you?"

"Mmmm." I ducked my head back and forth. "Kinda."

He sank his fingers into my hair. "You think I love you or something?"

"I do think that."

And I knew for sure I loved him. I loved that he accepted all of me. I loved that he saw me clearly. I loved that he would always be tender, and prickly, and hilarious, sometimes at the same time. I loved that in some ways he was my total opposite and in some ways he was my mirror image. I even loved that he'd kept Jayd's secret because it was the right thing to do. I loved him the way I loved my family, and the Key, and Marjorie—instantly and irrationally, not despite their faults, but because of them—except I loved him more.

He wasn't the soul mate I'd have picked for myself, but he was exactly, *exactly* the one I'd needed.

"...and I think you picked the name Goodman for another reason, too."

Toby's mouth quirked in surprise. "Do tell."

I spun him out, then reeled him back in, and cupped his face in my hands. "I think deep down you know you'll be a

Goodman, too, someday, so you weren't just thinking about naming it for *me*, you were thinking about naming it for *us*."

Toby's mouth fell open again, and he blushed. "Sweet, dimpled Adele, how did you know that?"

"Toby trivia king. Undefeated."

He shook his head and grinned like *he* was the lucky one around here, and I felt ten feet tall. "Okay, I admit, I hoped putting the idea of you and me being a permanent thing out into the Universe might be powerful. You're never gonna convince me to give up coffee, and I will only do yoga if it's sexy yoga, but this Universe business..." He shrugged. "I mean, it's worked out pretty damn well for us so far, right?"

"Right," I agreed. And Toby wasn't wrong—the law of attraction *was* super powerful. But Toby and me together? We were unstoppable.

Then I leaned down and kissed him, pulling him against me, because in every version of the future it would be him and me together.

Want to see what happens when two former friends end up on a crazy cross-country road trip? Grab Off Key, *book three in the Whispering Key series, here: https://readerlinks.com/l/1834952*

Want to know what Fenn and Mason were up to in O'Leary while Toby and Beale were falling in love? Check out the bonus epilogue, Unicorns Forever, *to see what happened when Fenn and Mason met Micah and Con here: http://readerlinks.com/l/ 1571315*

ABOUT MAY ARCHER

May is an M/M author who lives in Boston. She spends her days planning vacations, mainlining diet soda, avoiding the gym, reading M/M romance, and when all other forms of procrastination fail, writing it.

Visit her website at mayarcher.com to sign up for her newsletter to hear about sales and upcoming releases, freebies and behind the scenes info and more! Or join her Facebook group, Club May!

facebook.com/may.archer.author

instagram.com/mayarcherauthor

amazon.com/May-Archer/e/B075JQVGLX

patreon.com/MayArcherRomance

bookbub.com/authors/may-archer

ALSO BY MAY ARCHER

Get my <u>New Release Alerts</u>

Join me on Patreon

Follow me Everywhere Else

<u>Love in O'Leary Series</u>

<u>Whispering Key Series</u>

<u>The Sunday Brothers Series</u>

<u>Copper County Series</u>

<u>The Way Home Series</u>

<u>Licking Thicket Series</u>

(cowritten with Lucy Lennox)

<u>Champion Security Series</u>

(cowritten with Lucy Lennox)

<u>Honeybridge Series</u>

(cowritten with Lucy Lennox)

For a comprehensive list of titles, audio samples, freebies, suggested reading order, and more, visit my website at www.MayArcher.com!